ALONE ON ALTAIR

Shattered Alliance, Book 3

BENJAMIN WALLACE

ALONE ON ALTAIR

Copyright © 2023 by Benjamin Wallace.
All rights reserved.

ISBN: 9798768142513

This is a work of fiction. Names, characters, places, and incidents are the product of the author's imagination. Any resemblance to actual persons, living or dead, events, or locales is entirely coincidental.

Cover design by Benjamin Wallace Books.

JOIN MY READERS' GROUP and get a free book

From the pages of the best-selling Duck & Cover Adventures comes thirteen stories of those who survived the apocalypse. Some would go on to be heroes, others villains, some were dogs and will stay dogs, but they all must contend with the horrors of the new world and find a way to survive in the wasteland that was America.

Get this laugh-out-loud collection of stories from the Duck & Cover Adventures post-apocalyptic series now when you sign up for my Readers' Group.

To get your copy of TALES OF THE APOCALYPSE and be the first to know about new releases and other exclusive content, you just need to tell me where to send it.

Visit
http://benjaminwallacebooks.com/join-my-readers-group/
to get your free book now.

ONE

Fire in the Sky

From the surface of the planet, it may have appeared as though a shooting star was blazing across the heavens.

Perhaps somewhere a mother sat outside, bundled with her small child in an itchy blanket on a cool evening, sipping some kind of cider and watching the stars when she spotted it against the dark canvas that was the night sky.

"Look, my love. A shooting star," she'd say, and point to the sky. "Make a wish."

"I wish for…" the child would begin aloud.

"Shhh," the mother would say calmly. "You can never tell anyone what you wish for."

"Why not?" the innocent child, who had apparently never had a birthday cake, would ask.

"Because then your wish won't come true," she'd say with a smile. And, if she was being honest, she'd add, "And nobody cares what you wish for, so don't go boring people with your wishing nonsense."

So, the child would nod, close their eyes tight and wish hard, silently to themselves, but still moving their lips, because that's how kids work. Maybe the wish was for a puppy—or perhaps a kitten, if the child was a girl. Or a snake, if they were a future arsonist. Or a goat, if the kid was weird and needed therapy.

The wish didn't have to be animal related, of course. It could be a wish for wealth. A lot of people were greedy like that, staring into the heavens and wishing for the universe to deliver them a fortune. Wiser children wished for power because where power went, wealth followed, and you could score a twofer without violating the 'no wishing for more wishes' rule.

Or maybe it was none of those things. Maybe the kid was stupid and wasted this powerful opportunity on something immediate and fleeting like an ice cream cone. Only an innocent child would think nothing of asking all of existence to bend fate and physics for a simple dessert, provided it had sprinkles.

In the end, it didn't matter how greedy that child was or what their hypothetical wish may have been because what they were seeing wasn't a shooting star at all. It was an Alliance ship named the *Galahad* streaking across the heavens. And the only reason it looked like a shooting star at all was because it was mostly on fire.

Another blast from the Hama pursuit ship rocked the *Galahad* hard enough to throw Captain Antarius Thurgood from the pilot's station. He crashed to the deck and started sliding headfirst toward the front of the ship as it dove toward the planet. Experience had taught him long ago that hitting things with your head wasn't always ideal, so he dragged his arm and spun himself around. He was still plummeting, but at least he would crash on his feet.

Beyond his toes, the purple- and red-hued planet grew larger as he and the *Galahad* sped toward it. The viewport was coming at him fast, and while he was fairly confident it wouldn't break when he crashed into it, he was also fairly confident it was going to hurt like a mother.

"I've got you, sir."

Antarius's plummet slowed as the floor beneath him leveled out and the viewport filled with the void of space. The *Galahad* was turning away from the planet.

Gravity loosened its grip and Thurgood's slide came to an end. The captain turned back to his seat to see his first officer at the *Galahad*'s controls. Antarius got to his feet and rushed back to the pilot's station.

"Stand down, Higlee."

"It's Hinkley!" The first officer twisted the flight yoke to the left to avoid a barrage from the Hama pursuit ship. The evasive maneuver nearly knocked Antarius off of his feet and back to the deck. He grabbed the back of the pilot's seat for balance.

"I don't care if your name is Oliver Wilbur Wright, I'm flying this ship."

"You were flying this ship," the first officer agreed. "And then you were on the floor sliding all over the place!"

"Stand down." Thurgood put his hand on the flight controls and shoved the man out of the seat with his hip as he took back his command.

Higlee stood and made his way back to his own seat. But he wasn't done whining. "Well, excuse me for taking the controls and trying to save our lives."

"I've excused a lot of things, Higlee," Thurgood snapped back. "Your insubordination. Your contempt for Alliance protocols. Your damn whistling nostril."

"I don't have a—"

"Oh yes, you do. It's the right one and it never stops. It's like an off note played by an amateur grade school flautist with a combination of asthma and performance anxiety. Over and over and over like a damned mosquito with tinnitus."

"Wow, that's really specific. I never knew you—"

"Yeah, well, I've had a lot of time to think about it. You've been giving performances ever since you came aboard. But don't try to change the subject. I will not excuse this latest insubordination. Consider yourself reprimanded and remind me to reprimand you properly when I'm done saving our lives."

Thurgood leaned forward and put the *Galahad* back on course. Once more, the planet filled the viewport.

Higlee jumped back into his seat at his station and fastened his harness before turning back to the navigator's console. "No wonder your last first officer left you."

"You watch what you say about Stendak, Higlee. She didn't leave me. She quit. For love. Maybe that's a little difficult for someone like you to understand since you're so wrapped up in your own thing and can't consider the feelings of others." Thurgood turned his attention back to the planet.

"Are you serious?"

"I am serious and I am ordering you to keep her name out of your mouth. If you were half the first officer she was, we wouldn't be in this mess to begin with. And you'd damn sure look better in a uniform."

"You're blaming this on me? '10 pushups says I can get right off their bow without them seeing us.' Those were your words, Captain."

"Oh, I do not care for the way you just said Captain."

A shot from the Hama cannon struck the *Galahad* on the bow and knocked them off course. Thurgood corrected and put the planet back in front of them. Leaning into the throttle, he demanded more power from the engines. But they had nothing left to give. Somewhere in the back of the ship, the engines whined that they were at their breaking point. That would be going in his report.

"So, do you want to tell me your great plan?" Higlee whined. "Since it's not going to work and we're both going to die in the process, I think it's only fair that I know."

Nothing on this ship worked right, Thurgood thought. Least of all the crew. Stendak never would have questioned his plan. No matter how desperate it appeared. Well, she would have questioned it. Then she would have tried to talk him out of it. And it was that kind of level-headed thinking that they needed right now. Unfortunately, First Officer Sarcasm was no Stendak.

"Captain?" Higlee was as impatient as he was annoying.

"You want to know my plan? I'm going to fly to the surface of whatever planet that is and lose them in the canyons. That's my plan."

"What are you talking about? What canyons?"

Thurgood pointed at the viewscreen. "The planet's canyons."

"You don't even know what planet it is. How do you know there are canyons?"

"There are always canyons!"

"So, step 1 of your great plan is to hope there are canyons?" Higlee sounded like a lawyer. Like each answer was being entered into the record as he was working his way to some damning failure of logic.

"No, step 1 is you shutting up. And then, step 2 is the canyons."

"But..."

Thurgood held up his shushing finger. "We're still on step 1." He turned his focus back to the controls. "And don't worry. There are always canyons."

It was a universal, undeniable and possibly scientific truth. There were always canyons. Every captain worth his captain's hat knew that. But he still had to reach them.

He pushed the throttles harder against the stops and turned the ship into a power dive through the atmosphere. Things started getting bumpy as soon as the *Galahad* met the air. The ship trembled and rattled as it attempted to shake itself apart.

The upside was that the jostling drowned out Higlee's complaining.

The *Galahad* wasn't built for maneuvers like this. Or dogfights, as he had just discovered. And, if he had time to look in the manual, he was pretty sure there'd be a section specifically about NOT flying through alien canyons at top speed. It wasn't ideal for a lot of things. It was a luxury pleasure yacht. But after the rescue mission to get Priscilla and those freak soldiers off of Mirada, it was what he had.

He cursed the Alliance for not giving him a faster ship when he had asked for it.

"Subtlety is more important than speed for this mission." That had been their reasoning when presenting him with the ship.

"I'd like to trade a little subtlety for some more speed," he had offered. "Not a lot of subtlety. Just a little. You won't even miss it."

Their answer had been no. They had insisted on subtlety before speed. And now that the *Galahad* was in flames and streaking across the night sky, he would argue it had neither. But there was little consolation in being right if you didn't get to live to say *I told you so*.

The Hama pursuit ship, on the other, more alien hand, wasn't subtle in the least. It was straight up mean looking. By the looks of it, the Hama had access to more angles than Humanity and they had used about a million of them on the ship. On the *Galahad*'s screen, it looked like a thousand knives were chasing them through space. It was designed for dogfights, extreme maneuvers and probably, most likely, for flying through canyons. The ship was incredibly nimble, and it stuck to the *Galahad* like stink on a Dolgrath.

The alien pilot had already proven formidable. They had

followed Thurgood through a flurry of evasive maneuvers that had, until now, never failed to shake a pursuer.

The Hama gunner was no slouch either. Several blasts passed the *Galahad* without contact, painting the black of space with crimson streaks. But the gunner had landed enough tricky shots to earn both Thurgood's respect and disdain.

With such talent and such hardware at the enemy's disposal, it hardly seemed a fair fight. On paper, the old yacht didn't stand a chance. But Antarius knew something even the original designers of the *Galahad* couldn't have known: He was an incredible pilot.

Three blasts of cannon fire cracked their hull and sent the ship spinning as it tore through the alien stratosphere.

"We're losing pressure." Even Higlee's status reports sounded whiny. And that whistle was back.

Thurgood's own console was lit with warning lights and flashing text. He wasn't going to tell Higlee, but pressure loss was the least of their worries. They were losing air, coolant, structural rigidity and ray shielding. In fact, the only things they weren't losing were temperature and speed. But it still wasn't enough. Thurgood leaned over the yoke and put the ship in a vertical dive while he thought of new ways to curse at the engine for more speed. Higlee pleaded for him to slow down, but he didn't let up until the *Galahad* reached the clouds.

The captain took a deep breath and held it as they entered the thick, red clouds that billowed over the planet's surface. He leveled the ship out and eased off the engines long enough for a few of the lights on his console to vanish.

A sense of calm enveloped him as the clouds wrapped around the *Galahad* and took the ship into their embrace. Time slowed and he flew silently through the formations until Higlee ruined everything by speaking.

"Why are you holding your breath?"

"I'm not holding my breath," Thurgood said while holding his breath.

"You are, though," the first officer insisted, and brought his hand to his throat. "Are... are we losing air?"

"No, we're..." Thurgood studied the console. "Oh, it appears we are losing air."

This sent Higlee diving for the emergency oxygen canister under his station. He was out of his harness and scrambling for the bottle before Thurgood could stop him.

"Relax. The planet's atmosphere is breathable. I was only holding my breath because it's that thing you do."

"What are you talking about? What thing?"

"You hold your breath when you fly through a cloud. It's like picking your feet up when you go over railroad tracks or touching a nail when you pass a cemetery."

"No one does those things."

"I guess that *no one* was never a kid."

"You are a grown-ass man!" Higlee was completely hysterical now. He heaved and grasped at his hair as if you could hold on to your sanity by plugging holes in your head.

Thurgood wasn't quite sure how to handle hysteria, but he assumed that arguing with someone experiencing hysterics wouldn't help. So, he decided to agree with him. "That's right."

"You're flying a starship." Higlee seemed to be calming.

"Right again." Talking down the hysteric was easier than he thought. His agreeing-with-everything plan was working.

"You are in the middle of a dogfight with a very concerned passenger."

"And a loud one at that."

"Now is not the time to be playing childish games like holding your breath when you enter a cloud!"

Thurgood exhaled as the *Galahad* blew out the underside of the cloud formation. The timing was optimal, as he was getting dizzy. "Just to be clear, Higlee. I exhaled because the clouds ended. Don't go thinking you've won."

"I'm not trying to win anything!"

"That's a good thing, because I just scored another point." Thurgood angled the *Galahad* toward the planet and the surface filled the viewport. Antarius pointed to a place just shy of the horizon. "What did I tell you? Canyons!"

TWO

A Wily Foe

The *Galahad* ratcheted right, throwing Higlee from his feet and sending the first officer sliding across the deck. He struck the opposite wall feet first but ended up splayed across the viewport. He rolled over and directed an accusatory—and insubordinate—finger at his captain. "You did that on purpose!"

"It's the Hama," Thurgood said as the alien craft shot through the clouds after them, spraying blaster fire across the sky. Another lucky shot drilled through the *Galahad*'s canopy and the planet's air began filling the cabin, whistling like Higlee's right nostril. Antarius shook his head. "That's going to get annoying."

The console in front of him screamed a thousand alarms as they flew closer to the canyons. Proximity alarms warned that the ground was too close. Hull integrity alarms whined about all the holes in the ship. And, apparently, a door was open somewhere in the back. It was all too much to begin with, and then the reactor filter light came on. Thurgood tuned out the chaos and stared into the canyon ahead. It was time to shut off his conscious mind and give his magnificent reflexes the stick.

A quick glance in the rearview camera confirmed the wicked-looking ship had fallen in right behind them.

"That's right, you bastards. Stay close."

"This is insane!" Higlee shouted, still plastered to the viewport.

"Fortune doesn't favor the cowardly, Higlee."

"It's Hinkley!"

Thurgood ignored the outburst. "It's time for a little Follow the Leader." He grinned and pointed the *Galahad* at the ground.

The computer had an absolute fit as he took the *Galahad* below the horizon line into the narrow canyons.

He banked hard as the canyon doglegged left, which sent Higlee sliding down the viewport. It made a sickly screeching sound as the first officer tried to hold on with all of his skin. It left a smudge.

A quick right changed everything, and Higlee grunted as the forces of gravity pulled him in the opposite direction. He skipped a bit before another left started the whole process over.

"Hold on, Higlee," Thurgood shouted as he wrestled the flight yoke back and forth. For millions of years, the river at the bottom of the canyon had meandered, carving through rock and minerals to form the massive rock walls. And in all that time, it had never once made up its mind as to where it was going.

Thurgood tried to predict the turns and did his best to think like a river. *Flow, flow, erode,* he thought, and began to sway like the river racing against its own banks. *Flow, slosh, crash, flood*. He became the river. Smashing against the canyon walls that formed his prison. Desperately rushing for freedom. Clawing at the ground beneath him. Upset that animals kept peeing in him. *Rage, rush, ruin!* The mental transformation was so complete that his hands grew wet on the controls.

The next series of turns came faster, and Higlee grunted

louder as his journey across the viewscreen's transparent steel intensified. The *Galahad* shot though the canyon like a twig on the current. And, just like that twig, it bashed against the rocks on nearly every turn.

Metal shrieked.

Higlee whined.

Thurgood was pretty sure they lost an engine.

But soon, the floating stick of a spacecraft emerged from the twists and turns of the ancient canyon into the widening mouth of a river that had found its way to peace.

Higlee dropped back to the deck and half-crawled, half-whimpered back to the navigator's seat.

Thurgood laughed triumphantly and checked the rear camera. The display showed only the canyon walls behind them and they were growing smaller in the distance. "Let's see them make it through that."

The blast drove the nose of the *Galahad* into the river. Thurgood pulled up as water cascaded over the viewport and started dripping into the cabin through the holes in the roof.

"Where the hell did that come from?" he shouted.

"They're above us." Higlee said it as if he had known all along.

"What do you mean above us? How can that be?"

"They are flying above the canyon and firing down on us."

"They didn't follow us into the canyon?"

"Of course they didn't follow us into the canyon!"

"Why the hell didn't they follow us into the canyon?"

"Why the hell would they? Did you really think they would follow your dumb ass into a canyon?"

"Yes!"

"Why would they do that? Why would anyone do that?"

"Because that's how it works, Higlee!" Thurgood screamed at

the first officer, and then sighed. "These Hama bastards don't even know what they're doing."

The blasts came faster, and the *Galahad* began to rock back and forth as the hull did its best to absorb the energy.

Higlee swore. "I'm trying to get a rescue signal through. But they're jamming everything."

Antarius smashed the console. "They don't even understand the rules of war! How is it they have the Alliance on its heels?"

A Hama blast passed through the ceiling and exited through the floor, leaving a glowing red hole in each surface and the distinct smell of ozone hanging in the air.

More alarms went off and started yelling at him. He wished the *Galahad* had a mute button. All the pessimism was distracting. Also, something was on fire somewhere behind him. That wasn't helping his concentration either.

Every blast created a new problem, and the Hama weren't letting up.

Higlee was still trying to get a distress call through, but Thurgood had had enough.

"What kind of pilot doesn't follow someone into a canyon?" he asked aloud. "A cowardly pilot. That's the kind."

"Would you get us out of here!?" Higlee was a wreck. He had forgotten everything they had taught him at the academy about listening to your captain. He had lost all professionalism. That would be going in his report.

Thurgood cut right and pulled the *Galahad* out of the canyon. The ship struggled to climb and he found himself skimming the treetops. He could no longer distinguish between shots from the Hama pursuit ship and brushes with the foliage below. Both continued to increase in frequency until the flight yoke went slack in his hands.

Thurgood released the controls and leaned back in his seat.

"What are you doing?" Higlee was in a full panic now. "Why aren't you flying?"

"I've got bad news, Higlee."

The first officer jumped out of his seat and raced across the deck. He dove for the controls and pulled back on the stick while yelling, "Pull up!"

"Yeah. Why didn't I think of that? Good thing you're here."

It was useless, but he had to give the man credit. Higlee did his best to fly a dead ship.

The engines went out next. There was no sputtering or exploding; they just suddenly stopped making that comforting hum that somehow kept spaceships in the air.

Thurgood checked his harness. "I think you're going to want to buckle up."

Higlee turned to Thurgood. "I hate you."

"I hate you, too, Higlee."

"It's—"

The trees below the ship rang out like artillery fire as they snapped under the craft's momentum. It wasn't long before all forward motion stopped.

Jungles don't have hands. Not Earth jungles, anyway. Nor any of the other jungles he'd seen in his adventures. But it was like the jungle below them reached up and grabbed the *Galahad* out of mid-air.

The stop was sudden and quite painful. Thurgood slammed against the restraining harness. There was just enough time for the bruises to begin forming before the vertical part of the crashing began.

It was the part of crashing he had always liked the least.

It always lasted longer than Antarius thought it would. And this time was no different. He didn't blame himself for the poor estimates. How would he have any idea how tall the trees grew here? He knew nothing about the planet, much less its vegetation. And his first officer wasn't much help. Higlee had managed to grab ahold of some equipment, but he was just screaming as they spun and toppled their way to the ground.

The *Galahad* finally hit Terra Firma, or Wherever Firma, ass end first. Thurgood looked up through the viewscreen at the sky and treetops above them. What limbs they hadn't snapped on their way to the ground had moved back into place and given them a moment's cover from their pursuers.

"Have we stopped?" Higlee asked.

"I doubt it."

The man was all but hysterical. He was almost shrieking now. "And what do you know?"

Thurgood did his best to remain calm. Panicking solved little, and calmness was reassuring. "I'm not saying I know. Call it a gut feeling. I've been in situations like this before, and I just feel like we're not all the way crashed yet."

"They are still out there." Higlee climbed down from the post he had clung to during the crash. He stood on the front of his console and examined the path he'd need to take to get to the door. "I've got to find a way down."

"I'd give it a minute." Thurgood tightened his harness.

The first officer dropped his legs over the side of the console and lowered himself down until he was dangling by his hands. "With all due respect, Captain, you're a moron."

"Well, I think it's clear that you don't know what 'with all due respect' means."

Higlee eyed his landing spot and dropped out of sight. Thurgood tried to see where the man had landed, but his safety harness prevented him from turning far enough.

"Higlee?"

There was no reply from Higlee, but the world outside answered with the snapping of one final tree and the *Galahad* fell flat against the ground. Flat-ish. There was still a severe list, but at least they were right side up.

"There. Now, we're all the way crashed," Thurgood confirmed with a nod as he unbuckled his harness and leaned forward to examine the console. "Now, let's see where we are."

The screen in front of him was cracked and wiggled funny when he brought up the query screen. As he entered his question, the computer interrupted to tell him about the hull breach. He swiped as many of the alarms away as possible and brought the query screen back up. His question was simple; where in the hell were they?

For a moment it seemed as if the computer wasn't going to answer him. It just hummed as it tried to figure out what the hell was going on. It finally returned a simple answer: Altair.

"Altair, is it?" Thurgood punched in another query. "Now, let's find us some allies."

The computer responded with a low squawk and red text.

"Uninhabited? That can't be right."

Another alarm demanded his attention. This one was new and gentler than the rest. It's the only reason he paid it any mind. He hit the associated switch and the display changed to an overhead map of the area. It was patchy, as if the ship's computer was missing information. An icon representing the Hama ship moved slowly over the area in a standard search pattern.

"Did you lose something, boys?" Thurgood watched the icon as it swept the skies. Eventually, the icon slowed. "Higlee, it looks like the Hama are looking for a place to land. I wonder how far it is to a clearing."

Thurgood punched at the keys, but the console sparked, caught fire and the screen went blank.

"Quitter." Antarius kicked the console before unbuckling his harness. "Well, it looks like it's just you and me, Higlee."

The first officer didn't respond.

"Oh, don't be that way, Higlee." He stood and stretched the crash out of his back. There were several satisfying pops and he sighed. "Yes, things were said in the heat of the chase. Hurtful things. But I'm sure you didn't mean them and... oh, damn."

His first officer was suspended a few feet in the air with several pieces of metal sticking out of his chest. He couldn't identify all of them, but some were electrical conduits because they sparked and sputtered with sharp cracks of electric blue, causing the man's body to twitch in response. Once Thurgood moved closer and examined the tragedy, he discovered that Higlee had become impaled on the ship's Emergency Response and Medical Aid bot.

"Poor bastard. Killed by irony," Thurgood muttered, and was almost overcome with emotion. But, instead, he straightened and adjusted his resolve. There would be a time to mourn Higlee and ERMA. But that time would come later. Now, it was time for vengeance. Higlee deserved that much. Sure, Thurgood hadn't been looking forward to an endless stream of *I told you so*'s. But that didn't mean he had wanted the man to die. An Alliance officer's life had been taken, and the only proper response was revenge. It was his duty as the man's superior officer.

Solemnly and reverently, he removed one of the man's dog tags and held it in his fist. "Take heart, my friend. I'll avenge your death. I swear on my station that you, First Officer Higlee, will not have died in vain." He touched his lips to his fist and nodded before opening his palm and studying the tag. "Hinkley? Oh, I was way off. I'm surprised you never said anything."

Thurgood dropped the tag in his shirt pocket. "I'm... I am sorry about that. Still, the revenge oath stands. Just with your real name in place of the other one I was using." An awkward silence followed the oath, so Thurgood excused himself from the conversation. "I need to go."

Antarius turned away from the dead man and patted the sidearm holstered at his hip. "It looks like it's just you and me. Let's go hunt some Hama."

THREE

A Clever Deceit

The *Galahad* had only been in Thurgood's charge for a short time while he awaited re-assignment of a new capital ship. Despite this short time together, he felt an attachment to her, and as he made his way to the cargo bay, he felt every hole in her hull as if it had struck his own self. He was starting to feel like he had let her down.

It was all nonsense, of course. The Hama were to blame for the ship's sorry state. He had done everything in his power to save her from those monsters.

Altairian air reached into the ship like some tentacled mist, replacing the stale but familiar recycled air of interstellar travel with a damp aura that smelled faintly sweet. He caught only brief hints of it as he passed through the ship, but when he lowered the gangplank, the smell overcame him as the alien atmosphere rushed in and filled the ship. The air was muggy and tasted like feet, and he hated the way it sat in his lungs. He spat and discovered that on the way out, it tasted like wet feet.

At least it was breathable and he could forgo the envirosuit. Those things were not only uncomfortable and unbecoming, but they would make kicking Hama ass all the more difficult. And, being outnumbered, he was already at a significant disadvantage.

Once the loading ramp settled into the planet, he got his real first look at the world. It looked purple. Like a deep bruise.

He stepped from the ship and felt his foot sink into Altair. The surface was spongy, and each step he took wrung water from the ground and released another wave of stench into the air. The smell made him wretch. "No wonder this stupid place is uninhabited."

Thurgood ducked back inside the gangway for cover as the Hama ship passed overhead. Wash from the engines blew back the leaves that formed the jungle canopy and sent a thousand birds flapping into the air and shrieking a confused song that sounded a lot like the planet smelled.

Antarius grunted. "Not uninhabited enough."

Once the ship passed, the branches and birds settled back into place and Thurgood moved back down into the jungle. One of the pouches on his belt held a standard issue scout drone. He removed the device and looked up into the trees. "Let's see where they're going."

Antarius tossed the drone into the air and watched as it reached its zenith three feet above his head. It peaked, plummeted and hit the ground with a wet, spongey splat. Thurgood prodded the machine with his toe several times, but it was soon clear that no amount of poking would get the device to work, and poking was pretty much the extent of his troubleshooting abilities.

"Quitter," he sneered at the drone. "This is going in my report."

And it would, but that report would have to wait. Without the drone, he was going to have to scout the old-fashioned way —by climbing to the top of his spaceship and looking around with his eyes like some kind of caveman. It certainly wasn't optimal, but it was necessary.

Scaling the outside of the ship wasn't much trouble. Thurgood had always been a gifted athlete, and there was no shortage of hand- and footholds on the hull. Access ladders and the angle of the crash made it easy enough to get to the top, and he made his way to the highest point of the crash site, roughly above the cockpit. Unfortunately, it wasn't high enough. The jungle had all but swallowed the craft and, even standing on his toes, he wasn't able to view the surrounding landscape. He would have to go higher.

Thurgood reached out and grabbed a vine he expected to feel like damp feet. To his relief, it was woody like an Earth vine, and felt solid enough. He tested it by lifting one leg off the ground and then the other. Then he lifted both of his legs at the same time. The vine shifted under his weigh but held to its anchorage point somewhere high above him. He climbed. Hand over hand, he moved up into the trees of Altair until he reached where the vine had draped itself over a limb.

Measuring several feet wide, the limb held his weight easily, and Thurgood wondered if any tree on Earth could compare as he walked out the branch's length. The air didn't smell as footy at this height. In fact, the tree leaves gave off a fresh scent not unlike a neutral bathroom spray. It was pleasant and a shame that the aroma never quite reached the forest floor.

He reached the end of the branch and got his first look at the Altairian countryside. It was mostly trees, but from here he could see the rim of the canyons and, more importantly, the enemy ship as it circled the area searching for a place to land.

The jungle made it difficult to land if you weren't a really good crasher, but the Hama ship finally found a clearing several klicks away and was beginning its descent. He'd spotted the open terrain on the way down and he could have crashed there if he'd wanted to but, as he would note in his report, he'd crashed into the forest instead because, to ships, trees were soft and cushioned the impact. It was simple physics.

Thurgood watched through a pair of binoculars as the enemy ship settled into the ground. He could only imagine the stench it was stirring up. Even with a controlled descent, the ship lurched to starboard as the damp ground beneath the craft shifted. But he had to give credit where credit was due—it was technically a better landing than his. Even if it was completely lacking in flair.

The alien craft was one the Alliance classified a Hama Declavar Class Scout Ship. The best estimates put the ship's crew at no more than four or five men from the Imperial Navy. Up until this point, a scout ship's operations were assumed to be entirely space-based. It was a surprising move for them to follow him down to the planet. Or maybe it wasn't a surprise at all. He didn't know. There was still a lot about the Hama that remained a mystery. The biggest of which was how they had avoided detection in the galaxy for so long. The Alliance's best minds had been working on it for some time, and together they had come up with a collective shrug.

This time, he was thankful the enemy had strayed from protocol. Their ship was his ticket off the foot-smelling rock of a planet. All he had to do was overcome a four- or five-to-one advantage, take out his opponents without getting himself killed, steal their ship and fly home. Those odds didn't bother him. As the son of the galaxy's richest man, he had faced hardships before and knew a thing or two about overcoming challenges.

His confidence was bolstered by the fact that they were navy troops. As far as the Alliance knew, there were no terrestrial operators assigned to the Declavars. The enemy would be operating out of their element.

The Hama gangplank lowered and the captain got his first look at his enemies. Three gray-faced men walked down the ramp and stepped onto the mushy planet. It was on. They were armed with Hama battle carbines and covered from head to toe in a modular armor. This would give them an advantage. Ballistic protection would be minimal against energy weapons, but the information fed into the helmets would be invaluable. There was every indication the Empire's tech was on par with the Alliance, and this made it safe to assume that sensor arrays would relay battlefield information directly to a display inside the helmets. And they wouldn't have to smell this place. Another advantage for them.

No other soldiers followed them down the plank. One or two would most likely remain behind to guard the ship. This meant he was only facing the three on the ground. His odds were improving, and it was time to develop a plan.

Thurgood had always believed in a strong offense. The sooner an opponent was neutralized, the better. Often, he tried to neutralize people before they knew they were his opponents. This strategy saved a lot of trouble and had proven quite effective in his days at the Academy. It was one of the reasons he had risen so quickly through the ranks.

Here, it would be different. The Hama were on their guard. They were armed. And, as of right now, he didn't know of any embarrassing stories or nicknames he could exploit to undermine their confidence, and he was pretty sure it was going to take more than a locker room towel fight to get them to cry and go home.

He had but one advantage. They knew the *Galahad* had crashed. But they didn't know if there were any survivors. Their first move would be to locate the ship and search the wreckage for survivors and intel.

Antarius couldn't hide the ship. It was too big, and much of it was on fire. But he could make sure they found what he wanted them to find. Misdirection was one of his specialties. Even his instructors at the Academy had noted this. They'd always referred to his way of thinking as counter-intelligence. He smiled to himself as he made his way back down the tree to put his plan into action.

Back inside the ship, he went to work. The computers were easy enough to disable, as they were mostly disabled to begin with. He found one of the few terminals that still worked and enabled a worm that would erase any data the enemy could find useful. He wasn't a technical man and didn't know exactly how the worm worked, but when he'd asked, he had been assured that the worm would survive any crash and still be able to eat away the data. It sounded like a remarkable creature.

Even so, it was his sworn duty to make sure that vital information never fell into the hands of the enemy, so he drew his sidearm and blasted what was left of the consoles. Smoke rose and several smaller fires began, but he was confident that between the high-tech worm and the good old-fashioned bullets, any information in the ship's computer would be inaccessible.

But counter-intelligence thinking wasn't just stopping one's enemy from gaining intelligence. It also meant making them dumber by making them think something that wasn't even so.

He tried to think like the Hama. It was a cringe-inducing process, but a necessary one. He had to put himself in their shoes and view the situation from their perspective. Sure, the computers were destroyed. But why? If there were no survivors on board, who would have done this?

Thurgood cursed. He had outsmarted himself once again. It happened often, and he assumed all great men often found themselves in such a predicament, but that thought was little consolation when pressed for time. He left his own pity party early and got back to the problem at hand.

If there were gunshots, there had to be a survivor, and the first officer was obviously quite dead. So the question was, why would a dead man shoot his gun at all? He stared at Higlee's body hanging on the wall and let several thoughts roll around in his head until one slowly settled like a die cast by Fate. The answer was suicide.

Thurgood dove into a nearby locker, produced a pen and paper and began to weave a sorrowful note of despair. This was counter-intelligence at its best. Misinformation was most effective when it left a paper trail.

Higlee's story was a tale of unrequited love and regret. It began with a crush and developed into a full-on obsession. The man lost sleep, thinking of his one and only. It was only recently he'd heard of her intent to wed another. This had sent the *Galahad*'s "captain" into a downward spiral of booze and narcotic abuse. These self-destructive habits led to his reckless decision to engage the Hama patrol ship. It was his intent to die in a blaze of glory. But duty overcame his despair as he realized the *Galahad* could not fall into enemy hands. So, he ran. And though he survived the crash, he could not live with the shame his life had become. So, he would shoot himself. The End.

Thurgood signed the note as Captain Higlee, folded it and tucked it into the first officer's breast pocket. He buttoned the pocket and straightened the metal name tag attached to the flap. He opened the pocket back up, removed the note, crossed out *Higlee*, wrote *Hinkley* and replaced the note in the pocket.

Satisfied, he turned to study the scenario he had created. It was important to look at it through the eyes of a skeptic. His confidence told him the picture he had created was ironclad, but he needed to remove himself from the situation and do his best to shoot holes in it. And he was glad he did.

A normal man wouldn't see it, but if the Hama had one trained eye among them, they might ask why, if a man was trying to shoot himself, did so many computers get hit by gunfire?

Possibly, to prevent the enemy from accessing the information within. Those would be the thoughts of a rational captain. But "Captain" Hinkley was obviously not in a proper state of mind, as evidenced by the suicide note. It would take further counter-intelligence to make the story bulletproof.

He pulled the note out one more time and added a P.S. where Hinkley lamented how poor a shot he was and what a disappointment it would be for his love to learn it had taken him nearly a dozen shots before he finally struck himself.

Satisfied, Thurgood saluted the first officer. He didn't like the man. He thought he was a coward, insubordinate and more than a little annoying. But that was no reason to disrespect the man. He tucked the note in the man's pocket and turned away.

Now that all of the "survivors" had been taken care of, it was time to plan his own survival. It couldn't be too hard. Surviving was just not dying, and he had been doing that all of his life. Besides, he had graduated near the top of his survival class at the academy.

He pulled open the emergency access panel and looked at the survival kits inside. He hesitated to take one at all, as the Hama may notice one missing. As a P.P.S. in a suicide note would be suspect, he decided to risk it without an explanation. He decided the risk was minimal as the Hama would have no way of knowing how many kits would have been stowed to begin with. It was simple math. Unknown minus one was still unknown.

Rifling through the bag, he took stock of the contents. There was a first aid kit, a water filtration device, an emergency blanket and a lot of other boring stuff that would be pretty useless in helping him fight the Hama. He could see maybe throwing the emergency blanket over one of their heads and hitting them with the survival machete while they struggled to get free. But other than that, the contents wouldn't be much help. Thurgood made a mental note to file a formal suggestion requesting that, in the future, all Alliance Emergency Survival Kits should include at least one survival bazooka.

There was a SERE suit folded at the bottom of the bag. He spread the suit out and smiled. "Finally. An edge."

The suit was a coverall of loose-fitting fabric designed to be worn over his uniform. At first, he looked like a gray sock with eyes, a cast member in the world's worst puppet show. But, once activated, the SERE suit's active camouflage would render him all but invisible and provide him with a distinct advantage over his enemy.

His next stop was the armory. It sounded a lot cooler than it actually was. As part of the Alliance's insistence on subtlety, there were no secret caches of weapons hidden behind false walls. But there was a sportsman's armory befitting the adventurous owner of the pleasure craft. The room was stocked with ornate hunting rifles. The weapons were more suited to hunting Grande Mals on Ryastar than engaging with the enemy, but they were his best option. He pulled one of the rifles from the display and slung it over his shoulder.

Draped in evasive tech, armed with an antique and satisfied with the narrative he had left on the bridge, Thurgood exited the ship through an emergency access hatch that closed behind him. Once the Hama found the ship, gaining access would still prove difficult. His ruse may not even be needed in the end. If all went according to his plan, the Hama would be dead or deserted on the planet before nightfall, and he would be halfway home in their ship. This was the most likely outcome, but it was a fool who left things to Fate.

Outside the ship, the smell hadn't improved. But now he was able to pinpoint it. The smell was strongest where the moss was thickest. This moss covered the forest floor and had been present in the trees, too. The whole area wore it like a dank fur. But where others saw a hirsute landscape that reeked like feet, he saw the upside. As he walked, the thick moss masked the sound of his footsteps. The planet had given him his second advantage. Thanks to the suit, he was nearly invisible. And now, thanks to the disgusting nature of the planet, he was all but silent.

Antarius pulled the hood down over his face and drew a deep breath. He had a lot of ground to cover to get to the ship. Being a man of science, he knew the shortest distance between two points was a straight line. He drew the survival machete and started into the forest.

FOUR

The Road to Ruins

Cutting through thick vines and small trees with the survival machete, Antarius hacked and hiked his way through the jungle forest for an hour. The growth was thicker in places where a starship hadn't recently crashed and the standard issue blade wasn't cut out for the job. It would have been more helpful if they had included a survival chainsaw or survival plasma logger. If they could fit a small lumberjack into the bag, that would have also been helpful.

There was little change in the terrain during that first hour. It was just tree after tree with the occasional small clearing where the moss grew inches thick and extra funky. The smell was still an issue, but these areas gave his aching feet a respite. It was like walking on one of the luxurious rugs that lined his family home back on Earth, only squishier. If he could only find a way to acclimate to the stench, the moss could serve as a mattress and offer a good night's sleep.

Altair's climate had proven hospitable enough. The air was mild if not a little muggy, but it wasn't so hot that the heat drained him. Thurgood wiped his brow and attacked another wall of vines with the hope he was still moving in the right direction. Parts of the forest were so thick he wondered if the Hama could ever find the *Galahad* at all. Or if he could find it again, if need be.

It didn't matter much. There was no turning back now. He had to take the Hama ship and report back to the Alliance. It was his only option.

Earlier in the day, he had come across something of a trail. It wasn't much of one, but if you squinted just right and believed with all your heart, then it was a trail. He couldn't say for sure if it had been made by man or by beast, but something had traveled its length long ago.

It didn't matter much to him who or what had made the path. It was going in his general direction. It was overgrown, of course, but less so than the rest of the forest, and the vines hung only half as thick. But they still hung. The survival machete was earning its place in the bag despite its poor quality.

The latest wall of vines fell after several blows and revealed a clearing in the jungle. It also solved the riddle of the trail.

"No beast blazed this path," Antarius said as he took in the ancient ruins before him. They filled the clearing, and even though they were riddled with vines and covered in that damn moss, the unmistakable alabaster of ancient architecture shone through.

They had been buildings once. Their roofs had collapsed long ago to be absorbed by the ground cover, and some of the walls had crumbled into piles, but their support columns still rose up into the forest canopy. Some were as high as the trees themselves.

Thurgood put a hand on one of the columns. It was smooth to the touch. The scalloped cuts in the stone were perfectly symmetrical, all of it the work of an ancient, master craftsman.

The machete made short work of some vines covering an

ancient bench, and he sat to catch his breath and take in the scene. He hated ruins.

Every planet you ever went to: "Do you want to see our ruins?" It didn't matter if you were on a diplomatic mission or just stopping in for some fuel, it was always the same. "Do you want to see our ruins?"

"No, I don't want to see your ruins. No one wants to see your ruins. Why would I want to spend my time looking at something that is literally ruined when I could be spending it doing something new?"

But, bagging on people's ruins was considered rude and sometimes "cause for interplanetary conflict," as was stamped on his personnel file. So, you had to see the ruins.

Even Earth—arguably the most successful planet in the history of ever—made a big deal about their ruins both locally and to any poor alien who stopped by for a visit to the Alliance's capital world. "I know you traveled thousands of light-years at a speed once thought unimaginable, possibly for the first time in the most advanced technology the galaxy has ever known... but do you want to see some old rocks that look kind of like the outline of a house?"

Thurgood had made several proposals that all Earth ruins be razed to the ground. Again. Or further. Or whatever it took. His plan was met with great resistance, but the only argument they had for him was nostalgia. He had nothing against history. And if those civilizations had succeeded, it would be a different story. But why would a planet want to brag about its missteps? It was a sign of weakness to be proud of such failures. "Look, here's where we couldn't make society work" was an odd boast in his mind.

Altair had the worst ruins he had ever seen. There wasn't even a snack hut or a Dippin' Dots cart. Not even an off-brand equivalent. That was the bare minimum for a local attraction if you wanted to be taken seriously as a planet. Planets usually went much further with it by including local delicacies and cultural mainstays like bathhouses or salting huts. The lack of amenities and crumbling, vine-covered state of things here told him he was dealing with a very uncivilized place indeed.

But, unlike most ruins, they weren't completely useless. Thurgood slung the survival pack across his back and made for the tallest column. The vines once again provided much-needed handholds and footing, and he climbed his way to the top of the tower.

It had been hours since setting out, and a view from the top could give him back his bearings. The column was taller than he had estimated. The top of the structure broke through the forest canopy and gave him the best view of the planet he'd had so far.

The Hama ship was closer than he had expected. He was at least halfway to the enemy landing site, and that meant he had made better time through the jungle than he'd expected. This knowledge put a new pep in his step as he climbed back down the column. If he applied himself, he could be there, conquer the enemy, steal their ship and get off this mossy rock in just a couple of hours.

He dropped the final ten feet back into the center of the ruins and found himself face to face with a figure clad in battle armor. The man's visor was down over his face, but Thurgood could tell the Hama soldier was just as surprised as he was.

Antarius hid his surprise better. They both shrieked their surprise and stumbled backward, but Thurgood's shriek wasn't as high-pitched, and the column stopped him from tripping like the Hama scout did.

Both men regained their composure in a matter of seconds and squared off in the middle of the ancient ruins.

Antarius unslung the hunting rifle. This gave him the advantage. The Hama was unarmed.

But soon, so was Thurgood.

It had to be some form of alien kung fu that had disarmed him so easily and placed him neatly on his back. Alien kung fu or extraterrestrial magic. The man had somehow disarmed him from several feet away and knocked him over. Thurgood was leaning more toward alien kung fu, but it would be foolish to dismiss the possibility that he was about to engage in a life-and-death struggle with a space wizard. They say you only make that kind of mistake once. Personally, he had made it twice before, and he wasn't about to make it a third time.

Thurgood scrambled out of the way as a Hama boot came crashing toward his head. He got back to his feet and planted his own foot in the Hama's chest. This sent the enemy flailing back across the ruins, pinwheeling his arms to keep his balance.

Antarius tried to draw his sidearm but found it trapped in the overly ornamental officer's holster. After struggling with the flap for a few moments, he panicked and drew the emergency machete instead. He held the blade tight against any potential spells. Then he saw it. It was a blur in the alien's hands, but the Hama twirled a rope in a figure eight pattern at a speed fast enough to generate a hum.

He was relieved it wasn't magic. Rope was much easier to fight than wizards. He assumed. He couldn't recall ever fighting rope before. Certainly not one this fast.

As if it was alive, the rope stopped twirling and shot toward him. It moved fast and struck hard. Thurgood felt its impact on the hand that was holding the machete. The blow stung enough to elicit a reflex and he drew back his hand. By the time he had assessed the situation and prepared to counterattack, the rope was a spinning shield in front of the Hama.

The scout stepped fluidly side to side. His body had a gentle sway that gave the rope its momentum. Antarius understood the physics behind it, but as he rubbed the bruise on the back of his hand, he wondered how rope could hurt.

It came flying at him again, and he ducked under the attack. It came again, and he stepped sideways as the rope struck the ground in an overhead swing. Thurgood dodged while the Hama leapt and spun to make the rope do his bidding. It became an almost obscene dance, and once Antarius recognized his part in the choreography, he decided to put a stop to it.

He stood his ground and, like a snake, the rope darted out for the machete. Unlike a snake, the rope used a small weight at the end to wrap itself around his wrist. So that's what hurt. It wasn't the rope at all.

The Hama jerked on the rope to pull the weapon from his hand, but Thurgood was ready for it, and the machete wasn't going anywhere he didn't want it to go.

The scout grabbed the rope with both his hands to jerk again. Before he could pull, Thurgood seized the rope and heaved. The force sent the Hama stumbling toward him.

By the time his opponent reached him, the man was pitched forward. Thurgood grabbed him by the back of the helmet and drove his knee through the Hama battle visor, shattering the screen.

He pulled the man back up. Some of the black material from the visor had found its way into the alien's face. Purple blood ran from the wounds and filled the creases in the alien's gray skin. The man screamed in a fit of rage and wrenched himself free of Thurgood's grasp.

Antarius let him back away. He unwrapped the rope weapon from his wrist and tossed it into the ruins. The Hama picked at the glass in his face, wincing as he pulled out the shards one by one.

"Don't worry, Scarface. I'm sure she liked you for your personality."

He couldn't be sure the Hama understood him, but from the look on the man's bloodied face, he'd definitely touched a nerve or two. The scout drew a blade of his own.

It was only half the size of the machete and this made Thurgood chuckle. He waved his own blade with a flourish fit for a pirate.

Then the scout drew a second blade and grunted as he performed his own flourish. His was much more elaborate. The display included a leap, a kick, several twirls and when it was all said and done, each blade was pointed in a different direction than it had begun.

Thurgood got the impression the man had done this before. He swung the machete once more for good measure and made sure he swung it hard enough to make that dramatic swooshing noise.

A scream preceded the scout's charge, and the man came at him with a flurry of feet and blades.

The blows came so fast, Antarius couldn't tell if it was a foot or a knife until it hit him. He let his reflexes take the wheel. It was all he could do. He countered what strikes he could with the machete but mostly found himself ducking under ruins to avoid the swiftly moving blades. Sparks flew as metal met ancient stone. It was all very frantic and exhausting. This use of blades was barbaric and another reason Thurgood believed the Hama Empire needed to be quickly relegated to a forgotten place in history.

He managed to stay ahead of the stabs until he rolled under a fallen pillar. He leapt to his feet on the other side and a knife dug deep into his left arm. He twisted away with the knife still stuck in his arm and demanded a minute.

His opponent was surprisingly accommodating.

Thurgood touched the knife's handle and winced. "Oh, that is… that is tender." He took a deep breath and pulled the blade out of his arm. A lot of blood came with it and he could hear the smugness on his enemy's face.

He looked up and, sure enough, the gray-face bastard was smirking at him.

"That was a lucky shot." Thurgood tossed the blade into the jungle and the fight was back on.

It was no less frantic than before.

The more he moved, the more his arm hurt. He realized he couldn't keep it up for long. It was crucial he end the fight quickly. So, he became the aggressor. He kept the blade moving and advanced, putting pressure on the scout and bullying him around the ruins. His slashes drew blood several times but failed to land a killing blow. His aggravation and boredom grew. He was losing time and more than a little blood chasing this loser around. It was time to take a risk.

Thurgood left himself exposed to draw a lunge from the scout. The blade cut through his side but it was worth the gambit. He connected with his opponent's wrist and the knife dropped to the ground. The scout backed away nursing a wrist covered in purple blood. The fight was his.

Raising the machete made his side hurt. His left arm hurt whether he moved it or not. It was time to finish this.

His killing blow cut only the air as his enemy rolled under the swing. Another slash and the Hama jumped back just enough to keep his stomach away from the blade's edge. This became something of a pattern. Slice, cut. Duck, dodge. It was getting tiresome.

"We all know how this ends," Antarius said after another failed swing. "Just let me kill you and we can both get on with our days."

There was fear in his opponent's eyes. It was satisfying to see.

"You're just drawing things out. You have—" he slashed.

The Hama leapt forward over the blade, rolled and came up with the rope weapon in his hand.

"Dammit."

The weighted end of the rope struck out and rapped Thurgood's knuckles.

"Ouch! Dammit, I hate that thing!" Antarius lunged, but that damn rope bit him again. It wasn't big but it was enough to parry his blows and cause his fingers to ache. Even worse, the Hama was getting his confidence back. The fear was leaving his eyes.

Every attack was countered by that damn rope.

Thurgood finally had enough. He threw the machete to the ground, grabbed a piece of ruin and heaved it at the Hama scout.

The rope flung out and struck the rock with a metallic *chank*. The rock struck the Hama with a wet *shunk* and the fight was over.

"Looks like rock beats rope," he said with a smile, and wished someone else had been around to hear it. But he was alone. "Stupid, uninhabited planet."

Despite the smashing victory, Thurgood realized luck had played a role in his triumph. He and Luck had always had a strained relationship, but he had never been foolish enough to dismiss the role fortune had played in his life. She was fickle, Luck. Just like all the songs said. And while he usually enjoyed tempting Fate, he was alone against the enemy and this savage world. The entire planet was literally against him. He would have to be more careful.

After examining his wounds, he found that most of the cuts were superficial and needed only a light dressing. Several items from the first aid kid provided almost instant relief from the wounds. He didn't want to exhaust the kit so early into his stay, but the wounds on his left arm and waist did require the use of a nanite injection. Science told him he couldn't feel the little buggers patching up the damaged tissue, but he always thought it tickled nonetheless.

Thurgood took stock of the kit's contents. There was still plenty left, but he couldn't afford to take any more chances. He would have to do his best to eliminate the rest of the Hama without being detected.

FIVE

Pray for the Predator

The forest grew thicker and his arm grew weary as he cut his way to the ship. The trail that had brought him to the ruins ended there as well, and his way forward was choked with vines and exposed roots that tripped him up as he made his way through. Progress had been slowed by half, and his frustration grew as he imagined spending a night in the wild. His was a body tempered for hotels and captain's quarters, not mossy forest floors that smelled like old leather shoes and pickle juice. The thought of lying down in that filth drove him on, and the machete swung with a new enthusiasm.

At least now he knew which way he was headed. The fallen Hama had yielded little of use in offense—Thurgood had not even been able to find the man's blade—but a transponder he found in the man's pocket was receiving a signal from the ship's beacon and guiding him to the landing site.

He followed the pulsating light on the screen for hours and saw it inch ever closer as the map's scale grew larger. Unlike some species he had encountered in his travels, the Hama language wasn't complete nonsense and the positioning device was quite obviously based on math, but the markings still looked like gibberish. But he figured as long as he made his way toward the blinking red light, he would find the ship.

A squawk from the device signaled a change. Three more dots appeared on the screen to indicate the position of the Hama crew. Another edge. And the best one yet.

Antarius felt his confidence boost as he activated the SERE suit's active camouflage. It was time to put his old survival training to use.

While the survival onesie did most of the work keeping him hidden, he liked to think he was doing his part. He remained perfectly motionless and stilled his breath to minimize his presence in the tree. Not breathing much didn't bother him because it also meant smelling less. Commanding absolute stillness from his body, he watched as the suit mapped the tree bark and replicated itself across the fabric. He was like one of those bugs that mimicked its surroundings to protect itself from predators.

No, that wasn't right. He was the predator. He wasn't hiding to keep himself safe. He was lying in wait—a trap set to spring. These weren't the markings of the prey, they were the markings of the apex killer. He wasn't some insect trying to look like a leaf, he was a leopard preparing to pounce.

He felt the muscles in his body coil as the metaphor crystalized in his mind. Picturing success was a vital step in achieving victory, and he envisioned his inevitable triumph. The Hama soldier would approach, clumsy yet vigilant, his black eyes keen and sharpened against the forest in front of him. But that vigilance was misdirected, for the threat was not before him, but above. The scout would undoubtedly stop beneath the tree, pausing to take in his surroundings—his last foolish mistake. For that's when the predator would strike. Not from ahead or behind but from above, the silent killer bringing instinct, strength and a survival machete to bear on his prey below.

Moving naught but his eyes, Thurgood checked the dot's location on the screen. It was dead center. That had to mean the scout was directly below him now. It was time to pounce like an apex predator.

With a movement that was all but imperceptible, Thurgood turned and spotted his prey. The man was peeing.

Thurgood paused. Did predators attack their prey while they were indisposed? He couldn't recall seeing a documentary where it happened. The prey was always eating. Not peeing. It would make sense to attack. Any advantage the predator could get, it would surely take. But it seemed a little unfair. Antarius was always up for a good fight, but he knew he wouldn't want to be sucker punched while doing his business.

It was kind of gross, too. He didn't want to get any on him. In theory, he would pounce, sail silently through the air like the apparition of death visiting the condemned, land on the Hama scout's back, knocking him to the ground face first, deliver the killing blow and move on to the next target. In theory.

But what if the guy turned? It would be embarrassing for all involved and someone was sure to get peed on.

The question *What would a leopard do?* was still repeating over and over in his mind when the scout spotted him in the tree. The man shouted something in Hameese and reached for his weapon. Thurgood screamed back in Leopard and jumped.

He hit before the scout could fire, and the two men crashed to the ground. The machete buried itself to the hilt in his opponent's chest, robbing the scout of the air needed to utter his final words. Their faces were inches apart. Antarius watched as his victim's lips worked in vain to form words as the last remnants of the man's life ebbed from his body, and his head fell back with a soft *phlurp* as it sunk into the moss.

Thurgood got up and looked down at the man. He felt no pride in what he had done. As it turned out, leopards were sneaky jerks. Out of respect for his noble prey, he decided to observe a moment of silence and hung his head in reverence. That's when he saw the wet spot on his survival suit.

"Oh, come on!" He'd been peed on. "I knew it was a bad idea."

He wrenched the machete from the man's chest, kicked the body and headed toward the next target on the screen while trying to find a way of walking where the wet spot wouldn't touch him.

***

Hanging from the side of the canyon wall, Thurgood began to feel like a local. He'd only been on the planet for a few hours and had already been someplace more than once. The woody vines provided a solid and comfortable perch over the lip of the canyon, and concealing himself in them had been more frightening than perilous. But, once in their embrace, he had the perfect place to lie in wait for his next target.

The icon on the locator was nearing his position, but this Hama scout was in no hurry. The dot on the device wandered around lazily. The wait was boring, but it gave Antarius time to admire the canyon from this new vantage. Racing through at full throttle with a Hama warship on your tail was no way to see the sights. One could also argue that hanging from a perch waiting to ambush and violently dispatch an enemy foot soldier wasn't a part of the ideal tourist package either, but it gave him something to do.

The more he studied the canyon, the more he wondered if it wasn't more of a chasm. Then he wondered if there was any difference between a canyon and a chasm at all. It could have been a gorge for all he knew. There was a river below him. Did that make it a ravine?

After a while, he decided he didn't care what it was, he just wanted to throw someone into it. The vines were starting to ride up in places.

The dot on the tracker meandered closer to his position often, but never close enough. He risked a peek over the canyon's rim and spotted the soldier. He pursed his lips to whistle.

No, that was stupid. There was nothing on the planet that would whistle. He didn't even know for sure if the Hama whistled. There hadn't been anything about it in the briefings.

If he couldn't whistle to get the guard's attention, he would imitate the local wildlife. He pursed his lips to make a sound like a bird but then realized he didn't know what birds sounded like on Altair. The last thing he wanted to do was make the sound of a robin or a goldfinch only to discover the scout was a junior ornithologist and recognized the calls as alien to the planet.

It was all becoming too much. Thurgood quieted his mind and listened. He listened to the planet. The river below. The air moving through the canyon. The trees swaying. And the birds. They were all around him. He heard their wings beat the air as they flew into the canyon and caught the air currents rising from below. And he heard their song. *Craw, craw.*

It wasn't wholly unfamiliar. The sound was much like Earth's crow but with a touch of an accent. Antarius repeated the sound softly to himself.

Craw, craw.

It possessed a calm and confident tone. This bird knew who he was and he wasn't looking to the world for validation.

Craw, craw.

There was sadness behind this confidence, however. A loneliness that only the successful could truly understand. Certainty was a trait many aspired to but still resented in others. They were ostracized and ridiculed when their backs were turned. Their success was both lauded as a worthy goal and loathed as unjust. Everyone aspired to be them but also hated them for their achievements.

Craw, craw.

It was a sound he knew too well. It was the same sound his heart made when he found himself alone with his greatness.

One of the birds landed on a vine near him and screeched. *Craw, craw.* It wasn't afraid of him in the least and its head flicked back and forth as it studied Thurgood.

"Craw, craw," Thurgood whispered. "I feel your pain, brother bird."

Craw, craw.

"Craw, craw," he answered back. "You and I are not that different. I, too, know the solitude of success. We are truly birds of a feather."

Thurgood reached out to his fellow majestic creature and extended a friendly finger for the bird to perch upon so he could unburden himself in the company of equals.

The little bastard bit him.

Thurgood pulled back his hand to find it was now bleeding. He put it in his mouth to stop the blood.

Craw, craw, the bird said before flying away.

"I am so sick of this planet."

Thurgood pulled himself up to the cliff's edge and cleared his throat. "Craw! Craw!" He shouted, perfectly capturing the nuance and existential pain of the local avian population.

It worked. The guard turned to investigate the sound and Antarius ducked back down out of sight.

"Craw! Craw!" He added a hint of sympathy into the call this time. It didn't hurt to tug at the heartstrings a little.

The icon on the locator moved toward him faster now. He could hear the scout's footsteps on the ground above him. Small rocks and soil fell as the man's boots sent the debris rolling over the edge of the canyon.

Antarius readied himself. He envisioned the man looking over the canyon for the bird that had summoned him. He would see nothing, dismiss the sound as a figment of his imagination and then turn away. That's when Thurgood would strike.

The man shouted something into the canyon that sounded like, "Gah!"

The translator in Antarius's ear deciphered the word as the equivalent of, "Hey!"

A half-second later, the call came back. "Gah! Gah! Gah!" The device in his ear repeated the translation. That settled it. It was a canyon after all. Ravines didn't have echoes. At least, he couldn't think of one that did.

The Hama scout laughed and shouted again. "Gah!"

Thurgood's ear said, "Hey."

The canyon said, "Gah! Gah! Gah!"

The translator said, "Hey! Hey! Hey!"

The man yelled again. The canyon. The man. The translator. The man. The echo.

"Gah! Hey! Gah! Gah! Hey! Hey! Gah! Hey! Gah! Hey! Hey! Gah! Gah!"

Thurgood screamed in frustration.

The translator said, "Wah!"

He pulled himself up the vines, grabbed the Hama scout by the belt and hurled the man from the ledge into the canyon.

"Gahhhhhh!" the Hama scout shouted all the way down.

"Heyyyyyy!" the translator screamed.

"Gahhhh, gahhhh, gahhhh."

"Heyyyy, heyyyy, heyyyy." The *heys* went on for a while. It was a long way down.

Another sound eventually reached his ear when the body landed on the bank of the river below. It sounded like *shunk*.

The translator beeped, "No known translation."

* * *

The third blip on his screen proved to be more of a challenge. The blip representing his target was approaching a small body of water, a perfect place for an ambush. Fashioning a crude snorkel from a piece of hollow vine, he moved silently into the water and grew still enough that the fish around him grew accustomed to his presence. He breathed through the stalk and waited patiently at the bottom of the pond, fighting buoyancy and boredom for nearly twenty minutes.

The blip moved closer and closer. But, just as his patience was to be rewarded, the target veered away from the pond and wandered back into the jungle toward the base of a cliff.

Concealing himself in a wall of mud, Antarius waited at the base of the cliff and wished he'd kept the snorkel. Breathing proved difficult as every exhale blew a bubble in the mud. But he was committed to the plan. It had not been easy, or pleasant, getting in there in the first place, and he marveled at how spas could charge for such treatment. It had taken some diligent wallowing to ensure he was covered from head to toe in the heavy soil. He had then backed into the wall and disappeared except for the whites of his eyes. He had tried rubbing the dirt in his eyes to cover them as well, but found it quite painful and counterproductive. With his eyes closed, he was all but invisible. Except for the bubbles.

Motionless, he stood like a very still rock, blending into the wall of mud as the dot on his tracker drew ever closer. He tightened his grip on the survival machete and prepared himself for the ambush that would surely come.

Twenty minutes later, the mud began to dry. And itch. He shifted, imperceptibly at first, trying to quell the sensation in some of the more sensitive areas. As it dried on his face, he felt the mud cracking and falling away from his lips. It left a tingling sensation which he at first dismissed as a trace amount of dirt hanging from the hairs on his face. Moments later he had convinced himself it was bugs.

Millions of bugs. Alien bugs crawling over his body. He didn't even like Earth bugs. Alien bugs were worse. Their feet felt different. They could be biters. And what if they had the ability to control minds? That was a stupid thought. But not completely unrealistic. Bug scientists could scoff at him all they wanted, but they had no firsthand knowledge of Altairian bugs. There wasn't as much as an amateur lepidopterist on the whole planet. So there was a chance he was right and those stuffed lab coats didn't know a thing. Or maybe they were just making him think they had mind control powers. He calmed himself. He was stronger than bugs. Even if they did try to take over his mind and force him to worship their bug gods, he was a man, dammit, he could fight it. He could outthink a bug. He had the bigger brain. He silenced his thoughts and remained still.

Until he thought about them getting into his pants.

Thurgood leapt from the wall of mud with a scream at the same moment the third target approached the base of the cliff.

This surprised both men.

The Hama soldier drew his pistol.

Thurgood slapped at it with the machete and knocked it from the man's hand. It landed on the ground. *Splurt*.

The scout turned and ran. It was the sensible thing to do. Covered in mud and screaming like a lunatic, Thurgood probably didn't even look human. And there was no telling what horrible creatures were hiding in the mud with the mind control bugs.

Antarius gave chase. It was a feat that proved more difficult than he had imagined.

It wasn't that the scout was faster than Antarius. Few people were. He had competed in track at the academy and had continued to run his entire life. He found that running helped relax him, and he ran often. His timed mile was that of a much younger man. But that much younger man was not covered in Altairian mud and, probably, mind control bugs.

Thankfully, the drying earth shed itself from him as he moved. First at the joints, and then bigger chunks fell from his chest and back. It was holding firm to his feet, however, and it made finding traction somewhat difficult. A giant clump also refused to let go from the seat of his survival suit and threatened to pull it down around his knees.

Still, he gained.

A quick glance at the tracker told him the enemy was heading for the safety of his ship. He couldn't let that happen. He reached deep within himself and found a final burst of energy he redirected to his feet. Antarius closed in on the scout, dropped the machete and dove.

Most of the scout slipped through the thick layer of slick mud clinging to his body. In one last desperate clench, Thurgood seized an ankle and brought the man down.

The Hama kicked Thurgood in the ear with his free foot and sent pain bursting through his head that exploded like static. This distraction and what was left of the mud on his hands allowed the man to slip through his grasp. And, to add injury to insult, the Hama's boot heel caught him under the chin and cut it open on the way out.

Mud. Blood. Bugs, probably. He'd had enough. He had to stop the scout and he didn't care who heard.

Thurgood pulled his sidearm and fired just as the Hama scout turned to gloat.

The chase was over, and the only marker left on the locator belonged to the Hama ship. Correction, his ship.

A looting of the body produced the scout craft's access module. If it was anything like an Alliance unit, it would give him full access to the scout ship's controls. As far as the ship was concerned, he was the Hama now.

Thurgood tossed the module into the air and caught it. "Thanks for the ride, chumps." Once his laughter ebbed, he heard a beep. It was faint, but it was real. And it wasn't natural. He searched the Hama again and found that the man had activated an emergency beacon.

"A cheater beeper!" In the coward's final moments, he had called for help. "You wuss."

The news was disappointing, but Thurgood wasn't overly concerned. It would take the Hama weeks to get to the planet. And by that time, he'd be long gone.

SIX

A Savage Landing

Calling for reinforcements was a coward's move, Thurgood thought to himself as he stripped off his survival suit and used the pond water to clean the mud from his body. The suit had done its job, but it was covered with mud and another man's pee, and he had no desire to wear it any longer than he had to. The mud alone had made the active camouflage inoperative. He'd have to talk to the Alliance scientists about a more resilient version that could handle a little dirt. Survival wasn't always the clean-cut business they assumed it was in their comfy labs. Out here it was life or death, and anything could happen. As evidenced by the panic button.

"A panic button," Thurgood grumbled to himself. That settled it. The Hama had no honor. They may fly around the universe in their advanced spacecraft and settle other planets like they were civilized, but they were nothing but a bunch of tattletales. That much was clear.

These thoughts consumed him as he walked back to the ship. He had been held prisoner by the Hama and spent that time under their watch studying them. The Rox Tolgath

Malbourne had presented himself as Thurgood's better, condemning Earth actions in the galaxy with a calm demeanor as if the Hama were above petty emotions.

Few things were as intimidating as an enemy that didn't feel. He'd fought a rock monster once. It was much like that. Cold and impervious to feelings and fists. Even throwing smaller rocks had no effect. It was an enemy that didn't know fear because it couldn't understand pain. Fortunately for Thurgood, the rock beast could not comprehend science either, and melted under a blaze of blaster fire. But if an enemy didn't know fear and couldn't be consumed by anger, they were unlikely to make mistakes.

That thought had kept him up at night in the first weeks of the fight against the Hama. But he had seen it now. He had seen it in the eyes of the guy that had peed on him under the tree. There had been genuine fear in the dark of his eyes. He had heard it in the screams of the man he had thrown off the cliff. And he had watched uncertainty flood the mind of his opponent in the ruins.

The Hama knew fear, all right. It was in their blood and pulsed through their veins with the steady rhythm of a coward's emergency beacon.

In all of his speeches and lectures, the Rox Tolgath had tried to convince Thurgood that the Hama were cold, calculating and possessed a civilized ruthlessness. But they were nothing more than...

"Savages!"

Thurgood ducked behind a tree on the edge of the clearing that held the Hama ship. Confident he hadn't been spotted, he drew back a branch and examined the scene before him.

The Hama ship sat at the top of a hill and was surrounded by what he could only describe as savages. They looked like men but were dressed like animals. Or, in animals. That may have been a better way to describe it. Their clothes were little more than rags and poorly cut pelts of oddly colored furs. They probably didn't know anything about bathing.

Worse yet, these savages were all over the Hama Declavar. Any fear they might have had at the appearance of such an alien object had been outweighed by their curiosity, and they stood around in groups, gawking at the craft. Some had scaled the ship and were standing atop it, marveling at how far they could see. They made odd grunts and pointed off into the distance as if they were seeing their world for the first time. It was possible it gave them a vantage they had never experienced before.

"I can see my filthy cave from here," they were probably saying.

Others ran their hands along the hull's surface, trying to make sense of what it was that had come to their world. One was poking it with a stick as if it were prodding an animal.

These stupid savages probably thought it *was* some kind of animal. Some great beast that had come from the sky and decided to rest upon their planet.

Antarius recognized that it was a foolish notion. As a civilized man, the whole idea made no sense to him. What animal could look like that? It had no head. What kind of animal had no head?

The cockpit kind of looked like a head, he supposed. He cocked his head and started to see a kind of head-like shape to it. The viewscreen could definitely be eyes, he'd give them that. Two sheets of varisteel dominated the screen and were split down the middle by a structural spar, so he could picture them as eyes.

And the way it sat on its landing gear did make the ship appear as though it were perched on legs. So it did have a head and legs. But that wasn't enough to make it look like an animal to anyone with a basic understanding of anatomy. Stupid savages.

The hull could obviously be a body. That was a given. So, it did have a head and legs and a body if you were willing to give the thought any consideration. But without arms or wings, it made no sense as an animal. What kind of creature waddled around all torso and head? A penguin, true. But even those had wings and it was foolish to think this ship was a creature since it didn't... oh, he saw the wings now. They had folded up for landing and he hadn't seen them at first. It really did look like an animal. It was difficult to unsee it now.

If he were a senseless savage, he'd call the creature a Starlight. A great beast that flew through the night skies and fed on the stars. It was this mighty bird's appetite that explained why stars, the steadfast rays of heaven, sometimes disappeared.

No, he corrected himself. That was stupid. Birds didn't eat stars. No one was that ignorant to the workings of the universe. Stars were too hot. So obviously, these savages would assume that stars were the Starlight's eggs scattered across the black of night. Through its grace, this majestic space bird gave light to the darkness. And when the eggs hatched, after millions of years, that star's light would go out as another great creature was born to fill the darkness with life and light the way of weary travelers.

But that was primitive thinking. It wasn't some great space bird. It was a space craft. And he needed it to get back to Earth. With the access transmitter in his pocket, it was essentially his ship. Now he just needed to deal with the locals.

Interacting with the savages shouldn't be too much trouble. After all, they surely wanted the great bird gone from their lands. No matter what mystical powers they foolishly ascribed it, no one wanted a 100,000-ton bird taking a dump on their lawn.

Thurgood stood and readied himself for the encounter. He

just hoped he wasn't mistaken for a deity. He hated it when that happened.

At first blush, it didn't seem like a bad thing. Being mistaken for a god was undeniably flattering. But there were always the ethical implications. Should you embrace their misconception and use it to your advantage? Thurgood didn't see the harm in it as long as you weren't abusing your power as a god. Words from the divine tended to motivate the locals into getting things done. And what was a little white lie as long as no one's feelings were hurt and no human sacrifices were made in your honor?

But even when you're a god, the best intentions can go awry. Inevitably, the locals started pegging you as an indifferent or neglectful god.

Answering prayers was easy at first. Technology solved a lot of primitive problems and looked enough like divine intervention to satisfy everyone involved. But, eventually, human (or alien) nature entered into things and you were presented with problems which even modern ray guns couldn't fix. It was almost always love. Love seemed to be at the heart of every true problem. And as soon as you couldn't fix something, the people turned on you.

Love wasn't always the problem, of course. Sometimes it was a lack of crops or a lack of rain that caused the catastrophe. One time it was soup. But it only took one thing to get the ball rolling and the next thing you knew, you were responsible for everything. It was all on you, so into the volcano you went.

In this case, however, it could work. He could duck in, be their god, duck out on the wings of a Starlight and be gone before the inevitable lack of faith turned anyone into a human sacrifice. He'd give them some mumbo jumbo about the future and be on his way. Everyone would get what they wanted and no one would get roasted. No harm, no foul.

No, pretending to be their god wouldn't be fair to the savages.

What had they called it in sensitivity training? Racist? Elitist? No, cultural appropriation. That's what they had called it. Although, he couldn't really see how pretending to be a god was stealing anyone's culture. He wasn't stealing anything. If anything, he was adding to it.

In the end, it didn't matter what they called it or why. He knew it would be wrong, so he decided to talk to the savages like equals. Even though they surely reeked.

Antarius straightened to his full height and walked with confidence from the tree line. The savages were focused on the ship and didn't see him until he was within twenty feet of the boarding ramp.

"Hi," he said and raised his hand to greet the tribe.

It was a simple enough phrase and he said it kindly. There was even a hint of warmth to it. But all Hell broke loose nonetheless.

Savages swarmed around him, shouting in some insane language of grunts and gibberish. It sounded repetitive, but then he realized they probably had very few things to talk about. One grunt for *rock*, two grunts for *tree* and three grunts for *giant spacefaring birds who lay eggs like stars* would probably cover everything.

He didn't know what they were saying, but he could tell from their actions it wasn't the friendly language reserved for the upper parts of their society. He smiled anyway as he waited for the translator in his ear to absorb and crack the language.

The translator didn't usually take this long. Even with an unknown language, it started guessing almost instantly and worked to refine the vocabulary over time. Thurgood put his finger in his ear and wiggled the device while hoping that digging in one's ear wasn't a sign of aggression to their people.

The device was completely silent.

Thurgood gasped lightly through his smile as he

remembered getting kicked in the ear. The blow must have broken the device.

"This is going to be a problem." He kept a friendly tone despite the admission.

The more they shouted, the more excited the group became. They grew closer. He was right about the smell. Hygiene appeared to be a problem. They were covered in dirt, their nails were poorly kept and the invention of the toothbrush was clearly several generations off.

But when he looked past their bathing practices, he was surprised to find something startlingly human. Take away the smell, the dirt and ignorance and these men could be one of his kin. Not any kin he would own up to, but kin in a metaphorical sense. Despite their appearance and actions, there was a sharpness in their eyes that denoted a form of intelligence.

The savages soon realized their grunts were useless and abandoned any attempt at verbal communication. It was time to mime. Thurgood soon found himself surrounded by several grown men acting like birds. They flapped their arms and bounced up and down while pointing to the ship.

Thurgood shook his head and wondered if the gesture meant no on this backwards planet. "No. It's not a bird," he explained.

They pointed at him and the pointed to the sky.

"Yes, it flies, but it's not an animal. Think about it. You'd be able to hear it breathing."

The tribe's frustration was growing. They pointed harder and grunted louder.

"No, it's not magic. It's a machine." He thumped his ear again hoping to kickstart the translator. There was no response. He was on his own.

Their pointing was getting more dramatic. More fingers were

coming at him and the grunting was getting out of hand. He had to do something.

"Okay," Thurgood raised his hand. "I didn't want to say this, but I'm a god. I mean, I'm your god. Or, some god."

One of the savages slapped him on the chest. It wasn't violent, but he still didn't appreciate it. The man left his hand there and pointed to the ship with his other hand. The meaning was clear. They thought he had come inside the giant space bird that laid stars as eggs.

"Yes!" Thurgood understood now. "That's right, it's my ship. It is my ship."

He knew it was a lie. But they didn't know that, and that's why lying was so useful. To cement the mistruth, he removed the transmitter from his pocket and held it up for the men to see.

"See, I've got the keys right here. Uh, my keys to my ship." He tapped the smooth pad on the transmitter and everyone jumped as the craft's boarding ramp opened beneath the cockpit like the beak of some giant space bird.

There was a grunting of awe from the savages as the access point lowered to the ground.

"Yep, see? That's my ship all right, and now I'm going to—"

One of the savages grunted something that got the rest riled up. There was a cheer from the crowd, and they all started making their way toward the ramp.

"Wait," Thurgood raced to get ahead of the group. "Hold on, it's... you don't need to go in there."

His words weren't working, and he started pulling on shoulders to slow the crowd. He pulled himself to the front of the group and moved up the ramp. He turned, held up his hands and shouted, "Stop!"

Maybe it was his tone or a total coincidence that they knew the word *stop* in English, but the crowd did as he instructed.

"Now, I can tell you're all excited. You've had a big day with the space bird landing and meeting your god and all, so no one's blaming you for getting all worked up. But this is my ship," he held the transmitter up to reinforce the point, "and I'm going to take it and fly back home now."

The savage at the front of the crowd grumbled something and charged up the ramp.

Thurgood's reflexes took over and he landed a right cross across the man's jaw. The savage went down and rolled to the bottom of the ramp.

The tribe looked at their fallen comrade and then back to Thurgood. Surely, they believed he was a deity now. Might as well embrace it.

"It is not my wish to hurt anyone. And don't worry. Though I leave you today, one day, I shall return. One day when your tribe has risen from the soil and learned to love their fellow man and developed some kind of soap and hair care routine. On that day, I shall return. Or, more likely, someone that looks a lot like me but who is less important and has more time on their hands. And they will arrive in a similar ship. It won't be the same because we don't make this particular model. But it'll have wings and stuff like this one. And on that day, I shall bestow upon your noble tribe the truths of the universe and civilization. You're going to love it. Civilization has things like clothes and buildings and Dippin' Dots. So look to the stars for my return, or, you know, whatever dignitary they send. And try and clean up before they get here."

The crowd was lost. He had dazzled them with prophecies and promises, and it should buy him just enough time to get inside and close the ramp. He turned to embark and ran flat into the sweaty chest of the biggest savage he had ever seen.

It was like being slapped across the face first with a warm fish, like a Kasplatchian Manghoof hanging from a vendor's stall. Although, he had to admit, the Kasplatchian Manghoof smelled better.

Thurgood tilted his head back for what felt like forever until he saw the head on top of the chest. It was higher up than he expected and quite grim looking. The man stood a half foot taller than Antarius.

"Excuse me." He tried to move around the living obstacle.

The savage stepped in front of him again.

"I really must be going," Thurgood said, and stepped the other way.

The giant moved again and blocked his path once more.

He tried one more pass.

The savage grabbed him and shoved him back down the ramp.

"Now look here." Thurgood pointed at the savage with the machete to make his point. This is my ship and I am leaving."

Before he could even raise the blade above his head, the machete had been stripped from his hand and he had been raised above the brute's head.

A cheer arose from the tribe as Antarius went flying over their heads.

He landed on his back with a *phlurt*, and it was the first time he had truly appreciated the foul-smelling moss. Antarius did his best to roll through the crash, but he was stopped by the feet of several tribesmen. They grunted and cheered and pulled him to his feet. His attempt to break through the huddle was stopped by a half dozen hands. They spun him around and shoved him back toward the ship.

Stumbling forward took him right into the path of the brute's fist. Hitting the ground had hurt less.

The strike sent him into the waiting arms of more tribe members, who seemed to be playing the part of ring ropes. They flung him back toward his opponent. The brute grinned and drew back to deliver a blow that would end him. It didn't matter how soft the ground was—if his head hit it without being attached to his body, it was still going to hurt.

Thurgood got control of his feet at the last moment and turned the stumble into a charge. The brute swung as Antarius dove. He threaded the man's legs and came to a quick stop on the damp and spongey ground. He started to stand, but the giant recovered first and planted a monstrous foot on Thurgood's rear and shoved. The kick sent him flying several feet and back down to the wet moss.

He was getting damp. And his face hurt. The tribe was laughing at him. Their gloating sounded almost human.

He didn't understand how this was happening. He was good in a fight. He sparred. He drilled. He trained. And he was stronger than most men. He worked out. He lifted. He told everyone he lifted. But, somehow, he was getting his exceptionally fit ass handed to him.

It was time to fight dirty. He hated to do it. He prided himself on being an honorable combatant, but he couldn't remember ever being this outmatched. This must be what it felt like for normal people to fight him. No wonder they always tried to kick him in the junk. Now that he was on the other side of it, he understood. It was their only chance. He prayed evolution had seen fit to put all the bits and pieces in the same place on Altair as it had on Earth.

As soon as he felt the shadow on his back, Antarius spun and launched an uppercut into the giant's animal skin. The strike stopped the giant in his stride. The savage backed away with a shocked look on his face. It was a long way to go from crotch to brain in a body that big, and it took a moment for the pain to arrive. Once it did, there was a flash of pain on the savage's face. But it disappeared quickly and was replaced by rage.

Thurgood went for his gun. He had hoped to best the man in hand-to-hand and win the respect of the tribe, but that obviously wasn't going to happen.

Since the outbreak of hostilities with the Hama, the Alliance had seen fit to arm every officer with a sidearm and a stupid holster. It was one of those leather jobs with the big flap that was designed more for keeping out spilled cocktails than it was for quick draws. Another grievance to add to his report. He barely had the thing unbuckled when the brute's hand wrapped around his throat. He grabbed the savage's wrist as he was hoisted from the ground in an effort to keep his head and body together as a set.

He kicked several savages in the head. It was less a strategic strike as it was a matter of luck as he flailed above the crowd. He landed in the arms of two more tribesmen and all three of them collapsed to the ground. Thurgood ended up on the bottom of a dirty dog pile with someone else's foot in his face and another person's elbow in his spleen.

Thurgood kicked one of the tribesmen off of him. This sent the savage flying into one of his friends and caused tempers to flare.

The giant was above him before he could stand and grabbed Thurgood by the ankle. With one heave, he was flung like an Olympic hammer into three more of the Altairian natives. The brute was relentless and after a few more trips through the air, Antarius had collided with and pissed off almost every single member of the tribe.

The last heave sent him outside the circle of spectators, but it looked like the effort of throwing Thurgood around was finally taking its toll on the beast. The man was starting to look winded and took a moment to catch his breath.

This finally gave Thurgood a chance to stand. He studied the group in front of him. The entire tribe eyed him with anger. But they were all in front of him. Somehow, he was no longer surrounded. He glanced over his shoulder. The jungle wasn't far.

By the time he looked back, the savages had figured out what his plan was.

They screamed and charged toward him.

Antarius turned and ran.

SEVEN

Run Through the Jungle

The forest welcomed him back with hesitation. It enveloped him with its shadows, but it also slapped him in the face with a couple of low-hanging branches. Thurgood welcomed the obstacles. They were now his friends. They would help him in his escape. Another branch caught him in the ear. That one wasn't his friend. But every vine that tripped him up and every branch he had to duck under was on team Thurgood now.

Behind him, the savages were in pursuit. They may have been primitive and simple and believed in stupid space birds, but they were much, much faster than him. The *splurt splurt* of his pursuers' bare feet on the damp moss reminded him he never had much of a lead to begin with. And, it was quickly shrinking. His machete gone and his SERE suit discarded, the jungle obstacles were the only edge he had left.

Thurgood ducked under a low branch and slalomed between the trunks of several trees. He was just starting to believe he had lost them when one of the savages jumped out in front of him and screamed.

Without wasting a step, Thurgood dove and speared the savage in the waist with his shoulder. He drove the man into a tree and let him fall to his hands and knees. A follow-up kick rendered the man unconscious as he dropped him to the moss-covered ground.

Shpwork.

He took a moment to appreciate the victory over the Altairian native. That was more like it. He could handle the smaller ones. It was only that one big bastard that gave him problems. He was getting his confidence back and that was another edge.

Several shouts behind him sent him running again. He knew he couldn't take them together. He had to get them one on one.

There were voices ahead of him and voices from behind. How had they gotten ahead of him? They knew the area too well. He wasn't even sure where he was going. A plan had formed in his head which had consisted of a lot of running and an equal amount of doubling back. Maybe he was sticking to the plan subconsciously and had somehow gotten ahead of himself. It hardly mattered now. He was trapped. It wasn't the first time his brain had gotten him into trouble without thinking.

Thurgood spun and examined the options around him. It was pretty much trees on all sides, and that wasn't much help to him. There was a hill on his right. It was steep, but it wasn't trees. He scrambled up the hill using exposed roots to pull himself along. The moss was thicker here and slick, and the handholds were the only thing that allowed him any progress up the hill.

Below him, the voices grew louder. The top of the hill was getting closer and he pushed himself harder to make the crest. Even if they spotted him, they'd have to climb to catch him and the task had not proven easy.

A final push got him to the precipice and he pulled himself

over the top. Exhausted and heaving, he rolled onto his back and looked back down the hill. It looked taller from the top than it had from the bottom. No wonder he was tired.

The voices that had been behind him and the voices that had been in front of him met at the bottom of the hill. He didn't know what they were saying but there was obvious confusion. It delighted him to see the looks on their savage faces as they tried to figure out how he had gotten past them. They must have decided he had doubled back because they all pointed the direction he had come, and off they ran in pursuit.

Once their shouts faded, he was alone in silence. He took a deep breath and visualized the oxygen traveling through him, feeding his tired body. He then rolled over on his back and released the breath out into the damp Altairian air. What light found its way through the dense jungle canopy warmed his face and he closed his eyes. He'd give the savages some time to "chase him" deeper into the woods and then head back to the ship, fly home, attend whatever awards ceremony they would arrange for him and then get on to the next mission. For now, he'd rest. Just for a minute.

The warmth left his face as something blocked the light.

"Aw, crap."

When he opened his eyes there were four of them standing above him.

He couldn't tell if they had been there all along or if they had snuck up on him while he was resting his eyes but he knew he didn't have the energy to fight four of them. All he could do was try and run.

Thurgood hurled himself down the hill feet first and the slick moss sped him on his way. He tried to sit up as best he could but struggled to remain upright. He could feel the seat of his pants getting wet as the moisture kicked up by his feet hit him in the face. Some of it got in his mouth, and it tasted as bad as it smelled.

Spitting and doing his best to scrape the taste off his tongue with his teeth, he hit the bottom of the hill, leapt to his feet and ran.

Cries carried from the top of the hill as the savages gave chase. He dug deep and ran harder. Physical fitness was one of the pillars of his personal belief system, and he had always prided himself on his condition. He worked hard to maintain a well-balanced physique of form and function. He ran regularly and pushed himself to greater distances with regularity. But after a day of crashing, hiking, killing and evading, even his impressive muscles were starting to fatigue.

The savages had no problem keeping up. They were right on top of him. He hadn't seen a single overweight savage among his pursuers. To a man, they had all appeared fit despite their primitive status.

He was running out of energy and options and had to find his way back to the ship before he collapsed. Thankfully, he could still rely on his sense of direction. It seldom failed him. No matter what planet or vessel he found himself on, once dropped in a new environment he had an innate sense of place and always found his way to where he needed to be. Most of the time. There had been "instances," as noted in his personnel file.

The woods brightened ahead of him. More light was getting through. The trees were thinning. The clearing with the ship was ahead. It had to be. His homing sense had served him well once more. He put what energy he had left into his legs and burst through the tree line and into the clearing. Then he stumbled to a halt. He didn't remember the cliff wall being there.

He ran to the base of the cliff and put his hands against the barrier. He slammed his fists into it, hoping that some swearing would move the mountain that now lay before him. But it wasn't going anywhere. It rose straight up fifty feet. Rocks and dirt formed the natural barrier, and nothing short of a monkey would see it as a viable escape route.

He turned to run back into the forest, but the savages had closed the distance and his path was blocked.

They knew they had him. The first man stepped out of the forest calmly and stopped at the edge of the clearing. Another joined him a second later and the two men stared down their prey.

Another two emerged a moment later at the other end of the clearing and stopped at the edge.

Thurgood put his full attention toward unfastening the flap on the ridiculous Alliance-issued holster. He finally managed to work the clasp but he still had to wrestle with the leather flap for a second before he was able to reach the weapon inside. By the time he drew the gun, several more tribesmen had stepped out of the woods to join the others. They formed a crescent around him, cornering him in the shadow of the cliff.

"I don't want to use this!" he shouted as he waved the gun. "It's a... it's a death pointer. Whatever I point it at dies. Do you understand? Can your primitive minds comprehend what I'm saying? It's like your spears or clubs except instead of wood, it throws a kaon ray where matter and anti-matter combine and decay in the blink of an eye to form a devastating eruption of subatomic particles that will blow a hole in your chest the size of a slightly larger than average mango."

The savages just sneered at his threat.

"Dammit, Thurgood," he hissed at himself. "Don't be stupid. How would they know what a mango is?"

He could tell he had lost them with the fruit reference as they inched forward.

"I said stay back!" He turned and fired a shot into the cliff. The blast blew a boulder the size of a man from the rock wall and created a small rock slide that gathered at the base.

He turned back to the tribe. That had done it. They were impressed. They stopped all forward movement and began to chatter amongst themselves.

"That's right," Antarius said, keeping them covered with the gun. "Talk it over. I think you'll realize it's best if we all just go our separate ways. I'll go back to the ship and fly home and you go back to your caves or wallows or wherever."

The tribesmen were rather animated in their discussion. They pointed to the wall and replicated the explosion of rocks with hand gestures and sound effects. One made the shape of gun with their fingers and play-acted gunning down several adversaries.

After a few moments, the tribe appeared to come to an agreement; they wanted the gun.

One of the savages threw a spear. It sailed past Thurgood's ear and stuck in the wall behind him.

"Hey!" He fired the gun. The blast hit the man in the chest, tearing a hole in his ribcage. The force threw the man back against a tree where he stood just long enough for everyone to see the damage inflicted by the weapon.

Thurgood pointed to the wound. "See? That's what I was saying. That's about how big a mango is."

The tribe erupted in grunts and growls that quickly turned into shouting once the dead man finally collapsed to the ground. *Schort.*

"I don't want to shoot you!" Thurgood shouted. "I mean, I don't want to shoot any more of you!"

The savages exchanged glances but didn't say anything. There must have been some nonverbal signal given because they all rushed forward all at once.

Thurgood backed up until he was abasing the cliff and prepared to fire.

The next roar didn't come from the tribe or his gun.

It came from above.

And it was deafening.

EIGHT

Reigning Cats

Something above him briefly blocked out the sun. The shadow passed quickly over him and landed in the form of a beast between Thurgood and the advancing members of the tribe.

And what a beast it was. It lit on all fours and stood six feet tall at the shoulder. One look at the muscle rippling under its purple-hued coat and you could tell it was powerful, like a cow. But it was agile as well, not like a cow, as it had landed without a sound on padded feet like a cat. The creature was filled with rage, also like a cat. He had no name for this mighty beast that was as strong as an ox, light and angry as a cat, graceful like a ballerina but free of emotional baggage unlike a ballerina. It was both majestic and menacing.

The beast's fierce roar transformed into a rumble that made the ground tremble beneath Antarius's feet and turned the savages' bold words into panicked screams as they turned to flee the clearing. There was no order to their withdrawal. Pure terror drove them away.

The ballerinacatox—no, that wouldn't work—pounced, trapping one of the retreating tribesmen beneath its paw. Fangs, rough like jagged stalactites, sank into its prey's back with a sickening noise that turned Thurgood's stomach.

Pinned, the savage shrieked, for he knew this was his end. The cries of pain drew the attention of a foolish friend who attempted to save him from the cowlgar—that was a little better. His spear held out before him, the savage came at the beast. The creature batted the man aside like a ball of yarn that no longer held its interest and sent him sailing into the trunk of a tree. The loud crack that followed could have been the breaking wood or bone, but the end result was the same; the man did not get up.

Another savage succeeded in drawing the beast's attention and fury as he raced for the jungle. This escape attempt came to an abrupt end with another deadly pounce from the predator.

Thurgood took advantage of the distraction and began inching his way along the cliff wall. He felt if he could just get back to the woods, he would have a fighting chance at running away.

The cowlgar—no, the name wasn't growing on him like he thought it would—must have sensed his presence just before he'd reached the edge of the tree line because the monster turned and fixed its sights on him. There was a keenness in the beast's gaze, but there was no mercy in its eyes.

Antarius froze and smiled. "Nice monster."

The calming tone of his voice did little to soothe the savage beast. It roared again and lowered itself, preparing to spring.

Fortunately, charm wasn't the only weapon he had left. Antarius fired the kaon gun.

The creature reared back from the blow. Howling and thrashing about, it tried in vain to pull its head away from the pain on its face. But that wasn't how pain worked, and the creature continued to writhe in agony.

Thurgood made his break for the trees, but the sight of its prey fleeing triggered a reaction in the predator. It shook off the pain and leapt in front of him, baring teeth and an obvious grudge for shooting it in the face. Its look had changed. The cold cunning of the predator he had witnessed in its stare had been replaced by the searing hate of rage in one eye and a mango-sized hole in the other.

"I'm sorry I shot you in the face, Mr. Cowcat." Cowcat was the worst one yet. "That was wrong."

The monster didn't like the name either, and it roared its disapproval.

Thurgood couldn't argue. Cowcat didn't work. But he couldn't think of anything better, so he pulled the trigger again and ran when the creature reared back from the blast.

He wasn't alone. Everybody was running.

Any animosity between himself and the tribesmen had been temporarily forgotten. Survival was their only concern now. Petty squabbles over whose starship it was and who shot whose friend would have to wait. Allegiances were formed just as quickly as the loyalty between tribe members evaporated. It was every man for himself as they raced through the woods, jumping branches, dodging trees and trying to get away. You didn't have to be faster than the Panthebull—no, that was terrible, too—you only had to be faster than your fellow savage.

As Thurgood could have predicted, the slowest ones fell first. Distant screams rose up behind him but were quickly stifled. He didn't know much about the predatory behavior of most Earth animals, much less the Dancing Bovilynx—no that was a mouthful and kids would have a hard time spelling it with the silent b. But it was obvious this creature wasn't hunting for food. It was chasing down everyone that had dared desecrate its territory or blasted holes in its home and face. The cat was out for revenge.

Antarius risked a glance over his shoulder. There were still a half dozen savages behind him running from the apex predator.

At least, he hoped it was the apex predator. The idea that there may be something more dangerous than this thing somewhere out there in the jungle wasn't an idea he was ready to entertain. If this wasn't the top of the food chain, things were worse than he thought.

The creature leapt back into view with claws extended and landed on the straggler. The man's screams were quick and final. The beast leapt again and took down another runner. From one body to the next, the cat-like, cow-like monster eliminated the savages.

Somehow, Thurgood had managed to stay out in front of the pack, but his lead was evaporating as one man gained on him. The tribesman pulled even alongside him and Thurgood dug into his reserves. There wasn't much left in the tank, but he wasn't about to fall behind.

For the next few minutes, the two men raced neck and neck through woods. The screams of the Predabullcelot's—that could work, he liked how it got the predator in there—victims continued. And those screams were getting more distant. Thurgood and his running companion were pulling away from the carnage. The other man realized this as well and the two men looked at each other with a newfound respect. They laughed together. It was that nervous laughter that only came after cheating death together. This shared bond drove them both on, and Antarius felt the tiredness in his legs fade momentarily. As a military man, he knew the feeling well. They called it the spirit of coors. It was nothing new, but he marveled at the fact that, no matter the planet, no matter the species, the spirit transcended boundaries and bonded people in times of duress. He was feeling it now, with this man, this alien as they kept pace. Their steps even began to sync and they ran in rhythm as one.

Thurgood shot him in the knee.

The savage screamed and collapsed to the forest floor with a mango-sized hole in his leg. A moment later, the man's final scream chased Antarius through the trees as the Predabullcelot —yeah, it was really sticking—landed on top of the alien native.

Now he ran alone. The beast moved silently somewhere behind him, but he knew it was there, gaining on him. It wasn't about to give up. He looked behind him as he rounded a boulder. He couldn't spot the creature.

He wasn't foolish enough to think he had outrun the predator. It was clear the game had changed. He was no longer being chased. He was being hunted. It wasn't a feeling he enjoyed. Why had the creature taken the pressure off?

The trees in front of him thinned. There was a clearing ahead. Had he made it? Had he reached the edge of the monster's territory? Is that why the beast had disappeared?

Thurgood burst out of the woods as if he had crossed a finish line and skidded to a stop.

He was at the edge of the canyon again.

No, this was something different. The other side wasn't too far away, this had to be a ravine. Maybe a gorge. Damn, the pioneers could have been more specific with their naming schema. It didn't matter what it was. It was a long way down to jagged rocks and a raging river and the distance to the other side was too far to jump across.

But it wasn't too far to swing across.

Branches from the massive trees reached out over the void from both sides of the chasm's walls. Vines hung from the limbs creating a web over the gap—the same vines that had enabled him to scale the tree near the *Galahad* and those stupid ruins. He put his gun back in the stupid holster. A plan was forming in his mind.

The ground began to rumble under his feet, and he turned to see the Predabullcelot crouched between himself and the path back into the forest. He was stuck between a perilous drop to the jagged rocks below and a scarred face. A face that was now grinning at him as the blood of its victims dripped from fur around its mouth. Its claws dug through the moss and into the ground, finding solid traction as it readied itself to pounce.

Thurgood wasn't going to give it a chance. He took what he knew could be his final breath, turned toward the edge of the ravine and dove into the abyss.

Reaching out with a desperate grab, he seized the nearest vine and swung. It would take several vines and a few lucky jumps to make the crossing, but he was confident they would hold his weight.

Pumping with his legs, he swung hard to create as much distance between himself and the Predabullcelot as he could. The swing carried him almost upside down, and he managed to lock his legs around the next vine. He looked back to the edge of the canyon and smiled as the beast paced the edge, unable to reach its prey.

This smile turned into a chuckle and was about to turn into full-blown gloating when he felt the weight at his hip shift. The flap on the top of his holster hadn't been fastened and his weapon was falling out. Twisting his waist, he tried to shift the weight back into place. He bucked his hips and wiggled anyway he could to try and seat the weapon but the effort went unrewarded and the gun tumbled out of his holster.

It fell in slow motion and he watched it turning, end over end, all the way down. It didn't happen quickly. It was a long way down. The gun was small enough by the time it hit the river below that he couldn't even see the splash.

"Well... dammit."

It was disheartening, but he was still in the fight. The creature didn't appear willing to jump, and he had already grabbed the next vine. His plan had worked. Moving from vine to vine would take him safely across. He decided to permit himself a touch of gloating.

"Sorry, pussycat! You're not going to make a meal out of me."

The predator roared its frustration but made no move to leap. It was smart enough to stay on solid ground.

Thurgood offered his enemy a quick salute and moved on to the next vine.

It snapped.

Thurgood cursed the vine's weakness on the way down and found he still had time left to curse the whole damn planet and the stupid Hama for getting him into this mess as well. He was about to curse the canyon itself when he finally hit the river.

He plunged into the frigid water feet first and immediately had his feet yanked out from underneath him by the racing waters. If he had the presence of mind, he would have been thankful for the current. It moved the river swiftly along creating swells and aerating the water. Had the stream been still, he may have lived, but surely would have shattered several bones.

But there was no time to appreciate the geography. He surfaced momentarily and managed only a gasp of air before the raging torrent put him in a headlock and began beating the hell out of him as it swept him downstream.

The river turned him over and around so many times he lost track of which way was up. He struggled to gain any kind of control. Direction was solely at the river's discretion and it shamed him to admit he was losing a fight to a body of water.

In his defense, the river wasn't fighting fair. If it was just him versus the water, he was pretty sure he could take it. But the rocks had taken the river's side in the fight. Every time the river went around a bend it slammed him into a submerged boulder or dragged him across a jagged piece of slate. He was outnumbered by water and rocks and currents and waves and he was pretty sure he felt a fish slap him across the face at some point.

Every toe and knee on his body hurt as they were constantly bashed about. Every time he tried to put his foot down, there was something to trip him up or thump him for daring to stand. He caught only flashes of the shoreline, but it was enough to tell him he was moving fast. The pace kept up, the rocks never stopped and by the time the river finally gave up its grip and he was able to drag himself to shore, he had no idea how far he had traveled.

He pulled himself by bruised and bloodied fingers onto a sandy shore and rolled over onto his back. For a moment he simply enjoyed the air and the sun on his face. Then he blacked out.

NINE

An Intense Encounter

Thurgood awoke confused.

This wasn't unusual. How anyone could go to sleep for several hours and still be expected to remember where they were when they awoke was beyond him. To be asleep one moment and to still be expected to be awake the next moment and knowing what was going on was asking a little much if you asked him.

Of course, if you woke up in the same place you went to sleep, you could make some assumptions about where you were. But this time he couldn't even remember turning in. He had a ritual he followed before retiring for the evening, and he couldn't recall doing a single pushup, much less humming his goodnight song.

The entire situation was a mystery, and it was up to him to figure things out. He would have to use context clues to piece it all together and do his best to remember what had happened, where he was, whose bed he was in and whether or not he was happy to be there. Thankfully, it wasn't the first time he had awoken in a strange bed with no memory of how he got there.

This experience would be helpful in determining the how, why, where and who—if there was a who involved. The answer to "how" was usually Jungarin Brandy, but his breath didn't taste like a stamp that had been licked by a fish, so he knew it wasn't that.

One thing he did know about waking up in strange places was that you didn't want anyone else to know you'd woken up in a strange place if you could help it. Experience had taught him this. You only opened your eyes to an ugly surprise so many times before you learned it wasn't good for the heart. Worse was an ugly surprise knowing you were awake. You wanted to make sure no one else knew you were awake until the moment you wanted them to.

Thurgood kept his eyes closed and held his breathing to a steady rate as not to alert anyone who could be watching. As soon as you opened your eyes, you were giving yourself away, so he would have to rely on his other senses to figure out what was going on.

He felt a presence in the room. Whether it was hostile or attractive, he couldn't tell. There was simply the sense of another presence. It could be someone set to guard a prisoner or a forgotten lover. Best not to chance opening his eyes yet.

He was in a tent. Antarius could always tell when he was in a tent. It's not a skill he remembered acquiring. There had been no special course at the academy. He'd had no mentor guide him. It was an innate ability. Maybe if he'd had proper training, he could better understand the skill. As it was, he couldn't explain how he knew when he was in tents. He just knew.

The space inside a tent felt different. Maybe it was the ventilation. Or perhaps it was the way sound worked. Normally, when you hurled a shout against a wall, it hit with a satisfying amount of force and came back for another go. In a tent it just kind of *pliffed* against the wall and dropped to the floor. That's why tents were poor places to have an argument. You had to yell twice as loud in a tent.

There was a fire nearby as well. He could smell a sweet wood burning and hear the crackle as embers popped. It was also extremely warm on one side of his body and a little cooler on the other. This led him to believe he was in a poorly insulated space. He knew tents were poorly insulated. His theory was holding up.

The last thing he noticed as he carefully took in his surroundings was that he wasn't wearing any pants. This wasn't as surprising as waking up in a tent, but it was still a cause for concern. He didn't remember taking his pants off or anyone else volunteering to do it. Further exploration with his senses revealed that it wasn't just his pants that were missing— he was completely naked except for something wrapped around his midsection, and his body was covered by a heavy, itchy blanket.

This was of some concern. His skin rated high on the sensitivity scale, and the longer he was trapped under coarse fibers, the longer the rest of his day was going to be.

It was time to risk a glance. His other senses had done what they could, but now it was time to get eyes on the situation and get some confirmation. He opened his right eye slightly. Almost imperceptibly. Just like he did when he was about to get a surprise and they told him to close his eyes. Since then, he'd mastered peeking without being spotted, thanks in part to a full set of lashes graciously handed down the Thurgood line.

Antarius employed this technique now. He wasn't in a tent. It was a teepee. Which was pretty much just like a tent. The only differences were semantics and animal skins so he wasn't going to beat himself up about it. The leather walls came to a point far above him where an opening provided ventilation. Smoke drifted lazily up through it and into the air. Where there was smoke, there was fire, so he gave himself another point for another proper deduction.

A face appeared directly above him. It was an ugly face covered in worry lines and dirt, and he found it difficult not to flinch at the sight. Another savage. He must have been captured.

"I think he's awake." It was a man's voice that expressed the thought.

Thurgood shut his eye quickly. So quickly they would never notice it was open to begin with.

"Yep, he's awake," the savage said. "I saw his eye move."

The savage with the ugly face was clearly talking to someone else. That meant there was someone else in the room. And that meant he was outnumbered.

"Fetch him some water." There was another voice in the room. It sounded like another man. "Why do you think he is pretending to be asleep?"

"He's probably scared," said the ugly face.

Thurgood wasn't scared. Far from it. His first instinct was to fight them. But they had his pants and he had rules about fighting while naked. Especially around a fire. There were some mistakes you only had to make once. No, he was going to play it smart.

It was best to wait and assess the situation. They hadn't killed him. That was a good sign. They hadn't eaten him... yet. It was difficult to tell from culture to culture how people liked to prepare their food. But he didn't feel any seasoning on his skin and wasn't sitting in a marinade, so he felt confident in thinking they weren't going to eat him.

"Yeah," the other voice finally agreed. "He did look pretty scared."

That did it. Thurgood opened his eyes fast enough to make the ugly one hovering above him jump. The savage let out an *eep* and stumbled backwards into the wall of the teepee. Thurgood sat up and glared at the man as he fought the soft wall for his balance. He then turned and located the other voice in the room. That man got a good glaring, too. Scared? Him? Hardly.

The second savage stood slowly with his palms raised and gave Antarius a slow and cautious nod.

They made no move to restrain him or even help him. They appeared too awestruck to do much of anything. Maybe they thought he was a god now. They had his pants after all.

Silence dominated the room as the strangers examined one another. Both men were thin and toned from labor and each was dressed in clothes made of an identical greenish gray cloth that looked as uncomfortable as the blanket they had placed him under.

There was a third savage in the tent with them who had wisely remained silent. This one was a woman. She had fair hair and dark eyes that studied him by peering deep into his soul and caused him to be ashamed of his actions. He dialed back the intimidation in his eyes as he met her gaze. If you could see past the dirt on her face and her ignorance of the modern world, she could be considered quite attractive. Of all of the savages present in the teepee, he hoped it was her that took his pants.

He smiled at her and nodded to reassure her that he wasn't about to smite anyone. Well, not her.

She gave a warm smile in return and made no move to flee.

"Where am I?" he wondered aloud.

The man who had stumbled stepped forward. "You're in the Village of the Shooting Star."

"Wait," Thurgood said with an outstretched hand. He had understood every word the savage had said, and that didn't make sense. He pointed at the man who had spoken the words. "Say that again."

The savage looked confused by the command but complied with little hesitation. "You're in the Village of the Shooting Star?"

Thurgood had expected a series of grunts from the aliens, but their words, though heavily accented, were clear. He thumped at his ear. The translator must be working again. That would make things a lot easier.

"Who are you?" the woman asked.

Thurgood was still trying to piece together how exactly he had gotten to the teepee, but the rest was becoming clear in his memory. The *Galahad*. The crash. That first mate he was going to avenge. What was his name? The Hama and the savages. And that beast. The Predabullcelot. But how much should he tell them? He reasoned the truth couldn't hurt, but how much would they understand? He had to get back to the Hama ship. He didn't have a lot of time to be drawing diagrams in the dirt and trying to explain space flight or a heliocentric solar system. Though he regretted it, he couldn't be the savior they needed him to be. He needed to focus on his own mission, and that meant gathering crucial information.

"My name is Captain Antarius Thurgood and I have two questions for you." He spoke using his authoritative voice. It was the quickest way to ensure compliance. "One, how did I get here? And, two, how did my pants get somewhere else?"

One of the savages crossed the room and pulled Antarius's clothes from a drying rack set near the fire. He returned and handed Thurgood his clothes. "Reya brought you here after you fell from above."

"I knew it." Thurgood snatched his clothes from the man's hands. "You think I'm a god, don't you?"

All three of the savages exchanged confused looks. Their simple minds must have been reeling from it all. But what else were they to think when a man falls from above and lands in their village wearing strange garments and not covered in dirt. Could he really blame them?

"No," Reya, the woman said. "We think you are just a man."

"Oh? That's good," Thurgood said as he pulled his shirt over his head. "Well, I could be a god."

The man who gave him his clothes shook his head. "It is not likely."

"But you said I fell from above as if cast from the heavens. So, I can understand why you might think that. But the truth is... and how do I explain this so you can understand this with your limited knowledge? I crashed in a mighty ship." Thurgood made a crashing gesture with his hand and an exploding sound. "I come not from the aether but from another planet not unlike your own. I mean... it's better than yours in most ways, but I'm talking broad strokes here."

"We know," Reya assured him. "We meant you fell from above when you fell from the canyon wall."

"So, it was a canyon!" he shouted as the events came rushing back to him. "I knew it."

"You said you were trying to swing across but really 'screwed it up,'" Reya explained using air quotes.

They even had air quotes here. "I said that?"

"You were in and out of consciousness. At one point you said you tried to swing and you fell."

"Well, there was a mighty beast like a cat with the strength of a cow and..." he picked up his pants and looked to change the subject. They were still damp. He couldn't have been out for too long. That meant there was still time to get to the Hama ship and get off the primitive world. He unfolded the pants and then coughed slightly. "Um, would you—?" He made the intergalactically recognized symbol for 'turn around, I'm about to be naked' by twirling his finger like a ballerina. "Modesty forbids."

They all nodded sheepishly and turned their backs. At least they had manners.

Antarius removed the itchy blanket to find a bandage

wrapped around his waist and his body covered with bruises. The river had proven a formidable foe. He stood and pulled on the damp pants. It sent a chill through his body and he clenched his chest. "Oh, that's a little chilly."

There was something hard in his pocket. He reached in and pulled out a small device. "What the hell? How did this get here?"

Reya turned around and looked at the object in his hand. "It was in your ear. We weren't sure what it was."

"It's a translator," Thurgood said, touching his ear. It was definitely his translator. He'd become so accustomed to it he couldn't even tell it had been removed. But that meant that... he looked at the savages before him with a look that made them back away nervously. "How is it you've come to speak my language?"

"Maybe you speak our language," one said cautiously.

"What kind of savage witchcraft is this?" Confusion overtook him. It shouldn't be happening. There had to be another explanation. There was a pot boiling near the fire. He pointed to it. "Is that a potion? A spell?"

"What are you talking about, you strange man?" the man with his pants asked.

"Where am I? What is this?" He backed away in a panic until he hit the bed and sat.

"The Village of the Shooting Star," Reya said slowly.

None of this made sense. "You savages have hexed me with your—"

"We're not savages," she snapped. "Or witches. This isn't magic."

"Then how do you explain it? Do you know what the odds of two people separated by a million light years speaking the same language are?"

"Do you?" asked the other man.

"Don't get smart with me, Man Who Lives With Dirt on His Face! I'm on to you." He held up the translator as specific proof of his vague accusation. Even he wasn't sure what he was accusing them of. Magic? Is that what he accused them of? This wasn't Salem. He was just confused and he needed answers.

Reya smiled uneasily and crossed the room. She put a hand on his and lowered it. "I think it's best if I take you to the chief."

"Yeah. The chief. You're not savages but you have a chief." Tribal titles like that were a sure sign of savagery. No matter what they said. "You do that. You take me to your chief."

The woman stood and held open the teepee's flap. "Come with me, Mr. Thurgood."

He stood and straightened his shirt. "That's Captain Mr. Thurgood."

TEN

The Chief and the Captain

They stepped through the tent's entry flap and entered into a different time. Thurgood had woken up inside the skin of a dead animal, however, so what was outside the teepee came as little surprise. To say the village was primitive was being generous. There were no paved streets, no lights, no electrical devices of any kind he could see. The buildings surrounding him were a conglomeration of teepees, wooden huts and mud buildings.

Reya and the others led him down a dirt path to what a kind person might call the village's main street. It was a broad path laid with rough-hewn wooden planks that did more to define the trail than they did to keep the mud at bay. Despite this, it was heavily populated as the villagers went about their daily tasks.

The entire village was filled with activity. Carpenters cut at felled limbs and planed wood to create construction material, while others hammered away working on a new piece of furniture or an element for a new building or repair job. And animal hides were strung up all over the village. Nearly every home was stretching a dead animal on some sort of contraption outside their door. They must have needed the material to build more teepees.

One hut they passed was clearly the home of a potter, as two dozen jars dried in the sun outside their door. There was little artistry to the earthenware. It looked functional but it was as if the villagers wouldn't allow, or couldn't afford, even the slightest flair of color.

It must have been approaching meal time. Fires burned near every building and stew pots rumbled as steam rocked their heavy cast iron lids. He felt a stirring in his own stomach but hoped they had something better to offer than stew. Maybe they kept the good stuff for guests.

All of the villagers stopped what they were doing and stared at the man who had fallen from above as he passed by their homes. They ceased cutting, spinning mud, or preparing their food and gawked. He must be quite the oddity to them. Thurgood had been born into an age where seeing life from other planets was commonplace, and he found it difficult to imagine what it would be like to set eyes on an alien for the first time.

During his time in the Alliance, he had been a part of countless First Contact ceremonies. But it was never his job to make actual first contact. That was a task beneath his pay grade. But here he was, meeting another culture for the first time. He felt for these poor people. It would be quite a shock to discover you weren't alone in the universe. It could be worse, however. At least he wasn't an ugly alien. It would probably be more difficult to accept the truth if one was faced with an ugly superior intelligence.

For his own part in the encounter, he found it difficult to hide his own surprise at how human the villagers looked. Humanoids were quite common in the galaxy. Even the Hama appeared almost human. But there was often something distinguishing one planet's race from another. Usually, it was in the eyes. Thurgood always felt that subtle differences were the most dramatic, and that's where he saw it most. But when he looked into the faces of the Altairians, there was a sense of comfort… familiarity. He felt an immediate kinship with them.

Not that they looked like Earthlings. Not modern-day Earthlings anyway. They looked like something out of a history class. They were dressed in this planet's equivalent of buckskins and a heavy itchy fabric. They tended to basic chores like beating things on rocks and weaving. He saw more than a few people sitting in front of looms. He looked around, wondering what an Altairian sheep looked like, but there was no livestock to be seen in the village.

Despite his situation, a sense of calm settled over him. The village was peaceful. Quaint almost. Once he was able to see past the disgusting nature of it, he appreciated it for what it truly was. People living in tune with creation. The only sounds were of toil and hard work mixing with the sounds of the forest. The sounds of hand-operated saw blades blended with the wind. Boiling stew pots intertwined with the babbling of the brook that ran through the town. Villagers waded in the water, washing clothes and gossiping. Children giggled and splashed nearby. An elderly woman sat wrapped in an itchy blanket and rocked in a chair like elder women were wont to do.

Things were simple here.

None of the worries of an interplanetary alliance reached the banks of this river. None of the pressures of modern society burdened these pure and innocent people. Oh, to lead such a life. Serenity overcame him and he felt as if it was a gift passed from them to him.

Reya led him to a prefabricated metal building. It was a

structure out of time and place amid the wooden huts and stretched hide shelters. It looked almost like the hull of a ship, except it was covered with vines and moss. He stopped at the entry and ran his hands along the doorway. He brushed back a cropping of vines to reveal a text print on the exterior. The words Command Center were printed in Alliance Standard. He smiled as he pieced together the puzzle that surrounded him. Things were beginning to make sense.

One of the men began to speak but Antarius stopped him.

"No need to explain. I understand it all now. Why don't you introduce me to your chief?"

"The chief," the man said.

"That's what I said."

The heavy tarp that served as a doorway was pulled back to reveal an interior lit by electric light. Their color temperature matched the lights found on every Alliance ship in the fleet. A temperature that was optimized for focus and productivity. Thurgood stepped into the familiar glow of the cool white light and felt like he was home.

They led him through a series of tight hallways to an office door where they knocked before entering.

This made Thurgood chuckle.

"Why do you laugh?" Reya asked.

"It's nothing," Thurgood said. "It doesn't matter where you go, people are all the same."

"Come on in." It was a large but friendly voice that beckoned them from the other side of the door.

The savage opened the door and motioned for Thurgood to enter.

"There's our stranger." The friendly voice belonged to a friendly face. The chief wore a warm smile and a robe made from the woven material Antarius had seen in the village. He was a large, round man, which was probably why they had made him chief. Primitive societies often conflated strength and size and knew little of the dangers of heart disease.

He stepped around the desk with an outstretched hand. "It's a pleasure to meet you."

Before Antarius knew what was happening, he had shaken the hand and taken the seat offered to him next to an older man who smiled at him with a toothy grin.

The chief returned to his own seat behind the desk.

Thurgood fumbled his way through what he thought would be an appropriate greeting. "It is an honor to meet the great and mighty chief of—"

The chief started laughing before he could finish.

"I will say that's a better greeting than any of these ungrateful slobs give me." He looked up at the men who had led Thurgood to him. "You guys could learn a thing or two from our visitor."

"In your dreams, Chief," the man said as he and the woman took a seat.

"You let your people talk to you that way?" Thurgood asked.

"Oh, he's just playing."

"I imagined the position of chief commanded more respect than that."

"I get it. There's some confusion. I'm not their chief. I'm the chief. I'm the settlement's Chief Technician. The name's Durand."

"Chief Technician? That doesn't make any sense."

"Yeah, waking up in a strange place like…. You probably had a lot of questions."

"Just one really," Thurgood said.

"Maybe I can answer it."

"No need. I already found my pants."

The chief had a big laugh that filled the room, and Thurgood found it impossible not to smile along.

"Well, I tell you we have a lot more questions for you. I'm glad to see you're up and about. We feared the worst when Reya found you in the river." He nodded to the woman from the tent. "She pulled you to the shore and gave you mouth-to-mouth to get you breathing again."

"Really?" Thurgood smiled at the woman. "It seems I owe you my life."

She blushed and turned away.

"You sure do," the chief said. "She was able to keep it up until the doc arrived." He indicated that the man seated next to Antarius was the doctor. The man smiled again, revealing even more missing teeth. "The doc then took over the mouth-to-mouth until you were resuscitated."

Thurgood felt his stomach turn and did his best not to let it show on his face. "Uh, thanks?"

The chief nodded. "It was touch and go for a while, but everyone here did their part to make sure you lived."

"That's..."

"He had to keep pumping air into your lungs for at least... what, about half an hour, doc?"

The doctor confirmed the time. "I'm surprised his brain lived."

"All right," Thurgood snapped. "That's enough about you. Let's talk about me for a bit. I need your help. I need to get off this planet. I have information that I must get to the Alliance."

"What is this Alliance?" the chief asked.

"Oh, boy." Thurgood was exasperated. Yeah, quaint was nice but here's where ignorance stopped being bliss and started being a pain in the ass. "You don't get out much do you."

"I'm afraid not," the chief said with a smile. "What do you think of our humble village?"

"It's very… peaceful?"

"It wasn't always this way." The chief looked to the others in the office in a shared memory "We struggled for quite a while."

"All civilizations do. But I'm sure you got a real leg up when you discovered all this." Thurgood slapped the desk.

"My desk?" the chief asked.

"No, this Command Center manufactured on Earth. My planet."

The chief looked around his office like he was seeing it for the first time. "Yeah, that might take some explaining."

"I don't think so. I've got it all figured out."

"You do?" The chief appeared genuinely amused.

"I know why your society mirrors the history of my own people. And why your language and mine, despite being separated by light years, so closely resemble each other." Thurgood slapped the desk again.

The chief leaned back in his chair. "I'm afraid I don't understand."

Antarius stood and began pacing the room. "It's obvious, Chief. I've seen enough to know what happened. The people of Altair, your people, had once risen to a great society. I've seen the ruins. Perhaps equivalent to our own Bronze Age. Perhaps even something equaling Ancient Rome. But it was too much for them. It may have been greed or an exuberant fondness for human sacrifice. Maybe they couldn't handle their liquor, but for whatever reason, civilization didn't suit your ancestors.

"So, you went back to living like animals. Until…" Thurgood stepped to the wall and knocked on the building. "A gift falls from the heavens. You can't comprehend where it came from or how it got here. How could you? You know nothing of the worlds outside your own. Naturally, you claim it to be sacred. A holy place. For generations, holy men guard the doors while studying its secrets and using the knowledge found inside for their own gain. They use it to control the population.

"They learn the language they find inside and call it the holy language. The language spreads through required religious services, eventually replacing your own native tongue. It's been so long that now the ancient language has been lost to time. A shame… to lose one's heritage over a simple misunderstanding.

"This goes on for some time until one man… well, he had enough. He believed that all men and women should be privy to the sacred texts. It's a divine right, he says. It is unjust that any man should stand between a person and their god, and he leads a reformation. It's bloody, Chief. The old guard is not so quick to give up the influence it has enjoyed for generations. But eventually, the 'heretics' are triumphant. The old order is cast out. The texts are studied. Copies are made available. Literacy spreads. The secrets within are found to contain a knowledge that allows you and your people to leapfrog centuries of evolutionary development. Bringing you to this point in time.

"Well, I'm not sure how to tell you this and, believe me, I have no wish to destroy your belief system, but…" Thurgood took a deep breath. He didn't want to drop the truth on them like some kind of bomb, but time was of the essence. "This building is not some gift from heaven."

"No, actually," the chief said. "It's a colony command module from a ship called the *Shooting Star*. That was a colony ship that left Earth 150 and some years ago before it crashed here. We are the descendants of those who survived. My friend, we're from Earth. Just like you."

"Oh," Thurgood studied the people in the room. "And then, somewhere along the line, you reverted to savagery?"

"We are not savages, Captain Thurgood," the doctor said with a smile that said otherwise.

"You're wearing a dead animal," Antarius pointed out. He then pointed to the chief. "I'm not sure what you've got on."

"It's a textile we've learned to make from the moss that covers the forest floor."

"That would explain the smell."

The chief took the insult in stride. "We simply lack the resources to make consumer-grade products. So, we do what we can."

"I don't see how that's not savagery."

"It has not been an easy existence since our people arrived here," Reya said. "Most of the equipment that was supposed to make life on another world possible was lost in the crash. There were a couple of buildings like this, but we've been forced to improvise."

"Why didn't you call for help?" Antarius looked at each of them with renewed interest. Earthlings? Really? He couldn't see it.

"Damaged on arrival." The chief leaned back in his chair and put his feet up on the desk. "We've been told the distress signal worked for a while but even that was lost over time. It seems space travel has gotten easier in the last century and a half. Back then, it took a long time to send help."

"Most of our efforts have been focused on surviving here," another man said. "It's not much, but we're hardly savages."

"If you're so civilized, why did you attack me?" Thurgood asked.

"We didn't attack you," the chief said.

"Well, someone did. I didn't jump off that cliff for fun."

"I thought you fell," Reya said.

Thurgood deftly changed the subject. "The point is, it may not have been you in particular, Chief, but they were sure dressed like you. But also furrier."

The doctor and the chief shared a brief look before the chief sighed. "That would be the Volga."

"The true savages of this world." The doctor didn't think much of these Volga. That was clear.

"See?" Thurgood said. "Savages."

"Not quite," the chief said.

"But you just said… they were crazed, and their language was nothing but grunts."

"That was Russian," the doctor explained. "And they were always a little testy."

The chief took over the explanation. "They were part of the original crew. After the *Shooting Star* crashed, there were a lot of arguments as to what should be done next. Two factions developed. The Volga and what became our village. There was a falling out generations ago. We have been at war ever since."

"They raided our stores," one of the men said.

"They took our women," another added.

Reya looked embarrassed. "We have been at their mercy for years."

"Great," Thurgood said. "So, what you're saying is that I teamed up with the losers."

One of the men from the teepee took offense to the comment and began to stand. "Hey!"

"Hey, nothing." Antarius stood first. It was worse than he thought. These people weren't savages, they were wimps. "We've got bigger problems than your inability to defend yourselves. And I'd love to lead you and your people on a journey of self-discovery to help you build the self-confidence you need to stand up for yourselves instead of letting these Hussians kick your ass for sport."

"Russians," the doctor corrected him.

"Whatever. You've got bigger problems than some dirty bullies. I was pursued here by an evil race of assholes called the

Hama. You think the Volga are bad? Just wait till you meet these jerks. Before I wasted the last guy, he sent out a cry for help. There's a countdown ticking, and we haven't long before this place is crawling with his friends."

"But, why would they come here?" one of the men asked.

"They're looking for me," Thurgood said. "I'm a big deal back home, and we can't afford to have me captured by the enemy. So, we need to get me off of this planet as soon as possible."

The doctor pointed to himself and the others in the room. "What about us?"

"I don't think they know who you are. No offense."

"No." The chief was on his feet now. "What about getting us off the planet?"

"One thing at a time, Chief. Let's focus on the problem at hand. My problem. I need to get off this rock."

"How can you leave? You crashed your ship."

"But I didn't crash their ship. It will still fly. However, your big bad bullies have it surrounded. I think they think it's some kind of bird."

"Why would they think that?" one of the men asked.

"I don't know. They're your friends."

"They're not our—"

"It doesn't matter," Thurgood said. "We need to get me on that ship."

"But you said the Volga have it."

"Then we'll just have to take it back." Antarius finished his statement by pounding his fist on the desk.

"No, the Volga are too strong," the doctor said, and Thurgood could hear the fear in his voice. "They are too brutal. We have never been able to defeat them."

"Yeah? Well, things are different now." He slammed the desk once more.

"How?"

"Because now, you have me." How many times was he going to have to hit this desk?

The doctor pointed to the bandage. "You're bleeding."

Thurgood looked at the dressing around his waist. Blood was seeping through the bandage. "It's nothing."

"You have to rest," the chief said. "We'll talk about this later."

"I'm fine!" Thurgood hit the desk with his fist a final time and then collapsed from the blood loss.

ELEVEN

Sticks and Stoned

The captain was no stranger to passing out. Being a hero of the Alliance came with more than a fancy uniform. It came with its fair share of blows to the head and late nights of doing shots for peace. Everyone thought diplomacy was nothing but parties, a gentleman's game of manners and cautious phrasing. But the truth was, statesmanship had its rough side. If you spoke one wrong word, made one wrong gesture or slept with the wrong man's wife, you were in for a tough go of things. Thurgood had been in the trenches of diplomatic work for years and he was no stranger to blacking out.

But when he finally woke, he promised himself he would not make a habit of doing it twice in the same day.

He was in a tent again. There was no mystery around it this time, so he opened his eyes and once more saw a face staring back at him. But this time it was a beautiful face.

Reya, the woman who had pulled him from the river and given him the kiss of life, sat next to him on the bed running a cool, foul-smelling cloth across his forehead. He reached out and took hold of her wrist.

This surprised her and she looked into his eyes. She smiled to see he was awake.

"You're prettier than the last face I woke up to."

She blushed at this, took her hand back and dipped the cloth into a bowl of cool water.

"Much prettier."

"That's very kind of you to say." She wrung out excess water from the fabric and turned back to apply to it to his forehead once more.

He held her gaze as she wiped the cloth across his forehead.

"You worried everyone. You had a fever," she said.

"And you made me better," he said softly. "You sat by me until I was well. I don't know how I can ever repay you."

"We used the aspirin from your first aid kit. I just got here."

"Oh. Still, thank you." Thurgood sat up in the bed. Dizziness overcame him. It was another not-so-unfamiliar feeling, so he decided to push through it and stood. The feeling overwhelmed him and he stumbled.

But she was there, and she rushed to his side and took his arm to help him balance.

Her touch was warm and her hands were… well, they weren't soft. They were actually a little calloused, but that was to be expected given how difficult life on Altair could be. But her touch was still welcomed. He put his hand over hers and their eyes locked once more. But she was angry this time.

She scolded him for standing, and guided him back to the edge of the bed. "Sit! Before you fall down."

"I'm fine," he said, and pulled her hand away. "I must speak to the chief."

She placed her hand on his chest and pushed him back until he was sitting on the cot. "The chief has ordered you to rest. And that's what you're going to do. You need it."

She was probably right. But resting was a quitter's move. "I don't need rest. I need to take action."

"No, you need rest."

He was done pleading. It was time to take charge. He used his authoritative voice. "I have to get back to my ship so I can get back to Earth. Don't you see? They need me in this fight."

"They need you to get better. So you can get strong. Then you can fight. You have to rest."

"And what if I refuse?" Thurgood leaned forward to stand.

She put her hands on his shoulder and pushed him back with a strong shove. "Then I will make you."

This made Antarius smile. He wasn't used to being told no. People had tried. The first time he remembered it happening was when the butler had scolded him for kicking the other butler. He had been young and reacted poorly. He understood now what he couldn't then, that the man had only been looking out for Antarius's wellbeing (and possibly the wellbeing of the butler he had spent half an hour kicking). Thurgood now regretted having the man fired.

As a younger man, he had come to believe being told no was a threat to his identity and that anyone who dared speak to him was trying to rob him of his own truth. As he matured, he learned that sometimes it had less to do with him and more with the fact that people didn't like being kicked so much. He could understand that. But sometimes they told him no for his own best interest. That, he had understood less. How could being denied something he wanted be in his best interest? It didn't make any sense logically. Still, he learned not to harbor resentment against a person just for telling him no. He just ignored them and went about his day, as it usually meant they were envious and trying to steal his happiness.

But when she said it, it meant something more than it ever

had before. It was at that moment Antarius Thurgood fell in love.

He had fallen in love plenty of times. In fact, he was quite good at falling in love. Put next to any man from any planet in the Alliance, Antarius was convinced he could fall in, or out of, love faster than any of them.

This wasn't him boasting. Antarius had always been a man of passion and brave enough to follow his heart wherever it may lead.

He tried to recall the three fastest times he had fallen in love.

There was the instructor at the academy who had rebuked him in front of the other cadets mere moments after stepping off the shuttle. It was a classic power move; she had to make an example of someone and she had chosen him. Probably because of his good looks. He had never been accused of being a random face in the crowd. She had dressed him down right there in front of the others. She attacked his posture, his smirk and she had demanded he look at her. So he did look at her, and later that night it was his turn to dress her down. She was transferred the next day, and they lost track of one another, but they had shared something special—at least twice.

Then there was a woman in the diplomat's office on the planet Thryst. It was his first assignment with the diplomatic corp. She had been sent to fetch him at the star port and escort him to the embassy. They had taken a detour on the way that led to a passionate romance that lasted several months until she had been "relieved of her duty" because she had been "suspected of espionage" and "an enemy of the Alliance." It had all sounded like nonsense to him. He had never seen any suspicious behavior from her. All he knew was she loved him. He could tell it was real because of the deep interest she expressed in everything he did. Everywhere he went. Everyone he spoke to. She wanted to know all about his day in detail. Expressing such an interest in your partner's career was a sign of true love that he had only known a few times in his life.

Perhaps the fastest he had ever fallen in love was with a communications officer on the outskirts of the outer rim. His ship had been in distress and there was a calm in her voice he had needed to hear. And wasn't that what true love was? Finding someone who we could instantly connect with? Someone who not only understood us but could recognize what it was we needed and give selflessly to aid the other in their time of need? It had been the purest love he had ever known. Discovering it was only a computer program working its way through a decision tree was one of the hardest lessons of his life. It took him months to get over whatever her name was.

Love was perilous. But, still, he wept for the timid, for they would never know the throes of ecstasy that came with losing yourself to love. True, there was a risk of being hurt and with a heart that swelled so large with love as his, heartbreak was inevitable. But he never blamed love for the pain. He was always gracious for the passion it brought him and always looked forward to the next time.

And here was the next time. But this time if felt different.

Not different like the time he fell in love with the Bammonitian princess. That just felt sticky. This felt different like something more was happening. There was a dizziness associated with the realization he was falling in love. It could be the lack of blood and it could be that he sat up too fast, but he didn't think that's what was happening.

No, this was something unique. The way she told him no was magical. It stirred something in him beside his loins. Something deeper, on a more personal level. Like a layer of loins he never knew he had before. Emotional loins. But how could he tell her this? Would she even understand? Did women have emotional loins? He had to make sense of what was happening.

"I'm going to get up," he said, and started to rise.

"No," she said. Simply. Lovingly. Loin-stirringly.

Another wave of euphoria washed over him. She hadn't even touched him this time, but her words alone had the same effect. What was going on? He decided to test the situation and began making demands he knew would result in denial.

"I need to get up."

"No."

"I'm going to get dressed."

"No."

"Do you want to see me do a cartwheel?"

"No."

Wave after wave of dizziness and delight struck him every time she shot him down. And each time she denied him, he fell deeper in love.

Finally, he couldn't restrain himself. Mere words no longer satisfied him. He wanted to be physically denied. He had to experience the physical side of this emotional discovery. If her words were waves of emotional bliss crashing against him as a fool on love's beach, what would her touch be like? He had to know. He pulled back the moss blankets and stood.

She stuck him with a needle.

He said "ouch" and stared at the source of the pain as she wiped the blood away with a swab. "You're getting too excited. This should calm you down."

He hit the bed hard. Or the floor. He wasn't sure. He just remembered going down and then being sideways.

But he didn't black out. He knew what that was like and this was different. When you blacked out, everything just went dark. Black. He assumed that's why they called it blacking out. But that didn't happen. This time his senses exploded in color, and the strain it put on his eyes forced him to turn away from her.

And when he turned back, she was him.

Or she was gone and he was standing where she had been. But he was still standing where he was so it must have been her looking like him. How was she doing that? Or was it him doing it?

It was all very confusing. And then he was a lizard.

He knew because he was suddenly able to lick his own eyeball and he had never been able to do that before. Antarius had never tasted eyeball before and he wasn't sure how he felt about it. If someone asked him if he had ever tasted eyeball, he could now say yes, but if they asked him if he liked it, he wasn't quite sure how he'd answer. It was salty like tears but it had a sweet taste, too, like the outside of a jawbreaker before everything turned sour in the middle.

Thurgood the lizard skittered across a flat rock, looking for some clue to his whereabouts. He wasn't in the teepee any more. The world had changed around him. Sunlight beat down on him with a ferociousness he had never known.

Even for a lizard, it was hot and he leapt from the rock to the sand to escape the sun's wrath.

But there was no safety on the sand. It began to fall away beneath him. His little lizard legs scrambled, trying to find footing, but everywhere he placed his foot, the ground shifted beneath him, sucking him into the earth below.

The void grabbed his back foot and wouldn't let it go. He could feel himself losing the struggle against the quicksand. It had him up to the knee now and was pulling him under to some cold darkness he could only sense. He slapped his little lizard tail against the ground and burrowed it into the shifting sand. With a wiggle he didn't know he was capable of, he propelled himself from gravity's hold and onto the tarmac of the nearby road.

The cold of the unknown was replaced by the intense heat of a sunbaked blacktop. The sun had turned the road into molten tar. The viscous surface seized his toes and slowed his struggle to a crawl. The more he shook to free himself of its hold, the tighter its grip became. He struggled frantically to free himself, to make it to the other side of the road and freedom.

Then his legs fell off.

It was one of the back legs first. And it dropped off without any warning. There was no pain or discomfort or even a popping sound. It just shed itself as if it was part of some natural process.

He kicked with the other rear leg and made it another foot toward safety before leaving that limb behind as well.

He used his forelimbs to drag himself across the line but lost each in the process.

Through his own struggles or through some cruel trick of biology, he shed his limbs and found himself writhing on his belly like a snake. But he was free, and he hurried across the sand while it shifted beneath him.

High above him circled a mighty bird. He had no idea what kind. Antarius never had much interest in ornithology and never considered bird watching a legitimate hobby. He refused to acknowledge that standing and looking at things counted as doing something. But now, he had millions of questions about the creature overhead. What was it called? How big was it? But, most importantly, did it eat snakes?

He kept one eye glued on the bird above, not as a matter of fascination but as one of survival. He could feel it in his snake bones that the bird was gunning for him. The intuition drove him on, and he slithered faster and faster toward the shelter of a rock.

The bird attacked. It screeched as it dove, its cry carried

faster by the wind. Talons gleamed like knives honed for the sole purpose of gutting snakes. He could hear them shearing the wind as they came for him.

Antarius snapped his body as the bird reached the ground and dodged the attack. He made a dozen impossible shapes out of his body. It was a few simple esses to begin with, but as the attack went on, he found himself gaining more and more control of his body and was forced to be more creative to dodge the talons. He formed a lightning bolt, an ampersand and a lemniscate despite having no idea it was called that. These complicated forms foiled the bird's attempts to grab a quick lunch and it took back to the skies in frustration.

Thurgood formed the vague outline of a middle finger and made a final dash for the safety of the outcropping. Once there, he coiled up and heaved as he tried to catch his breath.

The rock's shade gave him comfort. It was damp. And quiet. But he wasn't alone. He could sense another like himself. There was another snake in the darkness. Sneaking up on him like snakes often do.

Antarius was tired of running. He remained still and acted nonchalant. It was something he had struggled to do in life as a man, but as a snake he found it easy. He focused on hissing a little and sticking his tongue in and out. His goal was to act oblivious to his enemy's presence and lull them into a false sense of confidence.

Grains of sand shifted around him and he knew his enemy was close.

Antarius struck!

It was better to be the aggressor than a snack. He got the other snake by the tail. His fangs sank deep into the scales and he began to swallow. He dislocated his jaw to make his mouth larger. He was surprised how easy this was, but still a little freaked out by the whole thing. He swallowed the other snake, taking his would-be predator in a half a foot at a time. He would be nobody's victim.

Everything vanished suddenly. The rock was gone from overhead. The melting road disappeared and the bird of prey circled no more. He was left alone, hanging in nothingness. It was only then he discovered he was eating his own tail.

That's when he awoke screaming.

TWELVE

Le Enfanthomme

Thurgood awoke with the taste of snake tail in his mouth. At least, he thought it was the taste of snake tail. Now that he was awake, he realized he had no real frame of reference for what snake tail tasted like. But what else could it be? It was a gummy, sticky sensation that tried to seal his lips together and made his mouth move in slow motion. The terrible dream had literally left a bad taste in his mouth.

Off the top of his head, he couldn't remember another dream that tasted so awful. Usually, his dreams were so unremarkable he rarely remembered them. He had always assumed it was because he was living the dreams of so many others in his waking life that it would hardly be fair if he was also amazing while he was asleep. It was a price he had become accustomed to paying. This dream, however, would haunt to him for years to come.

The whole experience had left him in a fog and he struggled to open his eyes. Once he did, he found himself alone in a strange bed. This was far from the first time he had found himself alone in a strange bed, but the blanket was itchier than normal. And it had a funk to it he couldn't immediately place.

The smell from the moss blanket soon seeped into his memory and he remembered everything. The crash, the Hama, his whole situation came rushing back to him. He bolted upright in bed and looked around the room.

Where was the woman? She should have been there, looking over him. He looked around for Reya, but she was nowhere to be seen. There was no one watching over him. The tent was empty but for him. What had happened? Where had everyone gone?

Antarius ripped off the covers and leapt out of the bed, fearing the worst. They had to be in trouble. It was the only possible explanation for why they would leave him alone.

Had some beast descended on the village while he slept? Had the Hama arrived while he slept and found them?

No, it couldn't be the Hama. Not now. Not this soon.

But how long had he been out? Thurgood remembered the needle and felt for the mark on his arm. There was no mark. He had been out for some time. What had she given him?

Panic overtook him. If the Hama had come, the villagers wouldn't stand a chance against them. The enemy was too advanced, too brutal. And the bastards wouldn't show any mercy. It would be a slaughter.

Antarius located his pants by the fire and pulled them on as he stumbled toward the door. He took only a moment to appreciate the warmth of the pants before running out into the square.

What carnage could he expect to find? Had they spared the children? It was doubtful. The Hama were monsters, bereft of conscience and basic decency. But even the children? How could they?

Antarius steeled himself for the worst and raced outside to face the carnage. He anticipated the burning structures and the foul smell that always accompanied pillaging. He knew it would be worse, however, since the village stank pretty badly to begin with. It was probably the moss. Or maybe the mud.

Thurgood startled a middle-aged woman who was passing by him with a bundle of sticks and almost knocked her over.

The woman caught a scream before it left her throat, but the bundle of sticks went scattering across the dirt path that ran through the village which was, surprisingly, not currently on fire.

The huts were not burning. The villagers were not smoldering in mass graves, they were going about their chores. The children hadn't been slaughtered, they were playing in the mud because it was pretty much the only toy on Altair. Everything was fine.

About the only thing out of the ordinary appeared to be him. His dramatic dash from the teepee had not only startled the old stick lady, it had drawn a crowd of gawkers—many of whom were also carrying bundles of sticks. At any other moment, Antarius would have wondered, "What's with all the sticks?" But the looks from the villagers were making him uncomfortable and he began to squirm under the stares.

He cleared his throat and addressed the crowd. "I was just... It was just that I... I thought... Um, yeah."

With everything explained, Thurgood stepped unhurriedly through the crowd, smiling at each villager that made eye contact. He gave each a nod and assured them it was a good morning. He kept this up until he reached the edge of the crowd. There he started jogging in place.

"Just heading out for a brisk run. Physical fitness is an important part of every day. Never forget that." Thurgood waved to the crowd, turned and ran toward the chief's office.

The chief was in his office with several other villagers when Thurgood burst in the door.

"Captain," the chief said. "I'm glad to see you're feeling better."

"Like I told you earlier, I'm fine." Antarius looked at the people around the room. "I told the woman I was fine. I told the doctor. I told everybody. So let's stop worrying about my health and start worrying about getting me back to my ship. We can't waste another minute."

"You've been under for a week," one of the villagers said as he rose from his seat. It was the doctor who needed a dentist.

"A week?"

"A week," Durand confirmed.

That couldn't be right. Although, it would explain the taste in his mouth. But how could he have been out for a week? "That's just not possible."

"I'm afraid so, Captain." The doctor stepped close and began examining the openings in Thurgood's face. Mouth, ears, eyes, each nostril.

Thurgood wondered what one nostril could tell him that the other couldn't.

"You appear... very well rested," concluded the doctor as he sat back down.

"A week?" Antarius rubbed his arm, remembering the shot Reya had given him. "What did she give me?"

He turned on the doctor and shouted, "What kind of witch doctor concoction did you put into me?"

The doctor remained calm. "It was only a mild sedative."

"Mild?" Antarius remembered the part in the dream where his legs fell off. "What's mild about it?"

"We give it to babies when they are teething," the chief said.

"You give this to babies! They must be tripping all over the place!"

The chief shrugged. "They never seem to mind. Everyone is calling you Enfanthomme."

"Enfanthomme." Antarius spoke the word to himself a couple of times. "I like the sound of that. What does it mean? Dashing? Brave? Hero from the sky?"

"Baby man," the doctor said.

It stung. But Antarius had been called names before and many were better than this. "Not very imaginative, is it?"

"They aren't calling you this because it's clever," the chief said. "It's because you are a man that reminds them of a baby."

Antarius felt his fist tighten. "And just who is calling me this?"

A villager near the door spoke up. "Who isn't?"

"It doesn't matter." Thurgood fought back the anger. It didn't matter what anyone on this backwater mud hole thought about him. There were more pressing matters at hand. Matters these bullying simpletons couldn't even begin to comprehend. He leaned on the desk, looked at the chief and said sternly, "I have to get back to that ship. Lives are in danger. Yours and, more critically, mine."

The chief stood and smiled. "Don't you think you're being a little overdramatic?"

Thurgood ground his teeth. He didn't like his emotions being questioned. "I am being exactly as dramatic as the moment necessitates!"

The chief stepped out from behind his desk and walked around the office. "You've been here a week. And in that time—aside from taking up our hospital bed—absolutely nothing has happened. No aliens have landed. No one has attacked us. It's clear that you are in no danger."

"Except from perhaps yourself," the doctor added, and turned Thurgood's head to look in his ear.

"You think this is all in my head?"

"We don't doubt your story, Captain. Obviously, you've crashed here and it's clear you're out of your element. But we wonder if you haven't perhaps embellished your importance to the enemy."

"I beg your pardon?"

"Maybe you're not worth the effort," the doctor said.

"What are you saying?"

"You may not be as important as you think you are," the chief said coldly.

"I'll have you know that—"

"More importantly, it is also clear the people of the Shooting Star are in no danger. I know you want to leave, but I simply can't risk antagonizing the Volga to satisfy your whims."

"Fine, I don't need you. Just give me a map, a few days' worth of supplies and I'll go by myself."

The doctor choked back a laugh.

The chief let his out. "You wouldn't last a day. You have no idea what dangers await you in the jungles."

"The hell I don't…. Big cats. Scary birds. Stupid Russians. Nothing I can't handle."

"It is too dangerous a journey," the chief said, finalizing his position. "Furthermore, your actions may be mistaken for our own. I can't in good conscience allow it."

"You can't keep me here, Chief."

"To let you leave would be like sending you to your death."

"That's a risk I'm willing to take. Death and I have an understanding."

"That may be, but it's not one I'm willing to take."

"Perhaps we shouldn't be too hasty," the doctor said. "This could be an opportunity to reach out to the Volga. To broker peace. Surely they would realize that it's their chance to escape Altair as well."

"Why do they deserve to be rescued?" The man near the door spoke with venom, or an accent. "After all they've done to us. They should rot here forever."

"Is it not worth trying if it would save us all?" the doctor asked.

"Do you think they'd listen?" Reya had come into the room while they were talking and remained silent, carefully considering everything that had been said.

Durand shook his head. "More likely they'd just abandon us here the first chance they get. But it doesn't matter. I can't allow it. We can't take the risk."

Some empathy entered the chief's eyes. He crossed the office and put a hand on Antarius's shoulder. "I'm sorry to say this, but I'm afraid you now share our fate. You're stranded here with us on Altair."

THIRTEEN

Clear as Mud

Thurgood sat on a rock at the edge of the village watching two children play in the mud. They squealed with delight as they dug their hands into the wet earth and flung handfuls at one another, laughing louder each time it splattered across their skin. Even here, in the most remote reaches of the middle of nowhere, when there was nothing but wet earth at hand, these children could find joy. As their laughter filled the air, he could only think one thing; "I've got to get out of this shithole."

That, however, was proving difficult. Before departing the command center, Thurgood had declared his defiance and his intentions to leave the village against the chief's orders. In response to the "outburst," Durand had assigned some men to ensure Antarius stayed in the Village of the Shooting Star. And these men had proven to be formidable guards.

Thurgood's first plan was open defiance. After telling them to go to hell, Thurgood had marched directly to the edge of town, where he found two of the sentries waiting for him. He laughed when they warned him to turn back and swore when they threatened him with violence if necessary. He laughed at their warnings and walked straight through them. When he woke up, he had a headache and had lost an hour of the day.

On his next attempt, he went on the offensive and rushed them. He was successful in defeating the two men who blocked his path. It was the other two he hadn't seen that had gotten him. The result was much the same, only this time the headache was worse because they were a little miffed he had beaten up their friends.

Sneaking around them didn't work. They were waiting for him in the forest.

Bribing them didn't work. He had little of value on him and they didn't believe him when he told them how rich his father was.

Escaping under the cover of darkness didn't work because he kept forgetting to get up in the middle of the night.

Even his elaborate disguise failed to fool the ever-vigilant guards because they said a pile of blankets couldn't move on its own.

Every attempt he'd made at escaping had been foiled. He had even attempted to construct a hot air balloon so he could drift above his captors to freedom. But it proved difficult to build a balloon when your supply list consisted of little more than mud and sticks.

He was about to stand, scream and run into the woods waving his hands like a maniac. Maybe, he thought, if he made it look like he was being attacked by a swarm of backwater-planet bees, he could get by and make a break for it in the confusion.

As quickly as it had come to him, he dismissed the idea. If his guards were too smart to fall for the "I'm being chased by a pack of alien dogs" plan, they would be too smart to fall for the "I'm being chased by a swarm of alien bees" plan. Even if the bees were more realistic. He cursed himself for not trying the bees before the dogs and returned to staring at the children playing in the mud.

Reya sat next to him on the rock.

He didn't look at her. He knew why she was there. She was there at the behest of the chief to dissuade him from further escape attempts. It would be just like Durand to send a woman to do his job.

But Reya didn't say anything. She just sat quietly, watching the kids sling mud at one another.

"Your chief doesn't know the first thing about freedom," Thurgood said. He kept his eyes on the kids. "Or anything about liberty, either."

She didn't argue. For a moment she didn't say anything. "He is only doing what he thinks is best for everyone."

"Well, it's not the best. It's the worst. If I don't get back to Earth, billions of people could die."

"Billions?"

"You don't know the Hama like I do. No one does. Earth needs me on their side to protect the planets of the Alliance."

"Billions?"

"Yes. Billions."

Reya's stare became distant. "I can't imagine so many people. I've only ever known life on Altair. The idea of that many people is hard to picture."

"Well, they're out there, believe me. Some of them are jerks, but most of them are okay, I guess. But none of them deserve to die at the hands of the Hama. Even the jerks. That much I know. I have to get back to them. And every day I delay my return, the danger grows." He drove a fist into his palm.

She put a hand on his back.

Her touch was comforting. He didn't even mind the rough palms.

One of the children in the mud had gotten the upper hand

on his friend. He lifted a massive ball of mud over his head and threatened to drop it on his friend who had fallen to the ground. The child on the ground giggled and squealed as he tried to scramble out of range. His hands and feet found no traction in the mud and he struggled as the threat loomed over him.

It reminded Antarius of his dreams, and a shudder ran through him.

"What is it?" she asked.

"I don't know what it was you gave me the other day."

"It was just—"

"I know, for kids. But that stuff gave me the weirdest dreams."

"Sometimes our dreams tell us what we are unwilling to hear from others. Or the things we're unwilling to tell ourselves." Reya appeared genuinely interested in it all. "Sometimes they hold the answers we are looking for."

Thurgood laughed. "I don't see how eating myself is the answer to anything."

"The meaning isn't always clear. Why don't you tell me about it?"

He didn't want to tell her. The dream embarrassed him. Flashes of it came to him and each one made him cringe a little more. Why was he a snake? And if he had to be a snake, why was he such a small one? He didn't want to talk about it at all. But something told him he could trust her. Maybe it was her gentle touch or her kind eyes. Maybe it was because she was pretty.

"I was a lizard pursued," he began after taking in a heavy breath. "Chased across a hostile environment that tried to consume me. There was a bird. A mean bird. A dick bird. I tried to run. But the harder I ran, the more legs I lost. The earth tried to swallow me, so I became a snake. I shed my last vestiges of humanity to save myself."

Thurgood hung his head. He had felt some shame in the dream but as he said it aloud, the shame grew stronger.

"I hid. Like a coward, I hid. But I was not alone. There was another snake seeking refuge from the dick bird and I saw it as a threat. So I ate it. But that snake ended up being me."

"Ouroboros," she said softly.

"Well, I'm sorry if I'm boring you. It was my dream after all. You're the one that wanted to hear it." Maybe she was meaner than he thought. Like that stupid bird in his dream. Maybe she was the bird! "Let's hear about your stupid dream and see how enthralling it is."

Reya smiled as she repeated the word once more, overpronouncing each syllable. "Ouro...bo...ros. It is a symbol that has been found all throughout human history—it's one of the oldest symbols, in fact. It's been found in texts and temples across cultures. Its shape is the snake eating itself."

"Well it's gross," Thurgood said.

"It's actually a good thing," Reya said.

"I had myself in my mouth, lady! Maybe that does it for you, but I try to hold myself with a certain amount of dignity."

"It is not meant to be taken literally. The Ouroboros is a symbol of growth and maturation." She picked up a stick and drew the shape in the dirt by the rock. "It represents life, death and rebirth."

"Rebirth?"

"Change," she said. "Maybe, if you're being honest with yourself, there are changes to be made. Maybe your being here is no accident. Maybe here is exactly where you're supposed to be."

"Change," he echoed her words, trying them out for himself. Could she be right? He had always known he was a man of destiny. He had come to accept that. But he had never known destiny to be so confusing. It was always pretty straightforward.

But maybe destiny was more mysterious than he thought. The answer dawned on him, and he leapt to his feet and repeated it again with more confidence. "Change."

Reya stood and smiled. "Perhaps you understand now."

"I do," Thurgood said. "It's still gross, but I get it. How does someone like you know so much about snake symbols?"

"We're stranded. Not stupid. Everyone here goes to school. We learn about the classics, the sciences and even a little about how to better ourselves despite our situation. Do you understand?"

"I do. And it looks like I've got some changing to do."

Reya put a gentle hand on his shoulder, smiled and left him alone with his thoughts.

He watched her walk away as the word rattled around in his head. Change was the answer. Change was action. Change was advantageous. He looked around the village and watched as the villagers made the most of their humble surroundings. Despite living in mostly mud and moss, the people of the Shooting Star smiled and laughed. Humanity thrived just beneath the dirt and mud-covered surface of the village. The men and women had dug deep and found it. It was nothing short of inspiring, and it made Thurgood smile for the first time in days. "Yes, it's time for a change."

FOURTEEN

Itching to Change

Change began the next day.

Thurgood felt relief wash over him. He had felt embarrassed by his snake dream, but now he realized it wasn't dirty or anything to be ashamed of. Reya had been right. The dream was telling him change was needed if he was going to make the situation on Altair work.

It was obvious to him now, and he wondered why the snake couldn't have just said something instead of being all cryptic and gross. Instead of gorging himself on himself, the snake could have just gone, "Psst, hey buddy, change is the answer." It would have been clearer and cut back on all the confusion and icky feelings he had experienced the last few days.

But what was done was done, and the message had now been received. Change was the answer. It was that simple. And since he couldn't change the chief's mind about helping him get to the Hama ship, Antarius would simply have to change chiefs.

Durand would have to go. He needed to be replaced by someone with the leadership skills, vision and courage to make the hard choices necessary to benefit the village and—more immediately—himself. That made the new candidate for chief obvious; it would have to be him.

It wasn't going to be an easy task. Durand appeared to be well-liked, and Antarius recognized that he was an outsider here. He realized the only way the people of the Village of the Shooting Star would follow him was if he won their trust, became accepted as one of their own and proved to them he was better suited to lead them into a brighter tomorrow.

It wouldn't happen overnight. It was going to take some time.

A week should do it. And that would leave him just enough time to get off the planet before the Hama showed up looking for him.

Laboring under no delusions, he set to work to become one of the village people. The first thing he did was strip out of what was left of his Alliance uniform and don a set of the local rags. The shirt was made from woven moss. Next to mud, it seemed to be the most abundant resource in the village.

During their time here, the villagers had refined the textile process to separate the moss fibers and pin them back into a fabric. That fabric was then used for clothing, bedding, bandages and more. About the only thing they couldn't seem to figure out was how to get the smell out of it.

The shirt began to itch the moment he pulled it over his head, but he took the discomfort in stride. If he was going to win their trust, he would have to be one of them. And when you were trying to be like someone, the first step was to dress like them.

The pants were something different. The elderly lady that had given him the clothes had said the moss didn't wear as well below the waist. Her concern had been durability, but Antarius imagined it had as much to do with the itchiness as anything else.

He pulled on the buckskins and instantly felt a little

disgusted. The pants had once been a creature. And he was now inside of it. He had questioned the pants lady about the material. Her defense was that people back on Earth used to wear animal skins all the time. Pants, jackets, car seats. She had gone on and on, but he had been disgusted by the whole idea. Wearing dead animals was something only another animal would do. It was murderous, immoral and surprisingly flattering.

Antarius caught his reflection in a mirror and admired himself in the pants. He wasn't a fan of the material, but he sure was making it work. He turned several times, admiring the pants from all angles.

The more angles he examined, the more he liked it. The idea of wearing an animal's skin was detestable and brutal but, at the same time, undeniably sexy. This moral wrestling match didn't last long, and Antarius quickly decided that once he got back to Earth, he would have to have a discussion with Thurgood Industries' fashion division about the idea. He wondered for a moment if there was some kind of Earth equivalent creature they could use to source the skins.

He did one last turn in front of the mirror, scratched at his chest and stepped outside the mud hut he had been told to call home.

Reya was just about to knock on his door flap when he exited. They startled one another. She recovered first.

"Good morning, Antarius."

"Good morning, Reya."

"I wanted to—" she studied his clothes. "What are you doing? Why are you dressed like that?"

He smiled and did a subtle modeling turn. "Not bad, huh? I decided if I'm going to be here for a while, I might as well start acting like I belong."

"Okay," she said with some hesitation. "That's... sudden?"

"I'm rebirthing, Reya. It was your idea. Well, and the snake's."

"Uh..."

"Change! The more I thought about what you said, the more it made sense. I've been famous and successful my whole life. I was important from day one. What if I finally got to take a break from all the wealth and popularity? What if I, Antarius Thurgood, could be a nobody? This simple life could be just what I needed."

"Are you sure you're feeling okay?" Reya asked as she reached out to feel his forehead. "Maybe I should get you more medicine."

"I'm fine." Thurgood ducked under the outstretched palm. "I'm just really excited to get started living a boring life here in the Village of the Shooting Star. What should we do first? Gather some mud? Or how about some sticks?"

Reya's lips tightened as she examined his smile.

She wasn't buying his sincerity, so he smiled a little more broadly to put extra sincerity into it. "Which were you on your way to do?"

She didn't answer the question. "There's someone I'd like you to meet."

"Great, I want to meet everyone. Really get to know them, you know? Like that old lady." Antarius pointed to an older woman that was passing by with a bucket, probably of mud, in each hand. Thurgood rushed to her side and tried to take one of the buckets from her hand. "Let me help you with those, Old Lady."

"I'm forty-five!"

"I know things can get tough at that age."

The woman snatched the bucket out of his reach and continued on her way with considerably more attitude in her stride.

He dismissed the old woman as grouchy and probably itchy as he raced to help a man who was sawing through a tree limb. Thurgood moved to the man's side and set a hand on the log.

The man stopped sawing and looked at him. "What are you doing?"

"I'm helping," Thurgood said.

The man looked around for a moment. "How are you helping?"

"I'm holding this still while you cut."

"Um... thank you?"

"Don't mention it, friend. I'm here for you."

Another three draws of the blade finished the cut and the end of the log dropped to the ground with a thud. Thurgood stepped back to admire a job well done while the man lifted the heavy timber and threw it on a nearby pile.

"Nice work, neighbor," Thurgood said, and exchanged a friendly high five with the man.

"What are you doing?" Reya asked.

"Whatever I can," he said with a broad smile. "I'm here to help."

A squeal of delight drew his attention, and he spotted the kids from the day before playing in the mud once more. "Oh, look," Thurgood said with a laugh. "Revelry. Let's join in."

Before she could beat him to it, Thurgood raced to the bottom of the hill, scooped up a handful of mud and slung it at one of the kids with a playful, "Take that."

The *schwack* of the wet mud was quite satisfying. The child's screaming was a bit surprising, as was his collapsing to the ground in agony.

"What the hell are you doing, you jerk?" the other boy screamed as he rushed to his friend's side.

"I'm... I'm just... I was just trying to play along." Thurgood was pointing as much as he was talking. "So, I threw the mud."

The boy on the ground sat up, holding a hand over his right eye. Blood flowed through his fingers. "There was a rock in there, you idiot."

"Oh, I am sorry. It's been a while since I've played mud war. For the last few years, it's just been regular war."

"Why don't you go back to your stupid planet?" the first kid shouted as he helped his friend to his feet.

"I would if I could, kid. We've got proper mud back on Earth."

"Earth?" The bleeding kid got up and joined in on the name calling. "Is that the planet where everyone throws like a girl?"

"Hey! That's... that's uncalled for. First off, that's not an insult. I know a lot of ladies that throw quite well and..."

"Is it your mom?" the bleeding boy asked.

"You leave my mother out of this! How would you like it if I dragged your mother into this?"

The kid went instantly silent. Then his lip quivered. Then he yelled, "You're such an ass," and ran away.

"That's what I thought," Thurgood shouted after him.

Reya put a hand on his shoulder and started to say something.

He stepped away from her touch and yelled after the boy. "You can start it but you just can't finish it. Is that it?"

The first boy brushed the excess mud from his clothes, shook his head at Thurgood and walked after his friend. "You just don't get it, off-worlder."

"What?" Thurgood asked. "What don't I get? I'm just a big dummy from a planet that has more fun to offer than mud. So maybe you can explain it to me."

"The boy's mother died last week," Reya said softly.

"Oh no." Thurgood's heart sank.

"He has no one. He's an orphan."

"I... I didn't know. They should let people know. Maybe some kind of special shirt. Oh, I just..." Thurgood sighed. "I'm not really good at fitting in. Am I? I'm going to have to face it. I was just born to stand out."

Reya didn't answer. She just waved for him to get out of the mud hole and said, "Come with me."

"Where are we going?"

"I'm taking you to meet someone important."

Thurgood wiped the mud from his hands on his itchy shirt and staggered back onto drier land.

FIFTEEN

Wise Guy

The "someone important" was a very old man named Monsieur Babin. Not old like the easily offended old lady with the sticks, but *old* old. His eyes were cloudy and grey, and the man used a stick to hobble around his hut. It was an age Thurgood had never seen in person. Back on Earth, science had taken the sting out of aging long ago.

Despite his feeble physical form, the man's enthusiasm had not waned. He welcomed the pair in with great excitement and set to making a pot of tea for his guests.

Thurgood took an uncomfortable seat next to Reya and watched the man as he worked in the kitchen.

"What's wrong with his eyes?" Antarius whispered to Reya.

"More than is wrong with my ears," the old man said as he filled the kettle. "My eyesight failed me long ago, young man."

"He's blind," Reya said softly.

"Blind? That's a real thing?" Antarius whispered back. "I've never heard of that happening outside of Greek myths."

"It happens," the old man assured him. He had a whimsical way of speaking that gave every word weight. "I'm afraid our doctors could only do so much once they were separated from their miraculous machines."

The kettle began to boil, and he reached for the whistling appliance.

This made Thurgood wince as he realized the man could not see what he was doing. But the old man found the handle safely and removed the kettle from the heat without burning himself. Antarius marveled at the act and wondered how it was even possible.

"Monsieur Babin has been here since the crash," Reya said. "Since the very beginning."

"You're from Earth then?" Thurgood asked.

"Not technically," Monsieur Babin explained as he poured the water. He didn't spill a drop. "I was born on the *Shooting Star* three generations into the voyage. My great-great-grandparents were the ones that set us upon this quest through the cosmos. I came along much later. You see, Captain, I'm not a child of Earth or Altair but of the stars. But, as sweet Reya said, I've been here since the beginning. Since the *Shooting Star* crashed onto the planet."

He finished pouring the tea and handed each of his guests a cup. Since he had arrived, Thurgood had been drinking out of crude earthenware cups made in the village. But this cup had a finish and delicacy to it that told him it wasn't from this planet at all.

"Thank you," Thurgood said as he brought the cup to his lips. He took a sip and grimaced audibly. The noise turned into a cough.

"You don't care for my tea, Captain?" Monsieur Babin asked, more amused than offended. The old man lowered himself into a recliner that squeaked as he settled in and put his feet up.

"It's not that, it's just that it tastes like you boiled leaves," Thurgood said.

"That's what tea is," Reya explained.

"Oh," Thurgood said, and looked into his cup. "Well, in that case it's great."

Monsieur Babin laughed, wheezed and started coughing. The fit shook his whole body, and Thurgood thought the man was going to die. Reya seemed unconcerned, so they just waited until the coughing finally stopped and Babin continued. "Many of the younger people here find it strange as well, my tea. I hoped perhaps it was still a thing back on Earth. Times do change, but tea had persevered for centuries. I couldn't imagine it falling out of favor."

Thurgood shrugged. Then he realized the man couldn't hear a shrug and added, "I'm not one to ask. I've spent more time in space serving the Alliance than I have back on Earth. It's those adventures that brought me here."

"Yes, I've heard a lot about the man baby who fell. I've very much looked forward to meeting you, Captain."

"And I, you," Antarius said, and caught an elbow in the rib from Reya. "I did. Though I didn't know it was specifically him. But an old person like him."

Reya was annoyed again. He could tell when a woman was annoyed with him sometimes. He turned back to the old man in hopes the annoyance would fade. "I have so many questions about the Village of the Shooting Star."

"Then I will do my best to answer."

Reya leaned in close to his ear. Close enough to send a tingle down his back. "Pay attention to him. He is very wise and greatly respected."

Her words echoed in Thurgood's mind. Not only because they were soft and aroused his hearing. If this man was greatly respected among the people of the Village of the Shooting Star, then there truly was a lot he could learn from him. If he could become just like the old man, it would be only natural for the villagers to respect him as well, and it would make it easier to become their new chief. He may be able to shave half a week off his schedule.

"You are too kind, my dear," the old man said as he sat in front of them. His hearing was remarkable.

Thurgood watched the man's every move. It wasn't until now that he noticed a slight tremble in the man. It was as if he approached his seat several times before he sat down. At first it seemed like a waste of time to Thurgood. He had always been a man of action, decisive in his moves, and this hesitancy to do something as simple as sit seemed like a way to broadcast uncertainty. But the more he thought about it, the more he saw the genius in the old man's movements. It wasn't uncertainty, it was a contemplative approach to everything. Every movement was considered, studied, and rejected or committed to. What appeared to be hesitation was the sign of an active mind, always thinking, always planning and always choosing the best path forward. That was true wisdom.

Reya sighed. "Sometimes, I forget how sharp your hearing is."

"And for that I'm grateful," he said.

It wasn't just his actions. Thurgood now heard the same contemplative approach in the man's words. He spoke slowly and deliberately, choosing his words precisely. Often, it sounded like he was going to use another word entirely, but his agile mind was always working and made decisions, mid-utterance, to change course and employ the better, more suitable and more impactful word.

Thurgood's annoyance at the slow speech soon turned in to a sense of awe as he watched this master at work.

"God gave us two ears and one mouth for a reason," he said slowly, stammering in all his wisdom. Afterward, he let out a satisfied breath and sipped his tea.

Thurgood waited for the old man to reveal the reason, but after a moment it was clear there was nothing more to the ear and mouth statement. Instead, the old man sipped his tea and shook with a barely perceptible tremble of wisdom.

Was this part of it? To state a simple fact as though it was some mysterious secret and then leave the room to answer the cosmic riddle on their own? Maybe it was on him to figure it out for himself. Maybe people respected you more when you didn't hand them everything and made them work a little. This whole two ears, one mouth thing was going to nettle at him though. It wasn't new information, obviously, but he'd never given much thought to it. He assumed humans had two ears, because if we had one, every time we heard a sound we'd have to spin around until we found out where it came from. You can't do much evolving if you're dizzy all the time, so being able to instinctively triangulate the source of danger made sense. As for one mouth, well he could only think of one use for two, and nature surely knew that kissing two women at once was going to always lead to trouble.

When Antarius finally returned to the conversation, he realized the woman and the old man were staring at him. Well, he was sure the woman was staring at him, the old man had that cloudy eye thing going on and could have been looking at just about anything.

"It's so we can listen twice as much as we speak," the old man said.

"I knew that," Thurgood said.

"Then why were you making kissy faces just then?" Reya asked.

Here was his chance to try out what he had learned. He spoke slowly and with purpose, mirroring the old man's speech pattern. "Because God gave us two lips for a reason."

He let the statement hang in the air and watched as they

worked out the wisdom in his words.

"What does that even mean?" Reya asked.

Monsieur Babin agreed with her. "I'm sorry, son, but I'm afraid you've lost me, as well."

Thurgood grunted and tried again. He spoke slower and put more tremble in his voice. "God gave us two lips for a reason."

They weren't getting it. He could tell by the looks they gave him.

Thurgood mimicked the man's shaky movements to add some extra wisdom to the statement. He figured it best to keep shaking until they got it.

This upset Reya for some reason. "What are you doing?!"

"What do you mean?"

"Are you making fun of his palsy?!"

"I don't think so. What's palsy?" Antarius asked her. When she didn't respond, he looked to the old man.

"Who would do such a thing?" Babin asked.

"Not me, that's for sure. I don't even know what it is."

"The shaking," she said. "The shaking that you're making fun of."

"I'm not making fun though!"

"You're still doing it! You're doing it right now!"

He was still doing it. He hadn't realized. "I didn't mean to—I thought it made me sound wise."

Reya made a noise Antarius could only describe as frustrated beyond words, stood and stomped to the door. "You're an idiot."

"I'm—"

"You're still doing it!" she screamed and left through the door. It was hard to slam a flap, but she managed.

Thurgood looked down. He was still doing it. What was wrong with him? He stopped shaking and began to apologize to the old man. "I didn't mean to offend. I was—"

The old man was trembling more now than before. His shoulders bounced and Antarius felt the first waves of panic take him as he had blown off most, if not all, of his mandatory medical training and didn't know what to do in a medical emergency. The panic passed a moment later when he realized the old man wasn't having a seizure at all. He was laughing. The laughter finally became audible and continued for some time until it turned into a giant wheeze.

"I'm glad you're finding this so amusing," Thurgood said.

The old man took a long sip of tea. "My great-granddaughter has always brought me joy."

"Your great-granddaughter?" He turned back to the hole in the tent and imagined Reya stomping off and the sound that stomping would make in the muddy streets of the village. "Oh, that's not good."

The old man continued to chuckle as he moved to the kitchen for more tea. "It will all be fine. Just explain to her that you're an idiot. She'll understand."

"I think she already knows that."

"Of course, she knew it the moment she met you. She just needs to know that you know it."

"Are you sure?"

"I'm certain."

The logic made as much sense as the two ears one mouth thing, so there must have been wisdom in it.

When the old man returned with his tea, Thurgood was still staring at the slammed flap. Somehow, despite his weird old man eyes, the old man could tell.

"She is something else, isn't she?" Monsieur Babin sat back down and sipped his tea.

"She saved me," Thurgood said. "I owe her my life."

The old man smiled. "She is a good person. Selfless. She is

the reason I can speak with confidence when I say the people here are going to be okay. For a long time, I wasn't sure."

"What do you mean?"

"Altair may have been our destiny, but it was never our destination. When the *Shooting Star* crashed here, there was an equal amount of chaos and hope among the survivors. As time went on, the hope faded. We had always known the chance of rescue was remote, but when it vanished altogether, the chaos reigned.

"The people, my friends and family, people I had known my entire life, began to reject their civility. They justified their cruel ways with good intentions of course, but cruel is cruel no matter the ends. Friends became enemies. Family turned on one another. The social order broke down. Some of us fought the encroaching savagery with everything we had. Sometimes it was in the smallest of ways."

He held up the tea cup as an example.

"For a long time, we felt it was hopeless. When you cling to law and order during a reign of chaos, it's hard not to think yourself mad. Why fight it? Why not give into the basic urges driving others if there don't appear to be any consequences? But the consequences of lawlessness were real. And they were worse than any punishment. We had to hold on to what we had."

Thurgood watched as the man's heart grew heavy. Antarius had little use for rules, but he had always respected law and order as two constants in the Alliance. It wasn't until a world lacked these things that they seemed truly alien.

"You do it for the children," Mr. Babin continued. "Sometimes an entire generation might stray, and they may shout that this new selfishness is the better way for all. But you have to have faith in the kids. They can always see the truth."

"Is that what happened with Reya?"

The old man nodded. "It started with her mother and others

her age. They were the ones that grew tired of living in fear and demanded things change. They wanted order back. They were the ones who kicked out the Volga. They were the ones that kept the hope. It continues with Reya.

"When I look at her, I know that good still has a place in this world. You see, Captain? When you look at people like my great-granddaughter, it's easy to believe that everything is going to be fine. I'm not as wise as they give me credit for. The good that happens isn't due to some prognostication. It's just my faith being rewarded. My faith in her."

"She really is something," Antarius said, staring at the doorway.

"She is," Monsieur Babin agreed.

The two men talked for what felt like hours. Antarius was told the history of the *Shooting Star*'s ill-fated voyage and the beginnings of life on Altair. It was a tale filled with adventure and political intrigue as the two factions formed and grew apart. The drama was thick until the Volga were finally cast out of the village and began their reign of terror on the remaining villagers. It was only recently that a fragile peace was brokered between Durand and the Volga chief. Monsieur Babin held out hope that peace would last, but he had little faith when it came to the others.

"My Reya deserves a better life than what Altair can offer her," he said. "Everyone here does."

"I'm trying to help, but your Chief Durand sees things differently."

"Durand is a good man," Monsieur Babin said. "But I'm afraid he's a little short sighted. His priority is the safety of the villagers. It's not an objective that welcomes risk. Sometimes life requires a little less safety. They need someone to show them that. They need someone like you, Captain."

Antarius sighed heavily. "I know."

"Help her. Help them all."

The old man closed his cloudy eyes for a moment and took a deep breath. He opened his eyes suddenly and added, "Not the Volga. Screw those guys."

With this said, he closed his eyes and lay back in his chair. He grew silent. And still.

Antarius sat quietly. He'd never watched an old man die before. He didn't know how to react. How long was he supposed to sit there? Normally he would say a couple of minutes seemed reverent enough, but the chair he was sitting in was quite uncomfortable. He counted in his head to thirty and figured that was enough, given the circumstances.

He stood up and approached the body of Monsieur Babin. "I promise you, strange old man, on your deathbed, that I will save these people. Or, at the very least, Reya. This I swear."

Thurgood reached out and put his hand on the old man's shoulder.

Monsieur Babin awoke with a start and a scream.

This caused Thurgood to shout. "Oh my God, I thought you were dead!"

"I was sleeping!"

"Well, you looked dead. And it just made sense if you said all those things and then just died. They really, really sounded like last words."

"I'm an old man in a recliner! I was sleeping. Until you scared the crap out of me."

"Well, I'm sorry for caring, okay?"

"Just... go after her," Monsieur Babin said as he struggled to get out of the chair.

"Fine."

"And let me sleep."

"Fine." Thurgood walked out of the tent and slammed the flap on the teepee. It just went *fwipsh*.

SIXTEEN

Sacred Waters

Antarius stepped out of Monsieur Babin's teepee hoping to find Reya waiting around to give him a further piece of her mind. He knew he was wrong and his plan was to apologize, but if she wanted to do it first, he wasn't going to stop her. It would make things easier.

She wasn't there.

Monsieur Babin's hilltop home commanded a view of the entire village, and Thurgood scanned the town slowly, looking for her in the crowd of people. It was a sea of strangers. He had lost track of how long he had been in the village—the drugs made time fuzzy—but he realized the only people he knew were Reya, the chief, that "doctor" guy and, now, old man Babin. The truth hit him. If he truly wanted to be chief, he was going to have to start meeting the people he wanted to lead.

A moment later, a lump of mud hit him. The wet ball of dirt smacked him in the face, releasing a rank smell in his nose and mouth. There was also a rock in the mud ball that rang his bell a bit. He wiped the mud from his eyes as evil laughter drifted up from the bottom of the hill. The two kids from earlier had ambushed him and were now pointing at him and rolling on the ground in hysterics.

Antarius flung the mud from his fingers and started after the kids. He hadn't gotten but a few feet when he lost his footing. The little bastards had covered the path to old man Babin's teepee in fresh mud, and he had stepped right into part two of their elaborate trap. The struggle was on. Antarius called upon his incredible sense of balance to fight against the combined forces of gravity and traction. Thanks to this effort and some impromptu flailing, it took him nearly a full thirty seconds to fall.

He hit the ground hard and started sliding.

In the brief time he had visited with Monsieur Babin, the little hellions had managed to turn the path to the old man's home into a mudslide that wound down the hill, up a ramp and into a bog. The boys stood on either side of the ramp and laughed at him as he passed. Thurgood tried to grab them while in midair but missed and landed with a *thwashunk* that drove the air from his lungs and replaced some of it with mud.

The boys ran away like the cowards they were as he pulled himself from the mud hole to give chase. They got a decent head start as the suction held him in place longer than he would like to admit. And the sides of the wallow were like ice, which made getting out difficult. By the time he got out, they were long gone.

Once free, he examined himself. He was covered in mud. His itchy shirt was now itchy and filthy, and his animal-skin pants were soiled. He stepped carefully away from the mire to prevent slipping back in and started asking if anyone knew where Reya had gone.

The people of the Village of the Shooting Star were hesitant to speak to him. Many of them ignored him completely. Others just shook their heads and quickened their pace to avoid the interaction. His nascent plan of meeting people was already falling apart. He wasn't winning anyone over. But he was persistent, and a woman finally pointed him in Reya's direction after he chased her halfway through the town and scared her half to death.

He tried to thank the villager for her help, but she fled as soon as he let go of her wrist. It didn't matter. He needed to talk to Reya.

The path the woman had directed him to wound through the forest for a short distance before ending at the bank of a river.

Reya sat on a fallen tree overlooking the flowing stream with her knees pulled to her chest. She didn't look at up him when he approached, but she knew he was there.

"Hi," he said. It wasn't his best opening line.

She still wouldn't look at him. She just watched the water flow by in silence for a minute. When she finally spoke, she said, "We don't know where the river goes."

"Downstream, I imagine." Thurgood took a seat next to her. She still wouldn't look at him but she made no attempt to leave in a huff. He took that as a good sign.

"But, where? What's downstream? What does it pass along the way? Where does it end? Does it feed into an ocean or another river? Does it pass other people or are we truly alone? We don't know anything about our home."

"No one's followed it?"

She shook her head. "Not anyone that came back. When the *Shooting Star* first crashed, people tried to explore the area. They found danger in every direction and decided it was best to stay close to home. Those that set out beyond the village never returned and were presumed lost to our savage new world. The loss of life was too costly to a community that was trying to survive, so exploration of any kind was eventually outlawed. We couldn't afford to lose anyone and so we will never know where the river goes. We only get to see what comes from upstream."

Thurgood watched the water flow and found himself wondering about its destination. The water moved gently here, but he knew firsthand how the river could turn on you. "Is this where you found me?"

"Right there," she said, and pointed a lazy finger to a spot near the shoreline. "I still don't know how you lived."

"An old habit, I guess."

This made her smile a little and her tone changed. "I'm sorry I treated you so harshly. I realize you're just trying to fit in. And that you're an ignorant moron. So, I know it can't be easy."

Antarius smiled as well. "I apologize for my ignorance. I'm not used to feeling so lost." He took a deep, sad breath and looked across the river. "I can't remember the last place I went where no one knew who I was."

"I'm sorry," she said with a fair amount of sarcasm. "Being stranded on our backwater planet must be hard for you."

"That's not what I'm saying. You were right, your great-grandfather is very wise."

"He told you?"

"Yes. He's very proud of you. We had a great talk. I learned so much about your tribe and what you all have gone through. I can't even begin to imagine the hardships your people have suffered. Being cut off from everything you know. Having all hope taken away. To overcome that is admirable to say the least. It's impossible for someone like me to understand. I've been sheltered from this kind of tragedy my whole life. The only thing I can compare it to is when I lost my ship."

"They took away your command?"

"No. The Hama blew up my ship. I'm getting a new one."

"Then it's not quite the same, is it?"

"No, it's not the same. This one will be bigger and better. And

I'm going to point it right at those Hama bastards and give them what for."

"That's not what—" She turned to look at him for the first time and saw that he was covered from head to toe in mud. She started laughing. "You're such an idiot."

"I am," Antarius agreed as he laughed along. He tried to wipe some more of the mud away. "I really am."

Reya stood up and held out a hand.

He just stared at it at first.

"Come with me," she said, and wiggled her fingers for him to take her hand. "There's something I want to show you."

He took her hand and marveled at how such a simple action could make him feel. In all his travels, in all his conquests, he had never met anyone like her. And it wasn't just the poor hygiene. There was something about her that made him crave her attention.

He let her lead him along the river and reveled in her touch. His hand was dirty, but she did not pull away. Now her hand was dirty, too, and they were dirty together. She could have insisted he wash in the river, but instead she took him to a path that led into the woods where they wound their way up a series of small ledges.

The higher they went, the less the world around them stank. The funk of the ever-present moss was replaced by a sweetness in the air that felt familiar, though he could not place it. Higher still and the dense growth of trees and vines turned to flowered bushes as the sun found its way through the heavy canopy. For the first time since he had crashed, he began to see the beauty in Altair itself.

And it was nothing compared to what came next.

A branch hung in front of them blocking their path. Reya smiled as she pulled it back like some magical curtain that had concealed a vision of pure fantasy.

The path they had followed had taken them to an outcropping that overlooked the majestic scene below them. The muddy color of the world he had known had been washed away by a series of crystalline waterfalls that streamed from all heights to fill shimmering pools of still blue water. Vibrant green plants marked by flowers of colors he could not describe surrounded the area.

"It's beautiful," he said as his eyes drank in the wonder of it all. He could feel the setting in his lungs as he breathed. He turned to Reya. "Is this what you wanted to show—"

Reya had stripped down to her underwear while he was momentarily distracted. It was a skill he had often practiced but never mastered. He almost always got caught with one pant leg stuck around his foot. That was usually when the questioning began. But she had shed her dress and stood before him as beautiful and exposed as the pools below.

"You're half naked."

"And you stink," she said with a playful grin. She stepped closer to him and started pulling mud from his hair. "You're covered in mud."

"It was those kids," Thurgood explained as he pulled off his shirt. He always felt it rude to be more dressed than present company. "I really should thank them."

"Not until you take a bath." Reya giggled and shoved him off the ledge.

Antarius's arms and legs pinwheeled as he plummeted a dozen feet to the pool below. He barely had time to register the fall before he hit the water with a splash. The water felt amazing. He opened his eyes and could see the mud leaving his body in a cloud. It drifted away in tendrils and swirls into a gentle current and disappeared over the edge of another waterfall. It was gone in an instant, leaving only the still water of the pool. It was the clearest water he had ever known and was filled with life. Fish more colorful than the flowers darted about him, regarding him as nothing more than a curiosity.

He broke the surface and looked back up at her on the rock. "That wasn't funny."

She leapt and time slowed. She didn't plunge like he had; she floated through the air like an angel approaching a desperate man whose prayers had been answered. She landed in the water next to him and resurfaced a moment later, still laughing. She shoved him playfully and then backed away.

"You enjoyed that," he said, pointing to the rock.

"Oh, I very much enjoyed that." She splashed him.

Antarius splashed her back.

This continued for a few moments before she started to swim away.

"Where are you going?"

"Follow me," she said.

It was hardly necessary. He wasn't about to let her get away. He swam after her with eager strokes and caught up to her.

Reya led them both to the edge of the pool where the water flowed softly over an all-but-imperceptible edge. Once there, she folded her arms across the ledge and leaned forward.

Thurgood met her at the edge and looked over. It took his breath away.

Below them were a dozen other blue pools cascading into one another to form an idyllic grotto from some forgotten poem.

Here there were also sounds of happiness as people from the village frolicked and bathed in the waters, free of their daily concerns and most of their clothes. He never imagined such a pedestrian existence would have so much partial nudity. Maybe he was cut out for simple life after all.

No, the Hama were coming. He couldn't let himself be distracted by the beauty of it all or lulled by the siren song of half-naked women bathing in the open.

"Look,' he said, still mostly distracted by the scene below. "Those two are about to do it."

Reya saw it, too, and pulled herself up higher on the edge of the pond. "Hey! Remi! Denise! Stop that!"

The two teenagers looked up, shocked to hear their names.

"I'll tell your parents," Reya threatened.

The teens scrambled to find their clothes and ran from what they had thought was a secret spot behind a flowering bush.

Once they had gone, Reya relaxed again and soaked in the scenery.

"This is beautiful," Thurgood said after a long silence.

She nodded. "I long to leave Altair and, like everyone in the village, I dream of a better life. But, when I come here, I feel at peace. I feel like I'm home."

"Thank you, Reya," he said. "Thank you for showing me your people's sacred waters."

"Our sacred waters?"

"Certainly, these are sacred pools, aren't they?"

"I mean, I wouldn't call them sacred, but please don't pee in them."

"But I'm the first outsider you've shown this place?"

"You're the only outsider. Ever. I mean ever."

"Thank you," he said. "That means a lot."

"That's not what I meant."

"I'm starting to understand why your people love it here."

"We don't love it here. This is nice, but don't get me wrong. I'd rather have a shower in a house in a city with a few conveniences than this. We make the most of it. But we've heard the stories of life on Earth. We've seen the life that awaits us back there or any of a hundred other places in the galaxy. If you can save us."

"I've been ordered not to by your chief."

"But you're not going to let that stop you. Are you?"

"Not the chief, no. I could take him. It's mostly the guards. Those are some big guards."

She swam closer. "You don't seem like the kind of man that likes to be told no."

"I'm not, but I kind of like it when you say it."

"Is that so?"

He nodded.

"No," she said softly.

He moved closer.

"No," she said again.

"Do you really mean that?" he asked.

She began to say no once more but he stopped the word with a kiss. She kissed him back and soon they had embraced and he was once again cursing the animal-skin pants. He couldn't deny how good they made him look, but they simply weren't practical.

"Hey! Reya!" The shout came from below.

Antarius scanned the pools below and found the source of the call. The two teenagers from earlier shouted, "Stop that or we'll tell your parents!" They laughed and disappeared into the woods once more.

"Little brats," she said.

He looked into her eyes. "You're not going to let them stop us, are you?"

"No," she said, and it was the sexiest no he'd ever heard.

Antarius started struggling with his pants. The animal skin wasn't easy to work with underwater and every time he took his hands off the ledge to take them off, he sank under the water. It was frustrating, but he was making progress and he was determined.

The third time he came up for air, Reya was giggling at his attempts to disrobe. She draped her arms around his neck and said, "We can swim back to shore if that would be easier."

He nodded. "It would probably be safer."

They started swimming back to shore where they could both work on his pants when a scream from below pierced the sexiness and totally ruined the mood.

The scream was shrill and filled with a terror like none Thurgood had ever known. He had seen men murdered in conflict, seen them tortured to within an inch of their lives, but he had never known a sound like this. It was as if a soul was being ripped from its body and both were wailing in protest.

Antarius pulled himself up to the pool's edge and looked below. The pools were emptying. The swimmers were racing back to the village. By the time he turned to find Reya, she was halfway back to shore.

Thurgood reached down to pull up his pants and sank. He came up with a curse and started pulling the pants back up with one hand. Getting them back on was even harder than pulling them off. By the time he got his pants situated and swam back to shore, he had to race to catch her.

Unfortunately, running in wet animal-skin pants was almost as hard as swimming in them. He lost her somewhere up ahead as his legs began to chafe and he was forced to slow. By the time he caught up to her in the village, he didn't feel like he could walk another step. He decided to skip the meeting with the fashion division and leave the idea of wearing dead animals in the past where it belonged. Except for maybe a jacket. That could look pretty sweet if it had enough buckles.

All work had stopped in the village. Looms were unattended. Wood was sitting uncut. Sticks weren't being bundled. Every soul had gathered in the middle of the village around a young woman who had fallen to her knees and wailed as everyone tried to console her. Thurgood assumed it was she who had screamed.

Reya was right next to the woman and had an arm around her shoulder. She rocked her gently and spoke softly.

Once she spotted Thurgood in the crowd, she waved for another villager to take her place and pulled Antarius aside so the woman couldn't hear them speaking.

"What's happened here, Reya?"

"A mardok stole her child," Reya said softly.

The woman continued to wail.

"What's a mardok?" Thurgood asked.

"It's kind of like a giant Earth ape, I guess."

"So why not call it a giant ape?"

"Giant ape doesn't really cover it."

"Then why compare it to one?"

"It's just the closest thing I can think of. If you were to see one, you'd understand. They're horrible."

"I get that, but you could have called it anything. Mardok seems a little—"

Reya snapped, "It just felt like it needed its own name, okay? The point is, it's big and horrible and it took her child."

Antarius stopped arguing about local naming conventions and watched the people of the village console the sobbing woman. In a matter of minutes, an orderly line had formed and each person in the village took a moment to express their sadness for the woman's loss.

The mood had gone from panicked to somber in no time, and Antarius found it all a little confusing. He leaned closer to Reya. "I don't get it. What's with all the 'sorry for your loss' stuff that's going on? Was the child taken or was it killed?"

"The child was taken. Mardoks take their prey alive."

"So why the grief parade? They're acting like the kid is dead."

"The child was taken by a mardok," she said slowly, as if he hadn't heard.

"So? Let's go take it back."

"You don't know what you're talking about." This came from

the chief. Durand had come to comfort the woman as well but had overheard their conversation.

Thurgood didn't care for the accusation. "I know enough to know that when a child is taken, you take it back."

"Not from a mardok, you don't," Durand said.

"I don't care if the child was taken to hell by the devil himself!" Antarius fired back. "You go after it… Chief."

Durand dismissed the outburst. "You don't know what you're talking about. Mardoks are too powerful." He turned to walk away.

Antarius wasn't having it. "Now who's being the man baby?"

Durand turned back and crossed the path to get in Thurgood's face. He whispered, but there was a lot of grit in his whisper. "You need to stay out of this, Earth man. Things here aren't like they are back on that pillow-soft planet of yours. You don't know anything."

"Is that so?"

"Yeah," Chief Durand put a finger in Antarius's chest. "That's so."

The chief must have thought that was the end of the discussion. Because he turned and walked away again.

But Antarius knew better. He raised his voice so Durand, and everyone else, could hear. "I may not know much about mardoks. You're right about that, Chief. And I may not know much about your planet. But I do know this—when a child is ripped from his mother's bosom, the just thing to do is pursue the thing that did the bosom-ripping, kill it and get the kid back on that bosom. It doesn't matter how big it is, how scary it is or what weird name you chose to give it. Yeah, maybe we're a little soft on Earth, but I can tell you this, if we had mardoks there, we wouldn't just sit around waiting for the beast to kill the kid. We'd do something about it." The crowd was hanging on his every word. The chief's logical and sensible approach to the situation was losing ground to Thurgood's passionate argument.

"You'll be killed." Durand said this to end the conversation. It was stated as a fact. And the man probably wasn't wrong. But that didn't matter.

"Then we die trying," Antarius said. And the crowd was his.

"We don't have the luxury of numbers here," Durand said. He knew he had to win them back. He was speaking sense to them now. Like a rational man. But rationality had nothing to do with the situation. Reason was all the chief had left, and even he knew it wasn't going to be enough. "If we're to continue here… If we're to survive as a people, every life matters."

"But not the kid's?" Thurgood asked.

By his own reasoning, the chief had been defeated. "We can't…"

"Can't is just a word that means you're scared to do what's right."

"You'll be killed."

"Better me than the kid."

"No, I mean you and the kid will be killed. And anyone foolish enough to go with you will be killed."

"It's a chance I'm willing to take."

He felt a shift in the crowd. A physical shift. Villagers began to move in behind him. They had crossed the metaphorical line in the mud and chosen to stand with him. Antarius didn't say anything. His father had told him long ago to never sell past the close. His silence, and Durand's stammering, was winning him more supporters by the second.

It was soon evident that Thurgood has swayed the village.

"Fine. We'll hunt the mardok," Durand relented, though he wasn't happy about it. He turned to one of his aides. "Gather a hunting party. We're going after the child."

A cheer went up from the crowd. The mother's cries turned

to sobs of hope. The villagers patted Antarius on the back, and they left to prepare for the excursion. Soon he was left alone with Reya.

"You are very brave to go after the child," she said.

"I know."

"You are also foolish and stupid."

"You're not wrong," Thurgood said. "But, sometimes, doing the right thing takes more than courage. Now, if you'll excuse me, I have to change these pants."

SEVENTEEN

Party On

Given a choice, it wasn't a party he would attend. Despite the enthusiasm his speech had created in the village streets, only a dozen men and half as many women turned up to join the actual hunting party. And those who had turned up weren't what he would call quality volunteers.

"What happened?" he asked as he looked around the group. "Where did everyone else go?"

Those present hesitated to answer. Most were busy avoiding eye contact while others fidgeted from foot to foot.

"Everyone was so excited earlier," Antarius said. "What gives?"

A giant man nearby raised a timid hand, and Antarius called on him to answer.

The explanation came in fits and starts, but he eventually got going. "What I think happened—and I'm just guessing, because it didn't happen to me and I don't know for sure. Because, I don't want to speak for anybody. There's nothing I hate more than having someone put words in my mouth, you see? So I'd hate to be guilty of doing it myself. So, that's not my intent here. But what I'm assuming, or rather what I think what may have happened is that all those people that were all like, 'Yay! Let's go hunt the mardok!' or 'Let's kill the beast!' Those folks—of which I am admittedly one. I'm totally on board with saving this kid. But those people, that were all for mardok hunting earlier but didn't show up... They probably went home to grab something before coming here, like thicker shoes, or maybe they were going to say goodbye to their family or something and then they stayed." The man took a much-needed breath.

"Stayed?" Thurgood asked, and cast a quick look to the chief before turning back to the man. "What do you mean, stayed?"

"Well, what I mean is that they just stayed. Like didn't leave. Just... they just stayed home. Instead of coming here. That's what... stayed. Like maybe they went home and said 'I'm just here to grab some things then I'm off to hunt a mardok' but then they looked around their house and thought, 'You know what? This is nice. I've got some good things going here. I think I'll just stay.'"

Antarius glared at the man until the villager turned away. He had never been one to shoot the messenger, but it was disappointing news that so many had chosen cowardice over courage once they had been removed from the moment.

The villager took a sharp breath and held up a finger to make another point.

Antarius signaled for him to stop and spared him the breath. He knew the type. The man was nervous and talked to cover it up. It was an annoying trait, but for all his faults, the man had shown up to join the hunt and Thurgood had to give him that.

"Wait a minute," said another man in the crowd. He was sweating as if he were standing over a forge. "Are you saying we could have stayed?"

Antarius knew the type. The man was nervous, so he sweated to cover it up. It was a common strategy, but Thurgood had always found it odd as he never understood how it covered anything up. It was just gross.

"I didn't know we could have stayed home," the man said.

"No, you've done the right thing," Thurgood said. Cowardice clung to some of the volunteers, and it was important to stomp it out before it ran rampant through the crowd. "Those men may die in the comfort of their own homes with loved ones near and never know the taste of danger. But they will die cowards while you will die brave men in the service of another."

Two of the men in the party turned to leave.

"Get back here!"

The men turned back and shuffled back into their places.

Antarius studied the rest of the party. They were brave enough, but he could see the fear in their eyes. Only the man next to him seemed unconcerned about their coming adventure. He swayed gently back and forth, staring into the distance. He knew the type, a battle-hardened veteran who had known action and was intimate with the violence he had to visit on his opponent. He was familiar with the sound a man's last breath made as it escaped from his neck if you took his head. He knew the smell of death that flooded a battlefield full of rot. It was a weight that was hard to live with, and Thurgood admired those who could face it again if it meant doing the right thing.

He stepped closer to the man and put a hand on his shoulder. "Thank you for being here."

The man burped and a wave of alcohol breath told Thurgood he had been mistaken. The man wasn't a hero. The man was an alcoholic. He knew the type, a drunk who drank too much to cover his nerves, drown his fears or maybe forget a treacherous lover who ran off with your best friend because she couldn't handle your "condition" which was medical and totally addressable but she just up and left anyway but still sends

Christmas cards each year because she thought you bought the "No, it's totally not about your condition" line.

He stepped back and took in the party all at once. What he saw was a group of brave men and women who would put their own lives at risk to stand up for what was right. They weren't tough. They were brave. They weren't capable. They were just there. They weren't soldiers. They were fodder. And none of them stood a chance.

It wasn't their fault, of course. He didn't blame them at all, as fodder served an important role when it came to strategy. Fodder was often necessary. And, many times, it was the fodder that won the day. They were heroes. Sure, they didn't get the praise they deserved, because they were dead, but that didn't make their contribution to a victory any less important, just less exciting.

Looking at the crowd, Thurgood immediately identified two or three he'd throw in harm's way if it meant securing victory. But that didn't mean he didn't admire their courage. They were brave fodder and, if you asked him, that was the best kind.

Durand saw him studying the men and moved close so the hunting party couldn't hear their conversation.

"Remember these faces, off-worlder," Durand said. "Their deaths will be on your hands."

"You should have more faith in your people, Chief. Just by showing up today, they've earned it."

The drunk threw up at his own feet, and the crowd spread out to avoid the puddle.

"Not that guy," Thurgood said. "He's a drunk."

"I have faith in my people. It's you that has earned my doubt."

"I'm the last person you have to worry about, Chief."

"Your position in your precious Alliance has no doubt made you an elegant speaker. But you've worked my people up for a fight they cannot win. I wonder if your consolation speech will be as elegant."

"I doubt it," Thurgood said. "I've never had to give one."

Durand studied him silently. Thurgood didn't mind being stared at it. He was used to it. But he didn't care for being scrutinized and hurried the process along.

"Is there something you'd like to add, Chief?"

Durand put a finger in Thurgood's chest. "I'm not entirely convinced you're doing this for the right reasons."

Antarius didn't pull away. He didn't flinch. He stared back and stated plainly, "The kid is running out of time."

Durand held his gaze. "Sergeant at arms!" He shouted.

"Sir," replied a voice from across the crowd.

Thurgood leaned in a fraction of an inch and spoke through gritted teeth. "I'm not going to give you the satisfaction of looking away, but I do think it's pretty cool you have a sergeant at arms."

"Hand out the weapons,' Durand said, and turned away from Thurgood.

"Yes, sir."

Despite the serious nature of the situation, Antarius found himself getting somewhat excited for the hunt. It took an exotic weapon to hunt an exotic creature and from how they described the mardok, the kind of gun needed to kill it had to be something special. He pictured a double-barrel large bore rifle chambered for a nitro express round like the antique safari rifles in his family's collection or those back on the *Galahad*. Of course, given the Shooting Star's timeline, they would more likely have modified a mass driver to better suit hunting the beast. Stripping the battery to a supply suitable to single action operation would make the weapon more agile in the thick rainforest while still arming men with a round capable of felling their prey. He could only imagine what the streamlined weapon would look like. It would be an interesting sporting rifle.

The sergeant at arms handed him a spear.

It was brown and made of wood. A metal blade was affixed to the shaft with strips of hide. Several colorful pieces of cloth hung free near the base of the spear tip.

"This is it?"

The sergeant at arms handed him a knife. It appeared to have been made by industrial means, but the sheath that held the blade was worn from age and frayed in places.

Thurgood stared at the weapons in his hands. "Excuse me a moment. Are you kidding me here? What is this stuff?"

"This is what we have." Durand took a sword roughly two feet long from the armorer and waved it through the air several times.

"No, no," Antarius said as he handed the items back to the sergeant at arms. "You take these things back and I'll take a something with a little more firepower, please."

"We don't have any guns." The sergeant at arms returned the spear and knife to Thurgood. "We have these."

"Look I'm not going to judge anyone for being a pacifist, but if you live on a planet with giant ape monsters and the cat slash cow thing, don't you think it would be a good idea to keep a few guns around?"

"Yes, we do," said the sergeant at arms. "But, seeing as how we ran out of ammunition a generation ago, you get that spear."

"That's it?"

"And the knife."

"Well, that's just like a shorter spear, isn't it?" Thurgood asked.

"No, no, you see that's a special knife," the sergeant at arms said.

"Sure, it is."

"No, honestly." He took the knife back from Antarius and drew the blade from the sheath. "It's a lucky knife."

"It is?" A lucky knife sounded even more suspect than a special knife. But he couldn't refuse a good story. "How is it lucky?"

The sergeant at arms presented all angles of the blade as he explained. "You see, it actually belonged to one of the Volga. Its owner was not particularly strong, or fast, or bright. Or well liked for that matter. But this knife right here saved his life more times than you can imagine."

"How?"

"Well, as you can imagine. Slow, weak people that nobody likes get attacked all the time on a planet like ours. And every time he was tackled by an animal, an enemy or jealous lover, the attacker landed on the knife and killed themselves." The sergeant at arms returned the blade to the sheath and handed it back to Thurgood.

His skepticism was sending up signals, but he studied the weapon with a new fascination. "Really?"

"Yeah, sure, whatever," the sergeant at arms said.

"What was his name?"

"Who?"

"The guy. Who had the knife. The Volga man. What was his name?"

"Uh, Freddie."

Antarius felt his suspicious eyebrow raise. "Freddie? That doesn't sound very Russian."

"Chekov. Freddie Chekov."

"This is Chekov's knife?"

"Yeah, that was him."

"A little convenient, don't you think?"

"I don't follow."

"Are you not a literary man? You know who Chekov was, right?"

"I guess not."

Thurgood rolled his eyes. What kind of history were they teaching on these backwater planets? "Chekov was a famous starship crew member on a popular TV show."

"And?"

"And I'm famous for being on starships."

"You are?"

"I figured that's why you gave me the knife. It's poetic."

"I gave it to you because you complained about the spear."

"Sure," Thurgood said with a wink. But he had never really mastered winking outside of seduction settings, and it made the sergeant at arms uncomfortable.

"Um, good luck, fearsome hunter," the man said, and quickly moved on to arming the next man in line.

Every member of the hunting party was armed in due course and stood, nervously studying the ancient weapons in their hands, as it dawned on each of them that they were about to leave the relative safety of the village and enter into the dark jungle to pursue a creature that could tear them limb from limb while they had nothing to defend themselves with but a sharp stick.

This realization had a very specific look, and Thurgood could see their confidence waning. It wasn't surprising. Moments like this called for a supplemental pep talk. What was surprising was when Durand stepped up in front of the crowd and called for their attention.

"Thank you," he began. "Thank you for your courage and your bravery. I know it isn't easy. What we are about to do is… it's crazy. And I can see it on your faces that you're having second thoughts. And that's understandable. I won't lie. I've had them, too. But there is a child out there that is counting on your bravery. Counting on us. And if we all just hold on a little longer, we'll see this through."

Durand stepped down. There was no applause and no cheering, but the hunting party steeled themselves against their fears and grew determined to do the right thing.

The chief walked close by and Thurgood nodded. "Nice speech, Chief. I didn't think you were on board with this."

Durand stopped briefly and said, "If you won't do it for the right reasons, I will." With that, the chief moved on and led the crowd toward the jungle.

Antarius stared at his spear in one hand and the knife in the other and hoped he had not made a terrible mistake.

EIGHTEEN

Lair of the Mardok

The hunting party moved through the forest with an apprehension usually reserved for haunted asylums and dark, dank basements. Every member moved with hesitation, following only in the footsteps of the man or woman in front of them. Only the drunk dared to stray; he moved whichever way the world happened to sway at the moment. At this point, Thurgood couldn't tell if the man's insobriety was going to be a hinderance or a help. Of all the people, he needed the least convincing to move forward.

The mardok proved easy enough to track. It didn't move through the forest so much as it crashed through, leaving a path of destruction and debris that tripped up every member of the party. Snapped limbs littered the forest floor. Rocks, long covered in moss, had been unearthed in the creature's wake. Some of the smaller trees were simply uprooted, torn from the ground and left strewn across the path. From the wreckage, Thurgood couldn't attest to how apelike the mardok was, but he could tell they weren't lying about its size. The monster tore a path ten feet wide as it went.

It wasn't trying to hide. And why would it? An animal like this hid from nothing. Thurgood blamed the people of the *Shooting Star* for that. If they had spent more time putting the fear of man into the planet's fauna and less time playing in the mud, this may have never happened in the first place.

Instead, they had let the planet put the fear of the mardok into them. And it had worked. Every time they came across claw marks on a tree or a rock, or some slaughtered animal, the fragile hunting party threatened to fall apart. The members would cower and talk about how conventional wisdom always said to not hunt mardoks.

Throughout his life, Thurgood had found it good to go against conventional wisdom. He had always found it to be too timid. He quickly grew tired of their pessimism and ended up walking next to the drunk. The man was mostly quiet aside from some mutterings about killing and mardoks, and he found the alcoholic's optimism surprisingly refreshing.

"Hold," was cried out every five minutes or so. Durand would hold up a hand and bring the party to a halt. He did it one too many times, and Antarius refused to stop. He moved to the head of the pack and confronted the chief.

"What is it this time, Durand?"

Durand pointed to the ground. "Mardok droppings."

"So? Walk around them."

"It means we're close."

"About time. Let's speed this up."

"We need to—"

"We need to hurry," Thurgood cut him off. "The kid is running out of time. I mean seriously, with you grinding us to a halt every time you come across a pile of poop."

Durand gritted his teeth and spoke quietly. "We need to be cautious."

"We need to be more like Sir Drinks A Lot here," Antarius

said, grabbing the drunk by the shoulder and pulling him into the argument. "He may be blasted right now, but all he can talk about is killing the mardok. That's the kind of 'can do' attitude we all need if we're going to save the kid."

The party looked at the drunk, who kept muttering until he felt the eyes of the hunting party on him. Then he stopped and turned with them to see what everyone was staring at.

"He's not saying kill the mardok, off-worlder," Durand said. "It's a line from a poem we teach the children. As every child grows, every mother knows, there's danger in the woods so stay upon your toes. Watch the trees my daughter, watch the trees my son. You cannot kill the mardok. So you'd better run, run, run!"

The cadence of the final stanza sent a chill down Antarius's spine. "That's haunting."

"That's the point."

"I can't believe you teach that to children. How could you? It's scarring."

"It's so they remember to stay safe and not to wander from the village."

"I can't believe anyone would corrupt poetry—the language of the soul—to dupe children into obedience. It's unheard of. It's dishonest."

"It's been done since the dawn of time," Durand said.

"That's not true."

"It is."

"Liar, liar. Pants on fire." Thurgood said with a point of his finger and moved to the head of the group, barely missing the large pile of mardok scat.

A scream reached their ears before Durand could protest that Thurgood was now the leader. It was the scream of a child and it was close.

Pecking order was forgotten as the two men looked at one another before breaking into a sprint toward the sound. It was soon evident that Thurgood was the faster runner. It was one of the benefits of growing up in the academy and not on some malnourished backwater planet. Another point in Earth's favor. Durand struggled to keep up and began to warn Thurgood off as they got closer and closer to the source of the scream.

"Wait. Slow down. You don't want to charge in there, you might startle it into hurting the kid." Durand knew no shame when it came to losing a foot race and would resort to any tactic to cheat.

Antarius wasn't foolish enough to fall for the man's tricks and barreled on until he found himself in the middle of a clearing that had been trampled flat. The trees had been stomped into pulp, rocks had been beaten into the ground and the loose dirt had been compacted by sheer force into hardpacked soil. A nest built of tree limbs sat in the middle of it all. The screams were coming from inside.

"It's okay, kid. We're here to rescue you." Thurgood ran up to the nest. The wall that formed it was twice as tall as he was. He had just begun to climb when he felt eyes on him. They weren't human eyes. And no human could ever cast a shadow as massive as the one that now covered Thurgood in darkness.

Antarius lowered himself back to the ground, turned around and had to admit it did kind of look like a giant ape.

The mardok was at least fifteen feet tall. The creature slouched a bit, so Antarius gave it another foot or two with proper posture. It stood on squat legs and long arms, giving it the stance of an ape. It was covered in a blueish white fur that was in turn covered by Altair's moss. Patches of leathery skin showed through at its chest and shoulders.

The face was more alien than ape. It had keen eyes set above massive tusks that curved inward like those of a mammoth. He couldn't see it, but it had to have a nose somewhere on its face because Thurgood heard it snort.

The two foes, both large in stature, though one only metaphorically, stood frozen, eyes locked, taking the measure of one another. The mardok made no move to attack. Thurgood got tired of the stand-off and made the first move. "Attention, mardok. I command you to release the child immediately."

The mardok responded with tentacles.

No one had warned him about tentacles, but they lashed out from beneath the creature's fur and came for him. Now that he got a better look at it, the beast was predominantly tentacles, and he decided "giant ape" was a terrible description for the creature.

Antarius ducked one tentacle and tripped over another. This caused him to stumble, which helped him accidentally dodge two more wild grabs from the monster. He finally found his footing and rose up to his full height. "Now see—"

Another tentacle whipped across his chest and sent him flying across the clearing into the rest of the fashionably late hunting party. He knocked over most of them and considered himself lucky he didn't get a spear in the back.

Thurgood climbed out of the dog pile and shouted at the villagers. "No one, not a single one of you, said anything about tentacles!"

"We thought you knew," said the guy who sweated to cover his nerves.

"How? How would I know that an alien I've never seen from a planet I've never been to has tentacles?"

The man shrugged.

"In all the whining... in all the talk about how dangerous these things are, not one of you thought to say it's mostly tentacles."

"We tried to tell you—" Durand said.

"No. You said apelike. You said giant ape."

"Yeah, apelike," Durand said. "It's like an ape because it's got tentacles."

"Apes don't have tentacles!" Thurgood screamed.

"They don't?" asked the guy who talked to cover up his nerves. "I'm kind of surprised to hear that they don't because I thought they did, but you're saying they don't, but I thought they did."

"No! Haven't you ever been to the zoo?"

The man crossed his arms and huffed. "We don't have a zoo."

"Wait," Durand said. "Which one is an ape then?"

"Thurgood searched the ground and located his dropped spear. "You should have called it a squidape or apesquid. Or monktopus. That would have prepared a person for seeing a twenty-foot gorilla with octopus arms."

"Octopus!" The chief snapped his fingers. "That's the one."

The ape-shaped octopus roared like a lion as it charged the hunting party.

The party scattered.

The many arms of the beast slithered after the villagers. It found them as they tried to hide behind the trees outside the creature's lair.

Screams filled the clearing as hunting party members were dragged back into the clearing. They shouted pleas, they screamed for mercy and many of them feared for their lives or were grossed out by the slimy texture of the tentacles. It was not unlike being seized by muscular snot.

Thurgood looked at the spear in his hand and wished it was a more powerful weapon. With every day he spent on Altair, his argument for survival bazookas was getting stronger. But if a sharp stick was what destiny had seen fit to give him, a sharp stick was what he'd use.

Antarius ran toward the beast. He dove over a tentacle that swung at his chest, rolled and sprang back to his feet. This brought him close enough to the beast for a lunge, and he drove the spear tip into the mardok's chest.

The animal's hide didn't give. It was like shoveling into clay.

Antarius thrust twice more, probing for a weaker spot. All it did was further enrage the creature and win Thurgood its undivided attention and scorn.

The captain backpedaled as the beast turned toward him. It rose up on its hind tentacles, taller now than before, and roared.

The real problem with tentacles, aside from the gross part, was that there were always so many of them. He knew an octopus had eight, he could never recall how many a squid had, and he hadn't had a chance to get a final number on the mardok with any confidence. And that was hardly fair. When you stepped into the ring with a boxer, you knew you had to watch out for his left and his right. That was an even match. You had the information going in. But with tentacles... how did you watch for a half dozen lefts and a half dozen rights at once?

One of the tentacles wrapped around his waist like a damp rope and then tightened into steel coils as it threatened to crush him. It was only his amazing core strength that kept the life in him as the mardok pulled him closer to a mouth filled with jagged teeth and brutal halitosis.

It roared once more, blowing its foul breath at Thurgood and squeezing harder.

But it wasn't enough to stop him. Aiming right between the eyes, Antarius stabbed at the monster's face.

His mark moved and the tusk knocked the blow off course, but the blade sliced the side of the mardok's face. Blood as red as any Earthling's flowed freely from below its eye and the creature reared back.

"Behold!" Antarius shouted to the hunting party. "It bleeds! We can—"

Just before he hit the tree, Thurgood decided once and for all he didn't like tentacles.

It was a sapling, and the trunk snapped as he hit it. The break absorbed a fair amount of the force, but it still knocked the wind out of him, and he struggled onto his hands and knees while he waited for the air to fill his lungs.

He fought to one knee and surveyed the battle.

The mardok had all the upper hands. The hunting party was in complete disarray as the members panicked, screamed and pretty much bled all over the place. Men were flying everywhere. Those it couldn't grab with its tentacles were brushed easily aside by the beast's tusks.

If he was being honest, Thurgood would have to admit the fight wasn't going well. But that's not what great leaders did. They didn't admit defeat. They rallied. They motivated. They lied to inspire.

"We've almost got it, men!" he shouted.

One of the women volunteers screamed as she hit the ground at his feet.

"...And ladies."

His lying strategy was working. Every time they went flying, the villagers got back to their feet and came at the beast once more. That was the kind of persistence it took to take down a mardok. If it took a thousand stabs with their stupid wooden spears, that's what they would do.

He looked at the bloodied spear in his hand and wished he had more firepower. The thought sparked an idea and he pulled the moss-made shirt from his back and wrapped it around the tip of the spear. He pulled a survival lighter from his pocket and lit the shirt on fire. It burned steadily, and Thurgood rushed back into the fray, brandishing the one weapon all animals fear.

He was just in time.

The mardok loomed above the chief. Durand stood his

ground, but he was now fighting with a broken spear while trying to keep at least four tentacles at bay.

Antarius slid under one of the limbs and thrust the flame-tipped spear into the mardok's face.

The beast reeled back, and Thurgood finally heard a note of fear in its otherwise terrifying roar.

Several more thrusts put the creature back on whatever the tentacle equivalent of heels was as it retreated. Every push forward drove the monster back. Thurgood had the upper hand now and risked a glance back at the chief. "I told you we needed—"

He felt the tentacle seize his ankle before he could get the word firepower out of his mouth. The mardok flipped him end over end so many times that Antarius gave up trying to spot the ground and moved to a strategy of hoping he didn't land on his head.

It worked. He landed on his back. The spear was knocked from his hand, and the flame went out as the firespear stopped spinning, dropped to the ground and rolled around in the dirt. Thurgood struggled to get to his knees again and turned back to the fight.

He had put the fear of nature into the mardok, and it had forgotten about him already. The beast was focused on the chief once more, and the village leader had lost his broken spear. Thurgood watched as a tentacle coiled around Durand and lifted him from the ground. The chief was as good as dead.

His death was what Thurgood needed. But it wasn't what he wanted. He needed the chief out of the way so he could get back to his ship, but not this way. It wasn't right.

Durand struggled against the muscular tentacle.

Antarius picked up his smoking spear and ran.

The mardok opened its mouth as it pulled the chief closer.

The man's screams were lost in the mardok's roar.

Thurgood sprang up the back of the beast and drove the spear deep into the base of its neck. Fur covered the mardok's back, and Antarius had played a hunch that the hide was less thick beneath the blueish-white, green moss-covered hairs.

The mardok shrieked at the pain and forgot all about the chief.

Thurgood worked the spear around in a circular motion, forcing it deeper into the creature. Antarius was no doctor—in fact, the one time he had been entrusted with a syringe, he'd missed the patient entirely and stabbed a nearby sandwich—but he knew enough to know that if something had a brain, then it had nerves. And if it had nerves, it had one particular nerve that, if stabbed by a spear, would force the beast to drop its prey. It was basic science, so he twisted the spear and rocked it back and forth searching deep under the mardok's hide for that one nerve.

He was never certain whether he found it or if the mardok simply got tired of having a man stabbing him in the back, but the result was the same. The mardok's tentacles straightened as it roared, as if it was throwing its hands up and screaming, "Oh my God, what is stabbing me in the neck?"

Durand dropped to the ground and rolled out of the way as the beast turned its attention back to Thurgood.

"Score one for Science—"

A tentacle snuck up behind him and wrapped around his throat, cutting off the victory cry. Brute force from the appendage ripped him from the mardok's back and sent him tumbling forward through the air.

Converting the kinetic energy into several sweet ninja rolls before springing to his feet not far from the chief, Thurgood covered himself in bruises he was going to feel the next day. But he was still in the fight.

Thinking it had dispatched the pain in its neck, the mardok

turned its attention back to Durand, who was still stumbling around trying to catch his breath. The mardok charged.

Thurgood moved quickly and shoved the chief out of the way. Putting himself between the village leader and the creature, he drew the knife from his belt and screamed at the beast, doing his best to match the intensity and general phlegmyness of its roar.

The tentacles came for him in batches, but he countered each with a slash of the blade. The knife was old, but sharp, and the blade cut easily through the tentacles' thinner skin. Blood flowed from the cuts, and the tentacles pulled back as the mardok's reflexes took over.

It could be hurt. It could feel pain. That gave him a fighting chance, and after a few more successful slashes, it felt like he was winning. "I've got it distracted," Thurgood shouted to the chief. "Grab the kid while I lure—"

He felt the tentacle embrace his ankle like a lecherous string of snot and then tighten its grip until his foot began to go numb. Before he could react, Antarius was hoisted from the ground and hurled through the air. Tumbling head over heels, he hung in the air long enough to imagine more than a dozen painful landing sites: rocks, pointier rocks, a tree, a cactus patch, lava, a bed of nails, just the ground but the ground would be super-hot and scratchy. He finally decided that it didn't matter where he landed. He'd been in the air long enough that even the softest rocks were going to hurt. Thurgood closed his eyes and braced for a rough landing.

But the rough landing never came. Instead, he landed on a padded mass of grasses and twigs. He bounced slightly and hit an equally soft wall before coming to a stop. Thurgood opened his eyes to find himself in a bowl of woven reeds filled with several eggs and one small child.

Antarius quickly deduced two things: He had landed in the

mardok's nest, and this was probably the child they were looking for.

The kid was huddled against the edge of the nest, curled into the tightest ball a person could make without causing permanent back issues.

"It's okay, kid," Antarius said as he crab-walked over to the child. "We're here to help."

The kid didn't say anything. He just leapt at Thurgood and wrapped his arms around him. The child clung tighter than an alien tentacle and trembled in his arms. There may have been some crying.

"You're all right now, kid."

Thurgood stood and peeked over the edge of the nest.

Durand had rallied the remaining villagers and the force was advancing on the mardok. It was suddenly clear that, for all his flaws, Durand was a good and courageous man. Thurgood was overcome with regret for calling the man a coward, a yellowbelly and a pretty little girl in a frilly skirt that would rather play tea party than risk chipping a nail. It was clear now that Durand was none of those things.

Bravery like that was too precious to be wasted. Thurgood embraced the distraction, had the child move to his back and scaled down the outside of the nest until he was close enough to drop to the ground. Together, the pair ran across the clearing to the edge of the woods where many of the villagers had taken refuge from the fight. The boy raced to one of the women he recognized and hugged her tightly.

"Get him out of here," Thurgood barked to the woman. She nodded and headed back to the village with the child in her arms. Several of the wounded hunting party members followed close behind. "Godspeed, little one," Thurgood said softly to himself.

When they were out of sight, Thurgood turned back to the clearing. "Durand! We got the kid!"

Armed with the short sword and a broken spear tip, the chief was still engaged with the mardok and hacked away at the monster's tentacles. One particularly deep slash sent blood flying across the clearing as the monster recoiled, pulled the tentacle close to its chest and started backing away from the fight.

"Yo, Chief!" Thurgood yelled louder.

Durand turned toward the sound.

"The kid is all saved. Now, let's get me out of here."

A quick smile flashed across the chief's face when he heard the news. It was relief. Relief that one under his charge was safe. He sheathed the sword and started toward Thurgood and the rest of the hunting party.

The mardok suddenly abandoned its retreat and came for the chief.

"Durand!" Thurgood shouted. It felt like the world was moving in slow motion but everything happened rather fast.

The mardok caught up with Durand in two quick strides and struck the man in the back. The blow launched him into the air and drove him through a tree trunk and then another tree trunk and then into a boulder.

Durand landed a broken heap at the feet of the party. The villagers rushed to his side. But while they were focused on displaying compassion, Thurgood was more concerned with revenge.

Thurgood forced his way through the crowd that had gathered around Durand. The chief's gaze fell upon him. It was weak and fading.

Antarius pulled the sword from the scabbard at Durand's waist, quickly and quietly swore vengeance and raced back into the clearing.

The mardok was waiting for him there.

"I'm done with your games, you monkey octopus looking bastard. You just killed a good and decent man. Now, it's true I hardly knew him and I didn't like him very much until right at the end. But that changes nothing. You're going to pay."

As if the mardok understood, the beast roared and the battle was on.

What followed would go down in the annals of Altair's history. If they were even advanced enough to have annals. Filled with bloodlust and wielding the fallen chief's sword, Antarius clashed with the mighty mardok.

The beast was a confusing flurry of hairy arms and slimy tentacles.

Thurgood was a whirlwind of cold steel and colder nerves. He ducked and dodged the mighty blows while delivering cut after cut, drawing blood with each slash and working his way through the animal's thick skin toward the meaty and more vulnerable center.

Every cut drew a scream of rage from the creature, but the combatants were each determined foes locked together in a moment destiny had designated for them both. The alpha from Altair and the alpha from another world battled for dominance of the planet. And to the mardok's horror, the alien was winning.

Driven by honor, Thurgood was relentless, and he soon controlled the encounter. He cut and hacked with the sword and bloodied his fist with blows. He had the mardok on the defensive, and the pair was moving back across the clearing.

The people started cheering him on. Maybe. It was also possible Durand had finally succumbed and they were wailing with grief. The reality mattered little to Antarius as he let the crowd's noise push him on.

Thurgood had pressed his advantage until the mardok had its back up against a wall. It may have been a mindless monster, but the beast knew that it was losing and grew desperate. Every tentacle came for Antarius at once and he dove into their embrace. Their iron grip surrounded him and squeezed. He tightened his core against the assault and let it happen. The mardok's death grip was a part of his plan. It was expected. He knew the mardok would act according to Maslow's tentacle; when your only tool is a tentacle, every problem needs squeezing.

The mardok had enjoyed its position at the top of the food chain for too long to let any threat go unchallenged. Thurgood had embarrassed the beast in front of its eggs, and a simple death would not be enough. It drew Thurgood to within a few inches of its face and stared at him through devilish eyes.

Giving the creature no satisfaction, Antarius stared back and refused to show fear or pain. It was the last straw.

The mardok roared, revealing teeth sharp enough to slice bone.

Antarius struck. He drove the chief's sword through the creature's upper palate. Softer than other palates, the short sword pierced through the roof of the mardok's mouth and found the monster's most likely tiny and most certainly evil brain.

Everything went limp as brain function ceased. The tentacles released their hold and dropped Thurgood to the ground as the creature pitched forward.

"Oh no" was all he could say before the giant body collapsed on him.

Drowning in a dead animal would be a horrible way to go, and he didn't want that smell in his nose for eternity. Antarius clawed at the ground and tried to pull himself free of the corpse's weight. He was able to move his upper body, but at least one of his ankles was pinned. He couldn't even feel the other one. He shoved a tentacle out of the way and saw daylight. He pulled himself forward as much as his trapped leg would let him and gasped for any air free of the mardok's stench.

What fresh air he had gained access to was soon taken away by a cloud of dust kicked up by the remaining members of the hunting party as they arrived at his side. He looked up at the villagers. Bloodied and bruised, they looked at him in awe. He knew the look. He had finally won their respect. All it took was killing a giant apetopus in, mostly, single combat.

But it was a smelly giant apetopus, and he had run out of patience. "Get me out of here!"

There was a round of cheers as they pulled him from beneath the creature and helped him to his feet. The applause was nice, and he enjoyed a pat on the back as much as the next man, but there were other matters to attend to.

"How's the chief?" he asked the closest man.

The answer came in the form of a downward look and a heavy breath.

Thurgood followed the crowd to Durand's side. Despite being thrown through two trees and a rock, the chief was still alive, but his breath was slight, his eyes were unfocused and a few of his limbs were bent at impossible angles.

Thurgood knelt at the man's side. There was no comfort to be given, no medicine that could save him. Earth medicine had come far, and they could cure almost any disease, but there was no real medical procedure to unthrow someone through a tree or unsmash someone against a rock.

The man's dying eyes flicked toward Thurgood.

"You're a brave man, Durand. The child is saved. You can rest easy now."

Thurgood would never know if his words were appreciated or if the kind tenor of his voice sent the man off to rest in peace, but Durand's spirit slipped away to a place science had yet to follow.

The chief's death had drawn a crowd. The remaining members of the hunting party stood by reverently. Even the man who talked too much found himself at a loss for words. The event had changed them all. They were different people than they had been that morning. Some were wiser. Some were braver. One lady was missing a hand. All at once their world had become smaller. For generations, the Villagers of the Shooting Star had believed they were at the mercy of the world, prey to its tentacled apes. But now they had proven to themselves that Altair could be conquered.

NINETEEN

No Party for the Party
———————————

There was no party upon their return. No feast. No band. No banner draped across... well, he wasn't sure what they would drape it across, as there really wasn't much of a street. The truth was, there was no party because no one was expecting them to return in the first place.

It was for the best. The Altairian version of a ticker tape parade would probably involve mud and sticks and very little imagination. It wasn't something he was sure he wanted to see.

Their surprise return caused quite the stir. Some people cheered while others stopped working on the mass grave. The child they had rescued from the mardok ran into his mother's arms and was swept away home while being showered in joyous tears. Family members rushed to embrace their returning heroes. Wives wept. Husbands wept. Children made fun of everyone for weeping but then ran off to secretly weep themselves.

Once the reality of their success had sunk in, the people of the village began approaching Thurgood with outstretched hands and kind words like, "I was wrong about you," and, "I owe you an apology," and "You're not nearly the halfwit I took you for."

He accepted each apology graciously with a smile and a nod. "You're not the first person to tell me that," he said in response to each expression of regret.

The apologies came with praise as well. They thanked him profusely for standing up to the beast. They wanted to shake the hand that had slain the monster.

He spotted Reya through the crowd. She didn't rush to embrace him upon his return, she let him have his moment. But she never took her gaze off of him. The look in her eyes wasn't lust, unfortunately. But it was pride. And that was almost as good.

Slowly, the crowd's cheers were overpowered by the shouts of family members calling out for the fallen. The longer they went unanswered, the louder and more frantic the cries became. Joy was replaced by grief as the villagers began to understand that the victory had come at a cost. The shouts turned to panicked screams and soon wails as the family members were delivered the news about the death of their loved ones. Their reactions really put a damper on the mood.

The line to shake his hand dispersed as villagers went to comfort the grieving or return to digging the graves. Soon, he was alone in the street, and Reya finally came to see him.

She approached awkwardly, as if she was going to throw her arms around him, but she hesitated and it turned into a weak wave with a shy smile.

He mimicked the gesture and both of them laughed nervously at the display.

"I'm really glad you're not dead," she said.

"Me, too," he agreed. "It would have ruined my plans."

"You did it," she said. "You actually did it."

"Yeah, it looks like we did. The little tyke is safe, the mardok is dead. I guess everything worked out okay."

A small voice spoke up. "We hear the chief is dead."

"The chief is dead?" Reya asked, shocked.

"There were some kinks," Thurgood admitted. "A few deaths."

He turned to see who had interrupted them and found a small man he had never met before standing before him. The man didn't look happy. Thurgood couldn't tell if that unhappiness was directly related to the chief's death or if the man had spent his life not being amused. The man led a contingent of several others who also looked like they didn't like being amused.

"Can I help you?" Thurgood asked after a moment of silence.

"My name is Garnier. We are the village council," the small man said plainly. There was little fluctuation in his voice. It was all fact and authority. "Is it true the chief is dead?"

"It is. I'm sorry. He was a very brave man. Well, right at the end there."

Then men in the group looked at one another and exchanged a few nods before Garnier finally spoke for them all. "Then our village has no leader."

"Fine, I'll do it." Thurgood said with as much humility as he could muster. Admittedly, it wasn't much. He had just killed a monster and rescued a kid from certain death at the hands of said monster.

"You'll do what?" Garnier asked.

"I'll be your new chief and lead you into an era of prosperity and great technological advancement. I will be firm but fair, ruling with the wisdom of Solomon, the strength of Hercules, the, uh, courage of Atlas, and I'll be fast like Mercury."

"What are you talking about?" one of the grayer council members asked.

"It's an old Earth acronym."

"Sham?" Garnier asked.

"No, it's Shaz…" Thurgood replayed the phrase in his head. Something was definitely missing. "Wait, I did it wrong."

"We're not asking you to be the new chief," Garnier said.

"We've already decided that Claude is going to be the new leader," another council member said.

"Claude?" Thurgood was confused.

The council members all turned to reveal that Claude was among their ranks.

Antarius sounded it out. "Chief Claude?" It didn't have any kind of ring to it. Chief Claude didn't even sound right.

"Just Claude will do," Claude said.

"But I'm the one who killed the mardok," Antarius explained.

"That's not how we pick a leader," Garnier said.

"That's a pretty primitive way to determine a leader," one of the others chimed in.

"But I have the chief's sword," Thurgood said, and held up Durand's sword.

"Yeah, but it's not like it's a magic sword."

"I know it's not a magic sword. I didn't say I pulled it from a rock. I pulled it from the Chief. But it's the chief's sword. So doesn't that make me chief?"

"Just how backwards do you think we are?" Garnier took the sword out of Thurgood's grip and handed it to Claude.

"I think you're…"

Reya put a hand on his shoulder. "That was rhetorical. They don't really want an answer."

"But I avenged Durand's death," Thurgood said to anyone who was still listening. Mostly they were congratulating Claude on his new role as chief.

"Look," one of the council members started. "If it makes you feel better, we did talk about making you leader."

It did make him feel a little better. If it was true. "You did?"

"Sure, we did," another said. "Yeah, uh, we figured since you were already a captain, you had some leadership experience."

"That I do. I'd be a natural."

"You'd be a disaster," Garnier said with no regard for anyone's feelings. "So we're going to go with Claude."

"Fine," Thurgood said, and turned to the new chief. "Chief Claude, I know you're new to this thing, but I think your first priority as chief should be getting me off of this planet."

"Just Claude," Claude said, and then nodded. "And I couldn't agree more."

"Really?"

"Absolutely."

"I thought it would be more of an argument."

"Not at all. I think that the sooner you're off this planet, the better."

"I totally agree," Thurgood said, and reached out to shake the man's hand. It was as simple as that. "Wow, you're a way better chief than that last guy, Claude."

A series of gasps escaped the council members. Reya coughed.

"May he rest in peace," Thurgood finished. "Of course."

Chief Claude let go of Thurgood's hand and declared, "You leave tomorrow."

"Excellent. Now, let's talk strategy. The Volga have the ship surrounded so I'm thinking we sneak in under the cover of darkness, in the dead of night and show those damn savages why it's called the dead of night. I call it Operation: Dead of Night."

"No," Claude said.

"We can call it something else," Thurgood offered.

"It's not the name, it's—"

"My second plan is to build a giant horse and hide inside. The Volga will bring it into their camp because they're stupid. Then in the dead of night, we sneak out and kill them all. I call it Operation: Beaten by a Dead Horse in the Dead of Night."

"No. We... That's even worse. Where are we... We don't even have horses here."

"Plan C is called Operation: Dead Drunk of Night. We dress up as drunks and—"

"I'm going to stop you right there. We're not doing that either."

"Well, I don't know what to tell you, Chief, I only have one plan left and I can't say I have a hundred percent confidence in it because I'm not 100% sure what a doornail is or how to get the Volga to dress up as one."

"We are not going to do that either."

"Look, Claude, I don't want to tell you how to lead your people here, but if you keep crapping on everybody's ideas, they're going to start calling you Chief Craps on Everybody's Ideas. What's your big plan?"

"We're going to talk to the Volga."

"I love it!" Antarius shouted. "We act like we're going to talk to them and then kill them in the dead of night?"

"No, we're going to talk to the Volga."

"I don't want to criticize because you're new at this. But you might want to work on naming your plans. Plus, I don't know that the Volga will like what I have to say. I've been thinking of some pretty nasty nicknames since I met them."

"That's why I'm going with you. I'll be leading the expedition and I'll be doing all the talking."

"I don't think you'll like what *they* have to say, Chief. I know you all used to be friends, but I'm telling you, they've gone feral."

"Nonsense, they are still people, just like us."

"Yes, just like you, except meaner, gruntier, dirtier... well, not dirtier. Trust me, Claude, when I say they've changed. They've let the wild seduce them, or maybe it was the smell of the moss, I'm not sure how losing your mind works but they've gone savage. I still think killing them all is the safest plan."

"No. I'm the leader and I have spoken."

This sent chills down Thurgood's spine. It was a good line. He'd have to remember it. Antarius took Claude's hand once more. "It's a bold and stupid plan, Claude. But I like your spirit. You're a take-charge kind of chief and I can appreciate that. The best leaders lead from the front. It's one of the reasons why the Alliance puts the bridge at the head of the ship."

"What are the others?" one of the council members asked.

"To see better and because no one wants to ride in a butt," Thurgood explained.

Claude wrestled his hand free from Thurgood's grip and backed away. "We'll set out in the morning. Get some rest. It's a long journey." With his first official order given, the new chief turned and walked away. The council members fell in behind him and followed, leaving Reya and Thurgood alone.

"So, it looks like this is my last night on the planet." Thurgood took both her hands in his. "How do you think I should spend it?"

Reya smiled and kissed him. It took both of them by surprise, and it was over before anyone in the village could see.

They smiled awkwardly at each other for only a moment before they decided a simple kiss wasn't enough for either of them. She fell into his arms and they kissed for the whole world to witness. It was passionate and deep, and people started staring, and it became awkward for everyone. Everyone except for the new lovers. For them it was the only thing. The village melted away. Altair itself disappeared and she became his whole world.

They kissed until Thurgood felt a tap on his shoulder. He turned to see one of the hunting party members bearing a stretcher.

"Could I ask you two to move to the side for a minute? We're bringing the dead in and you're in the way."

It was a real mood killer.

Almost.

TWENTY

Hope Reborn

The sunlight seemed brighter the next morning, as if the planet's star had spent the night in the arms of a lover. The air was crisper, as if the breeze had found its happiness in the soul of another. A small mammal pranced by with a lighter step, as if it had gotten some and couldn't wait to tell the world. Sounds were clearer, colors were brighter and everything stank a little less as Thurgood stepped from his village home for what would be the last time. He inhaled the fresh morning air deeply and then coughed when he realized the stink was still there after all.

Reya joined him a moment later and took his hand. It no longer occurred to him that her hands were rough, and he welcomed her touch. Hand in hand, they strolled through the Village of the Shooting Star, smiling at everyone they met along the way and greeting them with the cheeriest of good mornings in a tone that contained an awful lot of subtext.

The expedition party had assembled at the approximate center of town, and the rest of the villagers had gathered to see them off. The force was smaller than the hunting party. The number of deaths from the hunt had caused more than a little hesitation in new recruits. The psychological forces at work were complex. Their victory over the mardok had steeled wills and given hope. But the deaths had made others hesitant to join. The deaths also meant there were fewer people left to volunteer overall. That was just math.

Thurgood had tried giving another rousing speech, but many in the town had called it derivative. Thurgood didn't disagree, but, in his defense, he rarely had to give two greater-good speeches two days in a row to the same audience.

Veterans of the mardok hunt filled the ranks of the expedition force. Victory over the beast had emboldened the surviving men and women, and he welcomed their experience and their courage. He counted the heads in the group. It wasn't many. But it would be enough. Antarius was confident the semi-feral Russians would present less of a challenge than a giant apelike creature with secret tentacles. If the Russians also had secret tentacles, though, all bets were off. Garnier and the others in the village assured him this wasn't the case, but stranger things had happened.

Despite the funerals from the day before, there was an electric excitement in the air. With the return of the child, the villagers had been given a taste of victory and it was clear they wanted more. Their confidence had grown, and they were willing to risk more than ever before for a chance at a better life. Victory for the expedition meant rescue. It was a way off the planet they had been forced to call home for far too long. It was a possible path to a life better than they had ever dared to imagine.

Thurgood could see the excitement in their eyes. They had heard stories of Earth from the village elders. They had seen images in the town's archives. But what they heard and what they had seen had to seem unreal to those who had grown up on the moss-covered Altair. What wonders were they envisioning?

"Excuse me, Captain." A pretty young woman in her early twenties spoke with a soft voice.

"Yes, my dear."

She refused to look him in the eye and stared at the ground as she asked her question. "Is it true that on Earth, people get to keep their teeth most of their life?"

"It's true," Thurgood said, beaming a broad smile back as proof. "As long as you take care of them and don't play hockey."

He could see a weight lift off the young woman's shoulders, and she looked at him with relief in her eyes. Her smile revealed several gaps and Thurgood quickly hid his own grin because he suddenly became aware it was a form of bragging.

The young woman raised her arm and covered her smile with her wrist as she disappeared back into the crowd. But she was hardly the last one with a question. A line had formed before him, and villagers took turns stepping forward to ask their questions about life on Earth.

"Is it true some people spend all their time making music?" one asked.

"Yes," Thurgood said. "Though some really shouldn't."

"Is it true we won't have to weave our own moss?" asked another.

"You'll be able to print the finest clothes with the push of a button," he said.

"Is it true we won't have to shit in the river?"

"Only if you want to, my friend. Only if you want to."

The line stretched on as the villagers waited to say goodbye to the man from Earth. They wanted to show their appreciation, to say thank you for bringing them the hope of rescue and to make him swear that he would come back to get them and not leave them to rot on this, as one sweet old woman put it, festering moss-covered shithole of a planet.

Their words touched him. Because it meant he had touched

them and this was their way of touching him back. And everyone liked being touched back.

A middle-aged man shook Thurgood's hand, offered a quick thank-you and stepped aside to reveal a young woman trembling before him. The woman tried to speak, but her mouth moved without words. It looked like she was trying to get the word "You" out when her bottom lip started quivering and messed it all up. She burst into tears and threw her arms around him, hitting him so hard that the embrace almost turned into a tackle.

With few other options available, Thurgood hugged her back and just held on when she began to sway back and forth.

The rocking must have helped her find her voice, for she finally started to speak actual words instead of sobby nonsense. She released the hug but held onto his hand as she took a step back and smiled. "Captain. I can't thank you enough for saving my child."

Of course, she was the child's mother. That explained her enthusiastic death clench of a hug. She may have bruised a rib or two, but it was hardly worth mentioning. "It was my pleasure, ma'am."

There was movement behind her, and Antarius looked down to see the child he had rescued from the mardok nest clinging to his mother's leg, sneaking the occasional peek up at his rescuer.

"And this must be little Antarius here." Thurgood smiled and crouched down and tussled the child's hair.

"Antarius?" the mother asked.

"Antarius," Thurgood repeated.

"I don't understand."

"Well, I'm assuming you named the child after me," Antarius said.

The woman looked at her child and back to him. Confused, she asked, "Why would I do that?"

"Well, for saving the child's life."

"I didn't... um, I..."

"Oh, you see back on Earth we have something called gratitude. So, I just figured..."

"I'm sorry... I am grateful, of course. But you want me to name my child after you?"

"I'm not saying you have to. I just assumed. Do you have any ideas how many kids are named after me?"

"I haven't any idea."

"Neither do I. But it's probably a lot. It's just something people do where I come from."

"But my child already has a name," she said, putting her arm around the child.

"And there's some kind of village rule against changing it? That's not a problem. I can talk to the new chief if you'd like. Claude and I are pretty tight."

"No. That's not necessary."

"Of course. Of course. There's no need to be formal. Maybe you could just make it a nickname then."

"We... we will think about it." The woman started to push the child away.

"I think your son would like it," Antarius said.

"She's my daughter!" snapped the woman.

"Oh? Oh! Well, don't worry. They're all kinds of accepting on Earth. They don't care how ugly someone is."

"Ugly? How dare you!"

Claude rescued the woman from the scene she was making as the chief called for everyone's attention. The crowd turned to listen as he addressed them.

Thurgood took a deep breath. "Well, it looks like it's almost my turn. It was an honor saving your child." Thurgood tussled the child's hair once more and joined the others.

Claude spoke with purpose. "Thank you to all of you who

have volunteered to accompany us on our journey. It won't be easy but, if we are successful, it could mean rescue. Rescue," he said, staring into the distance. "It's a word that our grandparents believed in. And it's a word that their children came to hate. The constant rebuke of hope taught us to reject the idea altogether. But now we have a chance at rescue. A chance to experience life in ways we've only heard about. To the members of this expedition, thank you for volunteering. And to all of you, thank you for trusting me. Now, it's time for us to leave."

It wasn't a bad speech, Thurgood admitted. The crowd applauded. Maybe he'd been underestimating Claude. Even he felt encouraged by the chief's words.

But would it be enough?

This brave band of warriors were being asked to trek across a violent wilderness, face untold dangers, engage with a group of savage Russians and retake an abandoned enemy ship, all so he could return to Earth where he would probably remember to mount a rescue mission for those left behind on the planet. It was a lot to ask.

He wasn't too worried about the Russians. Surely, they had to hate Altair as much as the villagers from the Village of the Shooting Star. As long as they would listen, they would no doubt jump at the chance to go home. He was sure of it. But there were still a lot of unknowns out there, and a little more encouragement never hurt. Thurgood stepped up on a rock just as Claude dropped to the ground.

"Before we set out on this, from what you tell me, perilous journey, I just want to say that I probably don't really need your help. But you volunteered all the same. And that means so much more than volunteering when you're needed. It shows a special kind of courage. And I am always proud to travel in the company of courageous men and women."

He looked at Reya, who had decided to join them on the

journey. In fact, she had refused to let him leave without her. Her presence gave him comfort.

"I don't know what it's like to lose hope. But I do know what it's like to lose other things. One time I misplaced my keys for a week. And that was terrible. But it was good when I found them. So I can only imagine what it would be like to misplace my keys for a generation and then to find them again. And that, I don't know what the emotion is called, but it's powerful and now we all share it. And when we're all feeling this... thing... together at the same time, nothing can stand in our way. I believe in us and I want to thank you all for believing in me. Now let's get me home."

They didn't applaud as much as they did before, but they were probably still tired from their previous bout of clapping. What mattered was that they were ready now. Thurgood stepped from the rock and moved to the edge of the crowd where Reya was waiting for him. Garnier and the council stood with her.

Garnier offered Thurgood his hand and a "Good luck, Captain. I hope we never see you again."

"That's kind of you to say," Antarius said as he shook Garnier's hand. "Don't worry. I'll get that ship or die trying."

"Those are suitable terms," Garnier said.

"I going to miss your wit, Garnier. Now, if you'll excuse me. I have to go rescue someone. Me." With this, Thurgood turned and walked bravely into the woods.

Claude called him back a moment later and pointed him toward the right path, and the group moved out into the unknown.

TWENTY-ONE

Making Friends

The first steps were taken boldly. Many of them had trod upon this ground before on their way to fight the mardok, and they found confidence in retracing the steps that had taken them to victory. As they went, they regaled those new to the party with war stories and recounting of the journey. Embellishments went unnoticed as the newcomers dared not call out the heroes on their version of the story.

But it wasn't long before the familiar path ended and the anecdotes ran out. The thick growth of the jungle swallowed all that was familiar, and the sights and sounds of home disappeared. The Village of the Shooting Star had been behind them one moment, gone the next. And with its passing, the expedition members were left alone in the savage wilderness of a world alien to them all.

Everything was foreign to them now. Even the birds sounded different on this side of the wilderness. Their songs were more haunting, and they seemed to be crying warnings from their perches in the limbs above. The haunting calls gave Thurgood pause.

Whatever it was he was hearing in the birdsong went unnoticed by the rest of the party. The men and women were too preoccupied by the situation they found themselves in. For every one of them, this would be the farthest they had ever been from the relative safety of the village. Even Claude was in new territory. He was forced to navigate from a map that had been handed down from leader to leader and would theoretically lead them to the Volga village.

They knew little of the path that lay before them. Where it would take them. What they would encounter. The only thing they did know was that they were in for a long journey. Thurgood's fall and subsequent trip down the river had taken him farther from the crash site than he could have imagined. He had fallen in more or less a straight line, while the return trip required a meandering path through the jungle. The trip would take them several days. Longer if they kept moving at their current pace.

The expedition leaders grew more cautious, and the stops came far too frequently. They had become as attuned to the birdsong warnings as he was, and every sound became a reason to pause, crouch and be wary. There they would remain, crouched until one of the expedition leaders called the all clear. The smallest sound or the most distant roar caused the party to freeze. They were getting nowhere, and Thurgood's knees were starting to bother him.

"This is foolish," Thurgood complained to Reya as they squatted once more.

"He's just being cautious," Reya said.

"His caution may cost us all."

"How can being careful cost us?"

"In lots of ways," Thurgood said. "The Hama could arrive before we get to the ship. The Volga might learn how to be pilots. My knees could turn to dust from all this crouching."

Antarius straightened his leg slowly, and there was an audible pop. He pointed to the joint as proof he was right.

"I'm sure you'll be fine." Reya placed a hand on his knee.

It tickled, and he fell backward into a bush. This drew a harsh shushing from everyone around him. Though it was not as harsh as every other time he had drawn their admonishment. It was obvious that even they were getting tired of the stopping and stooping.

"It's not helping morale either." Thurgood got back to his feet and crouched again. "He's losing the group."

"People are growing weary," she agreed. "You could help."

"Not with Captain Shushy Pants leading things," Thurgood said, and jerked a thumb toward Chief Claude at the head of the line.

"Talk to them. They admire you, you know?"

They did look up to him, and they needed him to distract them from the dangers of the jungle and the poor leadership skills. He decided to begin a campaign of camaraderie. Each time they were ordered to crouch, he would find someone new to squat next to and offer a hand and ask their names. Good leaders knew that people liked it when they thought others cared about them. And he was going to convince them all he cared.

"You're right, Reya."

"I'm going to get to know each and every one of them better than they know themselves."

"That sounds a little ambitious," she said. "Maybe just make friends?"

"Better than they know themselves," he reiterated.

"Are you sure you have time?"

It was a lot of people to get to know, true, but the Academy had prepared him for just such an instance. There was no shortage of situations in life when you needed to get to know someone quickly but didn't have the luxury of time or the desire to talk to them too much.

"It's simple, Reya. You see, it all comes down to asking them three questions."

"Three questions?"

She was skeptical. But he didn't blame her. He doubted her planet had psychology. "Three questions. I'll ask them to describe three things: their favorite color, the favorite animal and their favorite form of water."

"That's it?"

"That's it."

The "3 Questions" had been developed by either Alliance psychologists or a 21st century phishing scam. Either way, the answers revealed more about the respondent than simply "Are they dumb enough to fall for a phishing scam?"

Thurgood explained the deeper meaning behind each query. "You see, the words a person uses to describe their favorite color are how they see themselves. The words they use to describe their favorite animal are how they believe the world sees them. And the words they use to describe their favorite form of water are how they view love. And what more is there to know about a person?

Reya did not look convinced. "Okay. Well, good luck with that."

"I don't need luck when I have science, Reya."

Armed with the powerful mind trick, Antarius spent the rest of the morning engaging with every member of the expedition. To each, he posed the three questions, and from each, he heard their responses. By noon he knew each of their favorite colors, their favorite animals and their favorite form of water.

When they broke for lunch, he slumped down next to Reya. "I hate this stupid planet."

"So, the three questions didn't go well?"

"No. There are only two colors on this mudhole, I don't know any of the animals they're talking about and what the hell is smurge?"

"It's kind of a muddy, mossy and ice thing."

"That's smurge?" Thurgood was disgusted both by the definition and by the fact that every single person described it as their favorite form of water. "That's no way to describe love!"

"Oh really?" Reya moved close, until the two were touching, and asked quietly, "How would you describe love as a form of water?"

"Well, it's obviously the ocean, Reya."

"The ocean? Can you describe it?"

"It's powerful enough to overtake you, goes on forever and leaves you feeling sticky in the end."

She inched away and returned to her meal. "So, what are you going to do now?"

Antarius idly stirred the sludge that was his lunch. Science and psychology had failed him. The Academy had steered him wrong. There was only one way forward he could see. He sighed. "I guess I'll have to actually talk to people."

As it turned out, talking to people wasn't as bad as he thought it was going to be. He had spent a lifetime of diplomatic service in the Alliance, where socializing was often an assignment. To talk freely with others without trying to outwit them was almost relaxing. The more people he met, the more he found what they were saying to be somewhat genuinely interesting.

For example, the giant of a man who talked too much to cover his nerves and had thwarted many of Thurgood's escape attempts from the village was named Lance Petit, and he was one of the town's builders. Maintaining the villagers' homes was a role he took seriously even though he dreamed of one day building bigger things, like homes with two rooms.

Thurgood told the man about duplexes and apartment buildings and left the man dreaming bigger than before.

The man who sweated too much to cover his nerves was named Franc Simon, and he was one of the town's moss weavers. Producing textiles and welcome mats for the villagers to wear and wipe their feet on was a role he took seriously even though he dreamed of one day weaving bigger things, like a welcome mat that could welcome twice as many people at the same time.

Thurgood told the man about wall-to-wall carpeting and watched the man's eyes grow wide with excitement.

"From one wall to another?" he asked, envisioning the sight.

"From one wall to another," Thurgood said, and slapped the man on the back before moving on to make another friend.

The man who drank too much to cover his nerves was named Noel Leroy. And he wasn't drinking to cover his nerves at all. He was the village drunk. Drinking a lot, losing himself in a haze of moss-distilled booze and stumbling everywhere he went while making people uncomfortable was a role he took seriously even though he dreamed of one day being even more drunk and making even more people uncomfortable.

Thurgood told the man about the endless variety of liquors that could be found across the galaxy and social media platforms that gave everyone in the galaxy that ability to annoy millions.

Leroy just shrugged, stumbled off and threw up in a nearby bush.

"That man's going to be a hit," Thurgood said to himself.

By the time night fell on their camp, Thurgood had met and befriended every member of the expedition. He had listened to their woes and their dreams and offered them hope by sharing with them the hopes of a brighter future than they ever dared to dream for. It had put a new spring not only in their steps but his own. They all had moved with a new purpose toward the Hama ship and the realization of those dreams.

By the next morning, everyone was beginning to share Thurgood's impatience with the expedition's slow progress. With the new dreams playing fresh in their minds, even they tired of the constant stops. Every time they stopped, every time they were ordered to crouch, they began to grumble under their breath while they waited for the leader to call the all clear.

After Claude ordered them to stop for about the hundredth time, Thurgood refused to crouch. "That's it," he said to Reya. "We're never going to get there at this rate."

"He's just being cautious. Most of us never leave the village. This is the farthest many of us have been."

"Well, we're not going to get much farther at this rate." Thurgood stood and marched to the front of the group. Every crouched villager stared at him through wide eyes as he passed. He could tell they were nervous, but they had his back.

Chief Claude and another man spoke quietly to one another about a hanging branch that blocked their path. It was heavy with morning dew and thick with leaves, creating a screen concealing what lay behind it.

"What are you doing?" Claude asked with some bite when he saw Thurgood approaching. "You're supposed to be crouching."

"Why?" Thurgood asked, not trying to whisper in the least.

"Because that's... Because I gave the crouch signal," Claude whispered back, and demonstrated the gesture, which was two open hands pressing toward the ground.

"What is it this time? A twig snapping? Did a bird tweet? Did the moss do one of those burping things?"

"I... I don't have to say."

"You can't be afraid of every little snap, Chief." Thurgood

turned and motioned for the closest person to stand. "Come on, get up."

The man shook his head and stayed crouched. "What if there's danger?"

The villagers were excited, but they were so used to being timid, it was going to take some encouragement to get them to move. "There's always danger," Thurgood said. "Now stand up."

The villager looked nervously at his neighbor and back to Antarius. "I'm sorry but that seems like a bad reason to stand up."

Antarius stepped over to the man and pulled him to his feet. Then he turned to address the party. "Don't you all see? There is always danger. The world is full of it. All worlds are. But if we waited for safety to take each step, there would be no progress. There would be no duplexes," he said as he helped Lance to his feet.

Once standing, Lance nodded to himself to indicate that he had made the right choice.

Thurgood nodded back. He then pointed to Franc. "There would be no wall-to-wall carpeting."

Franc rose to his feet and shared a look with Antarius and Lance.

"There would be no bars filled with flavored whiskeys and infused vodkas," Thurgood said to Noel.

Noel rose to his feet, stumbled a bit and then threw up in the bushes.

"He's going to be a star," Thurgood said to himself before continuing. "It is only those that are willing to step boldly, despite the ever-present danger, that make a difference, that tame the wild and conquer worlds."

He pointed to another party member crouched farther along the line. The woman stood up. Antarius smiled at the rest of the party and stepped to the front of the group. He grabbed the branch that had blocked the path.

"Because when you walk boldly, danger moves aside." Antarius pulled the branch aside and was attacked by... it wasn't quite a monkey. It had more arms than a monkey, but it was furry and furious and clung to his head as it screeched and pulled at his hair.

His efforts to remove it were met with paws and even more screeching. He punched at the creature, but with so many arms, there was no real way through its defenses. Outrunning the creature was his only choice.

Unfortunately, as soon as he began to run, the beast used some of its superfluous arms to cover his eyes, and Thurgood ran both of them straight into a tree.

TWENTY-TWO

Lewis, Clark and Thurgood

Reya giggled as she wrapped the bandage around his head. He was bleeding from several shallow cuts caused by the monkey thing and one deep gash caused by the collision with the tree.

Thurgood grumbled while she told him tales of the mischievous monkey-like creatures. She told him how they would wander into the village and then wear things like hats. The kids would laugh at these silly animals putting all manner of things on their heads and acting like people.

"They should all be shot, skinned and their skins hung about as a warning to others," Thurgood said, and received a playful slap on his arm. "They're a menace!"

"They're cute," she said with a smile.

"They're not cute. They're dangerous."

"They're only dangerous if they're provoked."

"I did no provoking." Thurgood leered at the creature that was still sitting in a nearby tree taunting him and chirping like some stupid animal. "He started it. He did the provoking."

Reya smiled at the creature and then let out a laugh as it put a leaf on its head like a hat.

Antarius didn't care for the antics. "Stupid six-armed monkey."

"Moncheenie," Reya corrected him as if he was a poor student.

"How do you know that's what they're called?"

Reya thought about it for a moment and then shrugged. "That's just what we call them."

"Just like that?"

"I suppose." She finished dressing the wound and kissed him on the head for good measure.

"Interesting," Thurgood said as he stared up into the distance. A break in the trees allowed him a view of a mountain peak. They had been walking in its shadow all morning. He pointed to the snow-covered peak. "So, what's that mountain called?"

"Mt. First Time I'm Seeing It?" Reya said with a coy smile.

Thurgood smiled back. "But what do the locals call it?"

There was a laugh behind him, and Thurgood turned to see another one of the village moss weavers had been tickled by the question.

"What's so funny, Andreé?"

"We are the locals, you moron. If we didn't give it a name, it doesn't have one."

Thurgood looked back at the mountain through the jungle canvas as a new sense of purpose dawned on him. He had accomplished many great things in his time. He had set countless records at the academy. He had risen faster through the ranks of the fleet than any other officer. He had helmed the Alliance flagship right up until it was blown up. He had represented the Alliance in hundreds of first-contact ceremonies, attended a thousand diplomatic ceremonies and touched millions of lives. But he had never had the opportunity to discover a planet before.

Not from the ground, anyway. He had charted many new planets during his voyages using deep sensor arrays and other technical gizmos. But anyone could do that. All it took was a tube and a couple of glass lenses to discover a planet from space. But here, he was a true explorer. Here, he was blazing new paths and literally putting things on the map. And he was the first. He had seen the map Claude was using, the one that had been passed from chief to chief. It was drawn like a tourist's map with cartoonish landmarks and a dotted path, but it was devoid of names.

Thurgood stood with renewed vigor and decided it was time to take charge.

"On your feet, everyone," he said to the party as he shouldered his own supply pack. "Douse the fires and pack up. We're moving out."

The others weren't as enthusiastic about resuming their journey, but they began to rise and gather their gear as instructed. Their movement drew Claude's attention, and the new chief crossed the campsite in a huff.

"What's going on here? What are you people doing?"

"We're moving out," Thurgood explained. "If we're going to make the base of Mount Thurgood before tonight, we have to get a move on."

"What are you talking about? What is Mount Thurgood?"

"That is Mount Thurgood," Antarius pointed to the mountain peak in the distance. "Unless we find a bigger mountain later. Then that new one will be Mount Thurgood, and this will be Antarius's Peak."

"What in the hell are you talking about?"

"This little travel party just became a full-blown expedition, Chief."

"We are taking you to your ship," Claude stated. "Plain and simple."

"That was before, when I was Robinson Crusoe," Thurgood explained. "Now we're Lewis and Clark. And we've got some work to do."

"Wait. Who are Lewis and Clark and why do we have to be them?" Andreé asked.

"Who are Lewis and Clark? Are you serious?" Thurgood asked. He received nods and blank stares in response. "Don't they teach you world history here?"

"Our world history is 80 years long," Reya reminded him.

"Well, they were explorers. Men of undaunted spirit. Just like us. They set out into the unknown wilds and blazed a new path forward. They met strange and wonderful peoples and slept with those peoples. They named rivers and mountains and plants and probably stupid birds, too. They were heroes. And that's what we'll be. Someone bring me a journal. We're about to make history." Antarius once again pointed to the peak in the distance. "And we're going to start with Mount Thurgood."

Franc craned back his neck and looked up at the mountain. "Why are we naming it after you again?"

"Because I discovered it."

"You didn't discover it. It was just sitting there, big as a mountain, and you looked at it. That's not discovering anything. That's, I guess, seeing something?"

"Too late," Thurgood said, and snapped shut his recorder—since no journal had been provided, he had made the entry is his captain's log. "While you were whining, I was documenting. I've already recorded it. It's Mount Thurgood."

"I don't think that's fair," another man said. "I've seen that mountain before. Probably way before you. Why shouldn't it be named after me?"

"Because it already has a name. But don't worry, if we come across another, smaller, and less significant peak, we can name it after you."

This excited the man. "Really?"

"Sure, why not?"

"Wow."

"Now, let's get this expedition started for real."

With this newfound purpose, Thurgood pushed the party forward despite Claude's best efforts to exercise caution. Whenever the leader called for a halt, Thurgood simply moved by him and offered the reminder, "History doesn't remember the crouchers."

For the next three days, Antarius refused to stop for anything except meals and sleep. They were now on a march for knowledge, and he was recording discoveries in his captain's log at a pace that would make Meriwether green with envy instead of green with syphilis.

At one point, the trees thinned as Thurgood stepped into an expanse of rolling hills. He pulled the recorder from his pocket and snapped it open. "We came upon a meadow still and silent. The only sound was the dry grasses scratching upon one another in the breeze, playing a lazy rhythm to soothe weary travelers. It shall be known as Thurgood's Meadow."

Passing through the meadow, the jungle swallowed them once more. Thurgood pulled out the recorder. "The forest welcomed us back into its embrace like an old friend. There's a comfort in its strength and consistency. It shall be known as Thurgood's Forest."

The path wound through the trees and the scenery remained constant until they came to a precipitous drop. Thurgood spoke into the recorder. "We came upon a ledge within the jungle. Its height would mean a fatal drop to the rocks below. Calls into the chasm were answered with the cold efficiency of reflecting stone. It shall be known as Thurgood's Ravine."

The rainforest ended once more at the edge of a marsh, and out came the recorder. "We came upon a swamp, the turgid vegetation pregnant with water and ripe with odor. The moss here smells fermented and hangs in the nostrils. It shall…"

"Thurgood's Swamp," a voice behind him interrupted.

"I beg your pardon," Antarius said. "I'm trying to make a discovery here."

"Forgive me." It was one of the village builders. "Just trying to help you out there since we all know you're going to name it after yourself."

"No, I wasn't."

"Sure you were. You've named every single thing we've seen after yourself: mountains, ravines, trees, creeks, birds and even that pile of scat you thought might be some kind of mushroom. Why should this be any different?"

"I wasn't going to name it after myself."

"That's a load."

"I wasn't. I was going to name it after you, actually."

"Me?"

"Yes."

"Really?"

"Really."

The villager wasn't convinced. He folded his arms and smiled. "All right. Go ahead. I'll bet you don't even know my name."

Thurgood turned back to the recorder as he resumed the discovery process. "It shall be known as Whiny Bitchy Guy's Swamp." He turned off the recorder and dropped it back in his pocket. He patted the man on the back as he passed. "Congrats, Richaud. You're famous."

As the days went by, he documented countless plants and birds, and more than sixteen types of moss. At this rate, he could discover the whole planet in a matter of months. But that would have to wait. Though he pressed on for the sake of history and science, he knew they were running out of time. The Hama were still coming.

According to Claude's crude map, they weren't far from the Volga village and the Hama ship.

"See?" Thurgood pointed to the map in Claude's hand. "It should be just past Thurgood Basin."

Claude snapped. "I told you to stop drawing on my map!"

Thurgood pushed on despite Claude's sour attitude. But the closer they drew to their destination, the more timid the leader became. Even Thurgood's trailblazing spirit wasn't enough to calm the man's nerves. He called halts more frequently and even stopped Antarius from pushing forward.

Thurgood tried to push past him and lead the expedition on to their place in the Altairian history books, but a hand seized him by the collar and stopped him cold.

"I said halt," Claude scolded him in a whisper. He was serious this time.

"What is it now?"

Claude crouched and pulled Antarius down with him. "There's something out there," the chief said quietly and frustratingly slowly.

"It's probably another stupid monkey. I say bring it. I owe it one."

Claude shook his head slowly and turned his gaze to the limbs above them. "We are being stalked by a skydonk."

"Skydonk? Seriously? Skydonk? Are you guys ever lucky I'm naming things now."

The chief's response almost broke a whisper. "This is serious!"

"Fine. It's serious. So, what's a skydonk?"

"It is a ferocious beast," Reya said. "Not unlike a great cat."

"Great, first was great apes, now it's great cats." Thurgood rolled his eyes. "Skydonk. I hate this place and I swear if I ever leave, I am never coming back. Never ever."

Thurgood felt the gaze of the entire party on him. Lance, the giant of a man, rose to his full height and cracked his knuckles.

"I mean, of course I'm coming back to save everybody, yeah." Assurances made and nerves calmed, he added, "But after that, no way."

A low rumble filled the trees around them.

"Wait a minute," Thurgood said. "I know that rumble. That's no skydonk. It's a predabullcelot!"

A wicked roar surrounded them as the creature pounced from a tree above and blocked out the sun. Its shadow alone was terrifying, but when the beast landed in the middle of the party, it sent all of the members scattering into the thick woods for shelter. All except for the villager the purple beast had landed on. That guy didn't get very far.

The creature made short work of the villager beneath its claws and turned its attention to the others.

"Over here, kitty cat!" Thurgood shouted and readied his spear. "I've dealt with your kind before."

The beast snarled and turned toward the fearless captain.

The two locked eyes in recognition. Thurgood had no doubt it was the same beast he had encountered earlier. He recognized it as the beast he had tangled with by the scar tissue covering its eye. The beast recognized Thurgood as well because you never forget the person who shoots your eye out.

The roar turned from a hunter's tool to a howl of vengeance as the mighty predator attacked.

Thurgood dodged the first strike, came back up and thrust the spear in the cat's face.

The predabullcelot deflected the strike with the bat of a paw that sent the spear flying into the jungle. It roared once more and drew back its paw.

Thurgood braced himself for the attack, but it never came. Chief Claude tackled him out of harm's way moments before the predator's massive claws dug into the ground.

The pair rolled behind the safety of a tree as another villager drew the beast's attention.

"You've seen one of these things before?" Claude shouted.

"I've seen this thing before," Thurgood said as he got back to his feet. "This is the creature that chased me into the canyon."

The beast had its eye on Reya.

She backed away slowly as the monster lowered itself and prepared to spring.

Reya turned to run but caught her foot on a rock and went down.

Franc saw that she was down and leapt between her and the cat with a shout. Franc then screamed as the predator swatted him aside with a massive paw and moved in toward Reya.

The monster reared up to strike at the helpless woman like a coward. It stopped once it saw Thurgood standing in its way.

"That's right, Blinky. It's me. Why don't you leave the woman alone and let's finish our dance." Thurgood drew the Volga blade from his belt.

The gleam of the blade seemed to draw the beast's attention.

"Go now, Reya. This ugly one-eyed bastard and I have some unfinished business."

Reya scrambled to her feet and found cover behind a nearby tree. Once he was certain she was safe, Thurgood turned his full attention back to the mountainous predator. "All right, pussy cat. It's your move."

The predabullcelot pounced and landed on Thurgood, knocking him to the ground beneath its full weight. It was like being hit by a whole river and a mardok all at the same time, and he disappeared beneath its bulk.

But then everything was still. The beast no longer moved

and no longer roared. Thurgood wondered why it wasn't savagely ripping the flesh from his body. It was a surprisingly quiet killer. It didn't even hurt.

Maybe it was trying to suffocate him. He knew this was how cats killed babies while they slept, but it seemed an odd tactic for the fierce predabullcelot. He tried to get free, but the beast was too heavy. He began to call for help.

Soon, the creature began to move and he could see daylight once again. Several of the villagers were pushing the beast.

"Get it off me," Thurgood barked.

"He's alive!" Reya shouted to the others as she began pushing against the monster. "Help me."

More villagers came together in the small jungle clearing and heaved the massive creature to one side to reveal a bloody wound near the cat's heart.

Thurgood looked at the bloody knife in his hand. It was the lucky knife that had belonged to the Volga Chekov. The legends were true. The creature had tried to kill Thurgood and met his own end instead. It was fate that the sergeant at arms had given it to him. It had to be.

Chief Claude had a stunned look on his face as he helped Thurgood back to his feet. The man was filled with questions, but all he could manage was, "How? How? How are you not dead?"

"There's only one thing I can say, Chief." Thurgood smiled and held up the bloodied blade. "Thank God I had Freddie's knife."

TWENTY-THREE

Meeting of the Tribes

The waters of Thurgood's Brook were a welcomed feature at the evening's campsite. Filled with smooth stones and a gentle current, the water ran cool and clean until Antarius waded in to wash the skydonk's blood from his body. He sat on a submerged rock in the middle of the stream and watched as the carnage was swept away by the water and disappeared around a bend. Once it was gone, he was left alone for a quiet moment.

"Is this rock taken?" Reya asked as she sat next to him and joined him in staring downstream. "What's happening off in the distance?"

"Nothing. Nothing at all. You know, parts of this planet can be quite beautiful when it's not trying to kill you."

She hummed her agreement and put her hand on his back.

"Unfortunately, everything here is trying to kill you. Seriously, it's like Australia."

"I don't know where that is."

"Right. I keep forgetting you haven't traveled. Well, it's a beautiful place filled with monsters. Just like here. Spiders as big as your face."

"I didn't know spiders could be that small?"

He couldn't tell if she was kidding or not, and it was one of the reasons he loved her. A dry wit was indistinguishable from genuine ignorance, and he found both equally attractive, as far as he could tell.

Thurgood put his arm around her and they drank in the scene together. "I could be happy here forever."

"You said you never wanted to come back."

"That was a long time ago. When we were being hunted by a giant cat. But right here, right now, I'm happy and I never want to leave. What if I just stayed?"

"What do you mean?"

"What if we forgot about the ship and the Hama and I just stayed? I could run for chief; we could have a family."

She leaned in closer to him and whispered. "You're getting me off this rotten planet or I'm never speaking to you again."

"Yeah, I guess it would get old."

"There are too many places I want to see."

"Like where?"

"Australia. It sounds nice. You've opened my eyes to a bigger universe, and there's no way I'm giving that up now."

"You want the universe?" Thurgood looked into her eyes. "Then I'll give you the universe."

They were just about to kiss when Claude came sloshing through the water to ruin everything. "Our scouts found the village."

"Your timing is terrible, Chief."

Reya hummed her agreement.

"It was abandoned. They've moved everything to the landing site. They've turned it into some kind of shrine."

"They think it's some kind of bird."

"A bird?" Reya asked.

"A space bird," Antarius said, dismissing the whole idea of a space bird with a wave. "It's a whole thing."

"Well, they are all over it. The whole site is crawling with Volga."

"Don't worry, Chief." Antarius put his libido away and stood. "There's still time to enact my sneak in and kill them in the dead of night plan."

"No. The killing stops. We're going to talk to them like civilized people."

Thurgood rolled his eyes at the idea. "Okay."

"You two get some rest," Chief Claude said. "That's an order. In the morning, we meet the Volga."

Once he had sloshed back to shore Reya turned and said, "I think he just ordered us to go to bed."

"Well, if those are the chief's orders..."

The pair waded back to shore and did as the chief said.

When morning came, they saw that the Volga had indeed turned the Hama scout ship into some kind of shrine. It even had a face. Not a face Thurgood thought was worth worshiping, but a face nonetheless. They had painted markings on the Declavar's exterior to give it "eyes" and erected a wooden platform before it where a fire burned and several members of the tribe knelt and chanted. Others were scattered about the clearing, bowing before the ship.

"I'm not one to say I told you so, Chief, but you were clearly wrong here. That's some textbook savage behavior going on right there."

"This can't be," Claude said, peering through the dense foliage that bordered on the clearing. "I can't believe the Volga are doing this. They know better. How have they become savages in so short a time?"

"Are you sure you still want to talk to them?" Thurgood let

the bush he was peeking through settle back into place. "Because Operation: Dead of Night is still on the table."

"No, we must end this rift. The time for conflict has ended. And seeing them now... acting like this. They need our help." Claude stepped away from his own bush and pulled a brown rag from his pocket. He found a fallen branch and began tying the rag to the stick.

"What are you doing?" Thurgood asked him.

"In the olden days, warring parties spoke under a flag of truce. This was the symbol, a white flag."

"Yeah, I know all about white flags." Thurgood said, and poked at the rag with his own stick. "But that flag isn't white. It's filthy."

"It's the whitest flag we have," Claude snapped.

"This planet is gross," Antarius said as Claude finished fastening the rag to the branch.

The chief gave the flag a test wave and took a deep breath. His face hardened and he faced the clearing. He was focused. He was committed. He wasn't moving.

Antarius stepped in front of him. "Well?"

"Right," Claude said. But he didn't move.

"What's the hold up, Chief?" Thurgood asked.

"It's just..." It just wasn't anything. Claude just trailed off.

"Do you want to kiss and make up or not?"

"No! I mean, yes. Not kiss, but offering the hand of peace is the right thing to do. It's just..." He trailed off again.

"It's just... scary looking down the barrel of a valley full of savages?"

The words annoyed him, but Claude nodded.

"You're wondering just how far they've fallen," Thurgood prompted.

Claude bit his lip and nodded again.

"You're thinking, could they be cannibals?"

"I didn't think they could be—"

"And do they want to eat my manhood."

"No!"

"You worry that maybe they think a man's manhood is the source of his power, so they'll chop it off and say some weird savage prayer over it before eating it like a delicacy. All to absorb your strength."

"I wasn't thinking that at all!"

"And they'll be judging you the whole time they're chewing." Thurgood said, staring through the bush at the savage camp. "The animals."

"Good God, man, what is wrong with you? Do they not have therapists back on Earth?"

"Give me the stupid flag," Thurgood said, and grabbed the branch from Claude before he could object. "I'll go make peace with these stupid monsters."

He almost tripped going through the bush but was able to keep his balance after a couple of hops and started marching toward the Volga gathered near the ship. Grumbling as he went, he glanced up occasionally at the most disgraceful truce flag he'd ever seen.

It wasn't long until he was spotted. What sounded like warning grunts sounded all across the clearing. Even those who were busy worshiping the ship turned their attention to the man who was bold enough to march into their camp. He may have been mistaken, but some of the grunts sounded less like surprised grunts and more like grunts of recognition. Some of the Volga spat on the ground. So they did remember him.

"Yes, it's me, again. But I come in peace." He gave the flag a little wave. "My apologies. I'm sorry the flag isn't cleaner. To be honest, I'm more than a little embarrassed by it."

The grunting intensified. They started shouting back and forth, and the Volga that were closest to him started posturing and making rude gestures. Some of them, Thurgood even recognized. Maybe there was still some humanity left in them after all. When one of them gave him the finger, he started to think Claude's stupid plan might actually work.

"I know we got off on the wrong foot," he shouted as a *mea culpa*, as some of the misunderstanding may have been his fault. "But I just want to talk."

Several of the Volga shared a look and then began walking toward him. Once they came together as a group, they started moving faster.

Thurgood stopped, tried to look taller and waved the flag harder. "Hey! Hey! Peace flag! Peace flag!"

The Volga started running. Charging at him, snarling and probably smelling a fair bit as well.

"You stupid savages. I come in peace." They were testing his patience now. "I come under the brown flag of truce!"

Most of the group stopped about ten feet from him. But one of the members kept coming. The man was pointing and grunting something that sounded like, "Go! Go!" It could have meant anything, but it was obviously a precursor to attack, so Thurgood cracked him across the face with the makeshift flagpole.

The Volga went immediately limp and hit the ground. His friends watched him fall, then looked back to Antarius, who pointed to the flag and said, "Truce!"

They charged. Roaring like beasts, they came at him, punching and grabbing for him with fingers outstretched like claws. They closed the short distance in seconds.

He tried to explain the concept of the white flag as he beat them back with the branch. A call for the temporary cessation of hostilities, an armistice of sorts. But the concept was too much for them to comprehend, so he was forced to keep beating them with the stick.

Four or five of them were out of the fight almost immediately and littered the ground around him. But more were coming. The rest of the Volga had been watching from their village and the more people he beat upon the head, the more upset they became. Another dozen or so were already rushing him.

Thurgood backed away to give himself room and gripped the club tight. He pulled it back over his shoulder and seated his feet for the coming fight.

The group that was charging him slowed to a stop as Chief Claude led the others out of the bushes behind him.

"We come in peace." Claude said as he looked at the unconscious Volga. He shot Thurgood a tired look.

"They started it." Thurgood lowered the club. "I'm sure you saw it all from back there. This one..." Antarius pointed to one of the unconscious Volga. "Yes, this is the one. He tried to hit me and—"

"Men and women of the Volga!" More of the savage tribe members were drawing closer but Claude shouted so all could hear. "My name is Claude Masson, leader of the Village of the Shooting Star. You're old friends... and family. For too long, our people have been at odds. Today, we have come to make a lasting peace."

They were listening to him. They weren't grunting or trying to kill him. They were actually listening.

"With the arrival of this ship," he said, pointing to the Hama scout craft, "and this idiot," he said, pointing to Thurgood, "we have a chance to return to the home we never knew. A chance to live an easier life where we are not hunted by nature or forced to wallow in mud and moss. All we have to do is put aside our differences and come together in peace."

Claude finished speaking and let his words make their way through the gathering crowd. They were met with silence at first, but then murmurs began to ripple through the crowd. Thurgood did not understand the language, but he knew they were relaying the chief's message of peace to the rest of their people. Many of the Volga looked contemplative and began to nod until the message reached the last person in the back of the crowd, who grunted. This grunt was then relayed from Volga to Volga. The ones that had been nodding developed a scowl and began to nod harder. The message finally reached the men in the front, and the entire tribe attacked.

"Quick," Thurgood shouted to the Villagers of the Shooting Star. "Everyone get behind the peace flag!"

He took out two of the Volga before the club cracked in two and everything went to hell. The two groups rushed together, throwing fists and hurling insults. The Volga had terrorized the villagers for generations, and they were done being afraid. Even the meekest of villagers barreled into the fray, kicking shins and biting at ankles.

Lance, the giant builder, had shed his nerves and was throwing some of the smaller Volga around. The indiscriminate tossing and the intimidation it caused created a hole in the middle of the fight. On the other side of it was the Hama ship.

Thurgood raced through the opening. If he could get to the ship and awaken their "space bird," the Volga might finally listen to reason. Or he could pretend to be the space bird itself and start bossing them around. Savages came at him from all sides but he managed to sidestep most of the attacks and win the few scuffles that he couldn't avoid. With a few quick steps and a few more jukes, Thurgood had made it to the ship and activated the transmitter in his pocket.

Thurgood jumped onto the loading ramp before it had finished lowering and ran to the top. He glanced back at the fight. The entire area before the ship had become a giant donnybrook, and though it was too early to tell who would come out on top, his friends from the Village of the Shooting Star appeared to be giving as good as they were getting. Lance was still throwing tiny Russians about, Reya was using what was left of the flagpole to inflict blunt force trauma, and Noel the drunk was stumbling around so badly that no one could lay a hand on him. Antarius couldn't hide a smile. He was proud of his people. But they were going to get their asses kicked if he didn't get the ship started. There were simply too many Volga.

Though it was Hama in construction, the ship's interior was laid out in a logical arrangement and it felt no more alien than any of a hundred other ships he'd found himself on throughout his career. It only took a few wrong turns to find the bridge.

The consoles came to life in response to the transponder's presence. Everything was written in Hameese but the instrumentation was universal enough. He began pushing buttons, and systems in the ship started warming up.

An alarm caught his attention, and he located the sound coming from the ship's tracking system. The system was tracking several incoming ships. The Hama rescue team.

"No! Not now!" Thurgood screamed. "Not when we're so close!"

A hand set upon his shoulder.

Thurgood patted it and said, "You're right. Everything will be okay. We'll figure out something."

The hand squeezed. Antarius tried to wiggle out of its grip, but it was too strong. The hand spun him around and Thurgood found himself face to face with the big bastard of a Volga.

The reunion was brief as he was tossed from the bridge back into the interior of the ship. Antarius turned the crash landing into a roll and came up facing the giant savage. He backed away through the corridors as the Volga marched toward him.

"Don't you see?" Thurgood pleaded. "All of you will be saved. You'll have better clothes. Better food. We even teach you manners."

The giant savage charged with a wild right.

Thurgood ducked under the blow and continued to back away while trying to reason with the man. "You'll get ice cream, hot showers and someone will fix that unibrow you've got going."

The next blow caught him in the chest and sent him rolling through another doorway and out onto the top of the ramp. He came up angry. "Seriously? You're giving up ice cream?"

The savage screamed.

It was obvious that reason had failed. The only language the brute would understand—beside his own obviously—was violence. Antarius went on the attack. He unleashed an onslaught of blows with several finding their way past the Volga's defenses. It was when a left hook snuck through that his opponent seized him by the throat and lifted him clear off the ground.

Thurgood kicked and squirmed, trying to break free of the iron grip.

The giant smiled as he grabbed Thurgood by the waistband and lifted him higher into the air. The monster held him over his head long enough to prove his strength and then heaved him into the air.

Antarius closed his eyes as he expected to hit the ground but he went up more than he came down. This went against his understanding of most physics and old adages about what things going up did. Once his descent abruptly ended, he opened his eyes to find himself on top of the wooden platform the Volga had built in front of the ship.

The fight continued beneath him, and the odds were turning in favor of the Volga. Members of the expedition party lay scattered about the battlefield. He couldn't tell if they were dead or defeated, but they were no longer in the fight. And things weren't getting any better. The big bastard waded into the fight and bulldozed people out of his way until he and Lance faced one another. The two champions began trading blows. Lance was strong, but he wouldn't last long against the entire tribe.

"I'm afraid my people will no longer listen to reason."

Thurgood turned toward the voice. An old man dressed in robes and leaning on an ornate staff was standing behind him on the platform watching the fight below.

"You speak like humans," Thurgood said.

The old man smiled. "I speak Standard, yes."

Antarius got to his feet and pointed to the sky. "Tell your people there are invaders coming. They're coming right now and they're bringing a small army."

"They won't listen to me. They have all but forgotten the old ways. They've rejected education. They have forsaken learning and are slowly reverting to animals. They are nothing but brutes. Savages."

"Then tell them they've angered the gods and they are sending beings here to punish them."

"I said they were savages. Not idiots."

"Tell them whatever you have to. If we don't stop this madness, other more dangerous madness will get here and kill us all."

"It won't do any good. There's only one thing they respect now." The old man handed his staff to Thurgood.

"Is it... is it a magic stick?"

Antarius took the stick and examined it. Once he looked past the tribal decorations, he recognized it immediately. "My rifle!"

The old man nodded. "The only thing they respect is force."

"I didn't recognize it at first with all of the feathers and... look at that... you put paint kind of all over it. Is this a bone?"

The old man nodded.

"Well, isn't that creative." Thurgood pointed the gun into the air and fired. The shot split the air, echoed across the clearing and did nothing at all to stop the fighting below. He turned back to the old man.

The old man took a long and tired breath. "I'm afraid you will have to shoot one of them."

Thurgood drew a bead on one of the savages in the brawl. He took a breath and prepared to squeeze the trigger. Then he stopped. "Any one in particular?"

"Please, I already regret the role I have to play in this."

"I understand, but it is your idea. So if there's anyone you'd like to... you know."

"I love all my people."

"Yeah, but if *one* had to go?"

"Kirill," the old man said, and pointed to the big bastard.

"Oh, I was hoping you'd say Kirill." Thurgood aimed and pulled the trigger. The rifle bucked against his shoulder and Kirill dropped to the ground in the middle of the battlefield.

All activity below stopped as the crowd turned and looked up at him.

"Now that we understand each other..." Thurgood chambered another round. "I'm going to ask for your help."

The old man stepped up next to him and addressed the crowd. He shouted something in the broken savage language, and the tribe cheered. He then repeated his statement in Standard. "The Captain has killed your champion. He's chief now. We must do as he says."

"I'm the chief?" Thurgood asked. "Just because I killed Kirill?"

The old man nodded. "That's how it works."

"Well, that makes way more sense than the how the other tribe did it." Captain Antarius Thurgood, Chief of the Volga, turned back to the crowd. "Now that I'm your chief—we have some work to do."

TWENTY-FOUR

Laying Out the Welcome Traps

Thurgood pried open the doors to the *Galahad*'s armory, triggering the emergency power. Lighting inside the gun cases illuminated the collection of hunting rifles, to the amusement of the crowd. There weren't enough for everyone, but every little bit helped. Thurgood picked up one of the weapons and examined it thoroughly.

"Excellent," he said after a satisfactory inspection. The armory doors had kept the Altairian climate at bay and the weaponry free of moss and moisture.

Antarius pointed to one of the Volga and tossed him the battle rifle.

The savage caught the weapon and rolled it over in his hands. A smile grew on his face as he seated it in his hands.

"Now..." Thurgood started passing out the rest of the rifles. "I don't have time to properly train you on how to use these, so I'm just going to ask that you be really careful and try not to shoot each other."

A flash of light filled the room and a blast tore the air. One of the Volga grabbed at his chest where his heart used to be and then fell to the ground.

The Volga who had pulled the trigger stared at the smoking gun in his hands.

Thurgood stormed across the armory and snatched the rifle out of the Volga's hands. "What did I just say?" he shouted.

Antarius handed the rifle to one of the villagers from the Shooting Star and traded it for a staff she had been holding. He shoved the staff into the Volga's hands. "Because you didn't listen, you get a stick."

The Volga warrior looked at the gun he had just possessed and then the stick in his hands. He hung his head in shame and made a sad grunt.

"That's what I thought," Antarius said, and resumed handing out the rifles.

"Are you crazy? These are hunting rifles," Claude said as he examined the rifle he had been handed. "We will be going up against professional soldiers, with real weapons."

"True, it may seem that we're outgunned and outmanned, but our situation brings to mind the story of another group of scrappy fighters that challenged a great army with nothing but a few hunting rifles and the right attitude. They fought, not because they knew they could win, but because they knew it was right. They were fighting for something greater than themselves. And those patriots, they outfought, outshot, outsmarted and flat out outgumptioned that once-unbeatable army. So maybe we could take a lesson from those settlers on Lonock 7 and do a little less frettin' and a little more sweatin'."

"Or we could just fly away," Claude said. "Fighting them is madness."

"We wouldn't stand a chance," Thurgood said. "They'd shoot us out of the sky. Our only hope is to stop them here."

He handed a rifle to the chief. "Don't worry, other chief. This is what I'm trained for."

* * *

Thurgood stabbed the shovel head into the ground and wiped the sweat from his brow as he examined the giant hole they had just dug. "There. That should just about do it."

Members of both tribes leaned forward to peer into the pit they had just excavated together. They were tired and sore, but pleased with their work, and Thurgood could see the satisfaction on their faces.

"So, what happens now?" Franc asked.

"Now we cover it up with moss and leaves and stuff."

One of the Volga grunted a question in Russian. One of the older Volga translated into broken, half-forgotten Standard. "Tver asks why we had to move such dirt just to make look like we not move such dirt. He thinks it is stupid idea."

Tver grunted something else.

"Sorry," the translator said. "It you he thinks is stupid."

"Well, Tver," Thurgood said. "We cover it with moss and leaves and other ground litter so when the Hama come charging into the clearing, they fall into the pit. So, who's stupid now, Tver?"

The translator conveyed the message. Tver nodded in understanding and grunted a response.

"He still thinks it is you who are stupid."

"You know what, Tver—"

"He doesn't think it will work," the translator added.

"Well, ask Tver how many improvised warfare classes he took at the Alliance Academy and then when he says 'none,' tell him that's what I thought."

"Won't they just climb out?" Lance asked.

"Out of a mardok pit?" Thurgood laughed heartily. "I hardly

think so."

"What's a mardok pit?" the builder pressed.

"Well, obviously it's a pit with a mardok in it," Antarius explained as he pointed to the hole.

The Volga translator stammered his question. "Where are we going to get a mardok?"

"You mean where are *you* going to get a mardok?"

"Me?" The Volga stammered and looked to his tribesmen for help. Tver looked away and pretended to go back to shoveling. "Do you not have how much idea dangerous are mardoks?"

"Of course, I do. That's why we're putting one in the pit. It would be stupid to fill a mardok pit with puppies."

"I can't get mardok," the man said.

"Make Tver do it," Thurgood suggested. "He's so smart."

"No Volga get mardok!"

"Fine," Thurgood said, and studied the hole. "I guess a skydonk will have to do."

Some of the Volga gasped at the mention of the creature. Tver grunted something that was clearly not fit for mixed company.

The translator nodded to some of his tribesmen and then back to Thurgood. "No Volga get skydonk."

Thurgood pulled the shovel from the ground and stabbed it back into the dirt in frustration. "Well, what can Volga get? Huh? Because otherwise all we have is just a hole."

The translator and others from the Volga tribe chattered back and forth. They gestured to the pit and imitated the roar of several creatures before the translator answered Antarius's question.

"Volga get moncheenie."

"The stupid monkey things?"

"Volga get moncheenie."

Thurgood's head hurt. He initially thought it may be aching

from the frustration of the conversation. But he soon realized it could be the wounds inflicted by the moncheenie that had attacked him. He stuck his hand out to the translator. "Get me a dozen and you've got a deal."

* * *

"The rocks need to be rounder." Antarius stood at the top of a steep hill, shaking his head at an assortment of squarish boulders and disapproving of the entire pile.

"I don't know how you're going to get them to come up here anyway," Claude said.

"Trust me, they'll come up here, but we're going to need rounder rocks."

"These will be fine," the chief said.

"They're not fine," Thurgood pointed to the pile full of square rocks. "I can tell by looking at them."

Claude sat on one of the larger rocks and folded his arms. "They're good enough."

"Good enough?" Thurgood walked up to one of the massive stones and squatted before it. He placed his hands under the bottom and heaved. The heavy boulder flipped, rolled once more and then stopped, sending a thud trembling through the ground at the top of the hill.

"Does that look good enough?" Thurgood asked, pointing to the rock. "How are we going to flatten the Hama with rocks that don't roll? This should be bowling for bad guys not... not whatever that is."

"We've looked, okay?" Claude said. "We can't find any round rocks."

"Well, you certainly aren't going to find them with that attitude."

"What does that even mean?" Claude asked.

"Just find some rounder rocks," Thurgood said. "The pictures in my textbooks had rounder rocks."

"Why should I take orders from you?" Claude stood and stepped up to Thurgood. "You're not the only chief on this hill, Chief."

Thurgood stepped up and mirrored his tone. "That's Captain Chief, thank you."

* * *

"We need snares everywhere in here." Antarius dropped a pile of cable scavenged from the *Galahad* in the center of the ruins. It was here where he had encountered the Hama with the rope and it was here where they would spring their trap. "I want Hama hanging by their ankles all over the place."

"So there were people here before us," Reya said as she stared up at the columns.

She wasn't alone. Most of the group he had led to the ruins stared in amazement.

"Yeah, yeah. Ruins. Ooh, aah. We don't have much time." Thurgood started pointing to where he wanted the snares set, but no one was listening.

"What do you think they were like?" someone asked.

"Stupid," Thurgood said. "They were stupid. You know how I know? Because everything they did lies in ruins. They failed. Now can we get on with this?"

"Do you think they looked anything like us?" someone else asked.

"It doesn't matter!" Thurgood snapped. "The only thing that matters is that they aren't here to help right now, so I need all of you to get this fascination with one mysterious advanced alien civilization out of your system and get to work."

"How do you think they made these columns so tall without

machines?" another villager asked.

Thurgood sighed and sat down on his stone bench.

* * *

"The logs need to be rounder." Thurgood stood at the top of a steep hill shaking his head at a pile of felled trees. "Look, I just went through this with the rock guys. You can't turn the Hama into pancakes with all these branches on there."

"How are you going to get them to come up this hill anyway?"

Thurgood sighed. He never would have thought being a chief would be so exhausting.

One of the older Volgas crested the top of the hill and waved for his attention. "Chief Captain."

"Captain Chief," Thurgood corrected him.

"Captain Chief. There is questions at the not mardok pit."

A Captain Chief's work was never done. "Round out these logs," he said, and went to see what the issue was.

* * *

Several villagers and Volga stood around the mouth of the pit trying to communicate with one another.

"What's the problem? Could you not get the monkey things?"

"We got moncheenies," the translator said. "It is other orders that are problem."

"I'll bet Leiningen's ants never gave him these kinds of problems," Thurgood grumbled to himself. The Hama were going to be here soon and he felt like he was being forced to explain himself over and over. "What exactly is the problem?"

Tver held up a sharpened stick and let loose a string of

grunts while he shifted between pointing to the stick and his own rear end.

"I don't understand a word, Tver." Thurgood turned to the translator for an explanation. "What's his problem now? Does he not understand what I'm asking him to do?"

"Yes, he knows what you ask. But he says he doesn't know why you ask him to do this thing."

"Because it will give any gray-faced bastards that fall into the pit a festering disease."

Lance spoke up. "But won't they die before they have a chance to get sick?"

"Look. I'm the one that studied guerrilla warfare, right?" Thurgood said, and picked up one of the sharpened stakes. "And in class they teach you two things about punji sticks: they're sharp and covered in poop. So, get pooping."

Tver became very animated and fired off a string of grunts.

The older Volga nodded and then translated. "He says there must be better use of his time."

"Fine!" Thurgood picked up an armful of stakes and grabbed the one from Tver's hand. "If you want something done right… I'll take over here. You go look for some round rocks."

"This planet just doesn't have round rocks," Claude said. "Not anywhere near here anyway."

"Fine. Square rocks it is." Thurgood hated to admit defeat, but they were running out of time and he couldn't spend it arguing. There had to be another way around the square rock problem. He looked around. All they had to work with were square rocks, logs and villagers.

An idea struck him and he pointed at the giant builder from the village. "Lance."

"Yes, Chief Captain."

"Captain Chief. I need your help building something."

This caused the giant of a man to smile. "A hut?"

"No, something different."

"Yes, sir Captain Chief."

Claude looked lost. "What are you two thinking?"

"If we can't roll the rocks," Thurgood said with a smile, "we'll throw them."

* * *

The moncheenies weren't too happy about being in the pit, and with as much feces as they were throwing, Thurgood realized he may have wasted his time treating the punji sticks.

"They can't find anything to cover it with," the old man said.

"Tell them to use big sticks. And then smaller sticks."

The old man relayed the message and listened to the response from the Volga who were working on the hole. They didn't seem happy.

"He says then it looks like a pile of stick and the trap is easy to see."

"Use moss."

Again, there was exchange of suggestions and excuses.

"They say the moss is not big enough."

"Not big enough?" Thurgood rubbed his chin until the idea fully formed in his mind and then smiled. "Someone find me Franc, the moss weaver."

* * *

"The snares are all made," Reya said. "But they want to know where to put them."

"I told you."

"I don't remember you telling us."

"No, you were all a little too preoccupied with being all fascinated by history and these stupid ruins."

"Well forgive me for being a student of history!" Reya shouted. "Now where did you want these snares?"

"I don't remember."

"What do you mean you don't remember?"

"I mean I don't remember. I'm planning the defense of an entire planet here, I can't be expected to do everything. Just put them where the Hama are most likely to step."

"And how do we know where that is?"

Thurgood looked around the ruins to determine the Hama's most likely entry point. Noel stood at the edge of the ancient site and a game trail. "Perfect," Thurgood said.

"What's perfect?" Reya asked.

"Pay attention," Antarius said with a smile and called to the drunk. "Noel! Come here please."

Noel nodded and started walking. The man had been introduced to Volga Vodka earlier in the day and was more than a touch inebriated. He stumbled left and right as he made his way through the ruins, often using the walls for support. It took a while as he meandered through the site, but he finally made it to Thurgood and offered a drunken salute.

"Thank you, Noel. You can go back now."

Thurgood turned to Reya. "Everywhere he doesn't step. That's where we place a snare."

The ground started to shake beneath his feet and a distant roar grew behind him. Thurgood looked up at the tallest column in the ruins.

The man he had posted as lookout was waving down at them and shouting. His voice was soon lost in the roar of engines as the Hama ships flew overhead.

Thurgood took a deep breath. "They're here."

TWENTY-FIVE

The Final Battle, Finally

Thurgood watched the Hama ships set down from the top of the ruins. He smiled as they landed approximately where he expected they would. The clearing with the deserted Declavar hadn't enough room to accommodate the arriving ships, and they were forced to find a clearing on the far side of the ruins. It was perfect.

The rescue force was larger than he expected, however. There was another scout craft and two landing ships. He'd seen those before during the invasion of Shandor, and he knew there was a formidable force inside. Each ship would be able to deploy scout vehicles, gun platforms, mechs and possibly even a heavy tank. It seemed a bit excessive to retrieve a missing scout ship.

"This many to get one man?" the Volga translator said. "Who are you, off-worlder?"

"I told you I was important," Thurgood said.

"We didn't believe you," Claude said. "No one did. Not Durand. No one."

"I'm sure Reya did," Thurgood said, and turned to the woman.

She hesitated and then acted like she was going to hug him. "You're important to me now."

Antarius frowned and turned back to the invasion force. The loading ramps had lowered and the force was disembarking. It was pretty much what he had expected. Predominantly ground forces and support vehicles.

"What happens now?" one of the villagers asked.

"Now they'll head straight for us. And right into our trap."

"You never explained this," Claude said. "Why would they head for us and not for the ship?"

Thurgood reached into his pack and pulled out a black box that measured six inches on each side. A red light on top of the box pulsed a steady rhythm. "This is the ships transponder. Every time this light blinks it sends out a signal that is computer for 'Help me!'"

Thurgood held it up in front of his eyes and watched the light. Every time it flashed, he said, "Help me" in a whiny, high-pitched voice.

"Help me. Help me. Help me."

"Is that what you think computers sound like?" Reya asked.

"Computers, cats and babies," Thurgood said with a nod. "The point is, as long as this light is blinking, they'll come right for it."

Antarius bent over to put the box back in his pack. It slipped from his hands and tumbled off the edge of the column. He watched it drop into the open air, bounce off two shorter pillars, strike the top of a wall and land in the middle of the ruins.

"You can't see it from here, but it's probably still blinking. Those things are tough."

"They move," the Volga translator said.

Thurgood confirmed the news through his own binoculars.

The Hama force was moving out. And they were heading right for them.

"Everybody, get into position. Here they come."

Thurgood's position was back on the ground, and he stayed crouched behind a fallen wall when the first Hama soldier entered the ruins. As he expected, it was a foot patrol. Getting vehicles of any size through the trees would take time, and they wouldn't want to wait to reach the beacon. Two dozen men clad in battle armor entered into the ruins with weapons drawn and scanned the area.

The Hama solider walking point reached the flashing beacon and picked up the box. As Thurgood had predicted, the light was still blinking. But finding the device separated from its ship put the invasion force on high alert. Commands were given, rifles were raised and senses were heightened.

"Now," Antarius shouted as he rose from his position and fired.

The round from his hunting rifle struck the point solider square in the chest and knocked him off his feet.

Members from both tribes opened fire from positions scattered around the ruins. They fired from above and below. Those who weren't armed hurled rocks. Those who didn't have rocks hurled insults. The barrage sent the Hama force into disarray and they scrambled to seek cover.

"Snares!" Thurgood shouted toward the sky.

Men and women in the upper tiers of the ruins acknowledged they received the signal and sprang into action. Counterweights had been set high above the battlefield and secured to the ends of the cables. Now they were shoved from the perches to spring the trap.

"Careful, boys," Antarius shouted at the enemy. "You might want to watch your step."

One of the Hama soldiers heard his taunt and turned to fire.

But, before he could pull the trigger, the steel cable tightened around his ankle.

"Haha!" Thurgood shouted.

The snare ripped the man's legs off.

"Oh my God!" Antarius shouted. "That... that wasn't supposed to happen."

The Hama solider collapsed to the ground, screaming in agony as his leg dangled a dozen feet above him.

Thurgood turned away in disgust. "That's horrible!"

"You didn't know that would happen?" Noel asked, and then burped.

"No, I didn't know that would... I thought they would flip upside down and maybe get lightheaded."

"We used giant stones and steel cables!" Claude said.

"Well, I didn't want them to be able to cut their way out."

More snares were trigged and more screams filled the ruins as the Hama found themself either flung about the ancient stone works or dismembered by the overpowered traps.

Thurgood watched as another man was pulled from the ground. Thankfully, his limbs held. Unfortunately, he crossed paths with the counterweight on the way up.

Broken bodies and limbs were falling everywhere.

"Oh, wow. I feel terrible about this."

"It looks like we have bigger problems." Reya tapped him on the shoulder and pointed to the edge of the woods, where a half dozen mechs had made their way through the trees.

The powered suits carried heavy weapons and began opening up on anyone foolish enough to show themselves. Chain guns spun and threw streams of lead up into the high ground. Volga and villagers alike screamed as several were struck by the rounds.

"Activate step 2!" Thurgood shouted.

The words "step 2" were echoed through the site as the word was spread. Thurgood scrambled down from above, abandoning the high ground and falling back to his position. There, they assembled in teams and picked up several cables from the ground. On command, each team heaved as the mechs advanced.

Walls fell. Columns collapsed. The network of cables toppled whatever was left of whatever the building had been down on top of the powerful machines, burying them in the rubble.

Claude had not been privy to step 2. Thurgood felt the idea to destroy the site might lead to a disagreement and he didn't see that as productive. He had been right. The chief stood as the last rock settled and shouted. "You ruined the ruins!"

"Relax, Chief," Thurgood said in between congratulating the men. "They're still ruined. Even more so now. It you think about it, it's kind of the great thing about ruins."

The sound of grinding rocks ebbed as the rubble settled into place. One final piece of column fell and all was silent. But only for a moment.

The ground began to tremble and the rubble started to bounce. The sound of snapping timber fired off like shots from a rifle and the tanks came crashing through the tree line.

"Fall back," Thurgood screamed. "Fall back fast!"

Thurgood's army did as they were commanded and raced through the jungle just ahead of the collapsing trees. The tanks fired at the fleeing foot soldiers, causing the jungle to explode around them.

Antarius stayed at Reya's side as they made their way back to the clearing where the Hama scout ship and the next trap awaited. The heavy vehicles behind them rumbled along despite the dense forest, their treads wringing extra stink from the mossy floor.

Sunlight ahead told him they were close, and they quickened their pace.

They burst out of the jungle behind most of his forces. He and Reya ran to catch up with them and he smiled as the ground beneath their feet shook. Franc had done an amazing job on the cover. He was going make a great carpet one day.

The tanks crashed through the woods behind them and into the clearing. Infantry raced out behind them and opened fired on Thurgood's army.

"Keep moving!" he shouted to the others.

The Volga and the villagers responded and ran toward the base of the hill.

The tanks and the infantry followed across the clearing and into the mardok pits filled with moncheenies.

The heavy tanks were too much weight for the stick structure beneath, and they crashed into the pits below, taking most of their infantry escort with them.

"Now attack!"

Thurgood's fleeing force turned and dropped into firing position. What infantry hadn't fallen into the pits was quickly mowed down by their gunfire. It wasn't long before the shooting was done.

With the tanks disabled and the men inside trapped, Thurgood and his forces approached the pit.

The screams coming from inside were unholy.

Thurgood glanced into the pit and his stomach turned. The Hama were impaled on the sharpened stakes while the moncheenie tore at their flesh. Blood was everywhere. It ran down the punji sticks and collected in pools as the fierce monkey-like creatures tore the exposed innards from their victims.

"Oh, God, that is..." Thurgood turned away. "That is the

worst thing I've ever seen. That's worse than the snares. How could we?"

"How could we?" Franc asked. "How could you? This was your idea."

"I know but I didn't think... They never showed us in class how horrible it was."

"You filled a giant hole with sharp sticks!"

"It was... they were just to hold the poop!"

He stumbled away from the pit, but he still heard the screams of the men and screeching of the moncheenies as they tore apart the bodies. "Why are they doing that?"

"They eat the meat," the Volga translator explained.

"They're carnivores? I thought they were just mischievous!"

"What did you think would happen?" Claude asked.

"I mean, I don't know. I thought they were kind of like monkeys so it would be funny. Maybe they'd pull their hair or something like that."

A new sound interrupted the scene as a high whine grew within the forest. Like a banshee's howl or a bratty child's wail, it filled the woods and spilled into the clearing.

"What is that noise?" Reya asked as it grew louder.

The answer emerged a moment later as a swarm of vehicles sped out of the trees following the path the tanks had blazed. Everything that came out of the jungle hovered. Small, one-man scout craft and floating gunner platforms rode into the clearing safely above perilous pits.

"Up the hill!" Thurgood yelled, and fired his rifle.

One of the gunners on the lead platform took the shot in the chest and toppled over the rail.

Thurgood's army fired as they retreated, but their inferior numbers and firepower were starting to show. More Volga fell, and two of the villagers went down under the Hama assault.

Thurgood let the others get a head start before he displaced and made a run for the hill. He caught up to Reya and the others at the base of the incline and grabbed her hand. Approximately halfway up the hill, the men and woman began taking cover in vertical trenches the Volga had prepared for this moment.

Thurgood stood up in his trench and yelled to the top of the hill. "Lance!"

He dropped back down into the safety of the trench as the first log rolled over his head. He covered his head and closed his eyes. Bark and debris peppered him as the trees rolled over them. It was like sitting under an avalanche, and the sound it made was deafening—louder than any enemy tank or starship. Once the logs reached the bottom of the hill, it was over.

Thurgood uncovered his head. The thunderous sound of war had been replaced by painful screams and the wailing of the injured. He stood up and surveyed the battlefield.

It was absolute carnage. The scout craft had been crushed and twisted by their wooden artillery. The gun platforms had been either flipped or steamrolled. And broken bodies were everywhere. The screams of the dying came from amongst the scattered logs. Those he could see reached for help with broken and bloodied limbs. Exposed bones jutted through twisted arms and legs everywhere.

"Oh my God. It's terrible." Thurgood could barely find the words. What had he done? The textbooks never showed anything like this. Diagram C usually just had the enemy running away as the logs rolled after them. The screams turned his stomach. But it was over. The rest of the Hama were retreating.

"We did it," Reya said softly.

"We did," he said with no satisfaction. "It's all so horrible. I'm just thankful we didn't have to use the rocks."

"Fire!" Lance shouted from the top of the hill.

"Noooo!" Thurgood screamed as the catapults launched the

square rocks into the air. He was powerless to stop them, and he watched as they soared through the air and landed on the retreating forces.

"It's... so... so splatty," Antarius said, and then threw up for several minutes.

* * *

They watched the Hama retreat back to their ships from the top of the column. They had purposefully left the tallest one standing, and as Thurgood watched the end of the battle through his binoculars, he had to reluctantly admit that ruins had uses after all.

'They're back on their ships," he said, and lowered the lenses.

"You did it, off-worlder," Claude said proudly. "You saved Altair."

"But at what cost?" Antarius said as he watched the ships prepare to launch. "Who knew that war could be so horrible."

"You didn't know this?" the Volga translator asked.

"You're a soldier," Franc said.

"It's a lot cleaner from the bridge of a starship, I can tell you that. But down here when you're face to face with your enemy, you feel every bullet, every blow and every punji stick as if it was taking your own life. War is terrible," he said. "War is Hell."

Reya embraced him as the Hama ship began lifting off. "You did what needed to be done. Man has been forced to wrestle with the horrors of war since the dawn of time. Sadly, there are some times that only violence will end violence. You cannot be held accountable for the horrors of war."

"Thank you, sweet Reya."

A Volga scout climbed to the top of the column and grunted something to the translator.

"Tver says it is done," the older Volga said.

"Good work, Tver." Thurgood said, and pulled a black box from his bag.

"You did what needed to be done," Reya continued. "And you showed mercy to those that retreated. That kind of mercy makes you a good— What's done?"

Thurgood flipped a switch on the box, and the retreating Hama ships exploded somewhere over Mount Thurgood.

"Kaboom!" Thurgood said with a chuckle.

TWENTY-SIX

A Whole New World

"I've never seen anything so beautiful." Reya stared at Altair through the Declavar's viewscreen.

"Yeah, it's a lot prettier when you can't smell it." Antarius was studying the control panel. He wanted to make sure he had correctly identified the instruments before they left orbit.

"It's so peaceful from up here." Despite leaving such a horrible place, there was a sadness in her voice. Home would always be home. It didn't matter what it smelled like.

There had been many tears before takeoff. The Village of the Shooting Star and the Volga had been reunited, and the tribes promised not to kill each other while they awaited the Alliance rescue team. The new leader, Captain Chief Claude, would see to that as he organized the evacuation.

The scout ship accommodated few passengers, and it was difficult to decide who would get to accompany him on the flight back to Earth.

In the end, he brought Monsieur Babin from the *Shooting Star* and the old man from the Volga tribe. They had held on to the hope of peace through the darkest times, and Thurgood felt that faith of that caliber deserved to be rewarded. Also, they were old and probably weren't going to last much longer.

Lance joined them as well. And Tver insisted he had earned his spot by leading the saboteurs into the Hama ships.

Noel also joined them. Not because he had been invited, but because he had stumbled aboard and passed out in one of the storage lockers before they took off.

Thurgood stood behind Reya at the viewscreen and put his arms around her. "Are you ready to go?"

She didn't answer right away. She just watched Altair slowly turn. "It's strange leaving your whole world behind. My stomach is doing flips."

"That could be the gravity. I'm not sure I have all these buttons 100% figured out yet. Hameese is hard."

"No, it's not that. It's just that all my life I've looked to the stars and imagined leaving. Now that it's actually happening, I think I'm going to miss it. How do you do it so often?"

"It's easy when you realize the galaxy is full of wonders. And most of it isn't covered in moss." He turned her around slowly and looked into her eyes. "You see? There's beauty everywhere."

Thurgood kissed her long and hard.

And it was uncomfortable for everyone watching.

The End

If you liked how he treats space, read Benjamin Wallace's bestselling post-apocalyptic comedies, the Duck & Cover Adventures.

Check out the whole 5-book Duck & Cover series:
Post-Apocalyptic Nomadic Warriors
Knights of the Apocalypse
Pursuit of the Apocalypse
Revenge of the Apocalypse
Crossroads of the Apocalypse

It's the end of the world as you've never known it.

Also by Benjamin Wallace

DUCK & COVER ADVENTURES

Post-Apocalyptic Nomadic Warriors

Knights of the Apocalypse

Pursuit of the Apocalypse

Revenge of the Apocalypse

Crossroads of the Apocalypse

SHATTERED ALLIANCE

Shattered Alliance

Send in the Clones

Alone on Altair

JUNKERS

Junkers

Junkers Season Two

DADS VS

Dads Vs The World

Dads Vs Zombies

Dads Vs Zombies: Year 2

THE BULLETPROOF ADVENTURES OF DAMIAN STOCKWELL

Horror in Honduras

Terrors of Tesla

The Mechanical Menace

OTHER BOOKS

Tortugas Rising

SHORT STORIES

Commando Pandas & Other Odd Thoughts

UNCIVIL

UnCivil: The Immortal Engine

UnCivil: Vanderbilt's Behemoth

About the Author

Benjamin Wallace lives in Texas where he complains about the heat.

You can email him at: contact@benjaminwallacebooks.com
To learn about the latest releases and giveaways, join his Readers' Group. Click here to sign up.

If you enjoyed ALONE ON ALTAIR please consider leaving a review. It would be very much appreciated and help more than you could know.

Thanks for reading, visiting, following and sharing.
-ben

Find me online here: BenjaminWallaceBooks.com

 facebook.com/benjaminwallaceauthor
twitter.com/BenMWallace
instagram.com/benmwallace

Made in the USA
Middletown, DE
30 April 2024

53675431R00150